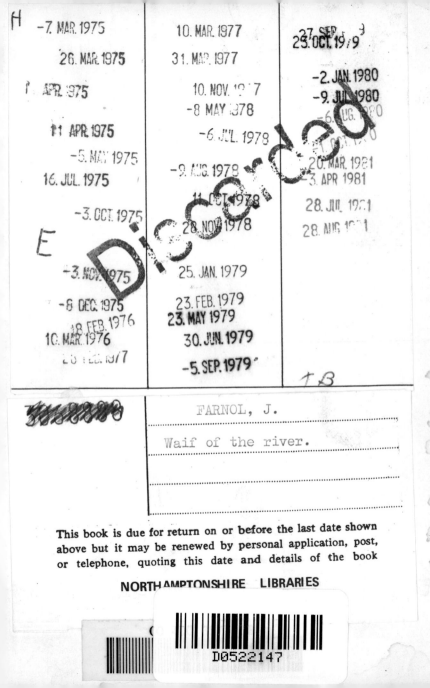

This book is due for return on or before the last date shown
above but it may be renewed by personal application, post,
or telephone, quoting this date and details of the book

WAIF OF THE RIVER

THE BROAD HIGHWAY
THE MONEY MOON
THE AMATEUR GENTLEMAN
CHRONICLES OF THE IMP
THE HONOURABLE MR. TAWNISH
BELTANE THE SMITH
THE DEFINITE OBJECT
THE GESTE OF DUKE JOCELYN
OUR ADMIRABLE BETTY
BLACK BARTLEMY'S TREASURE
MARTIN CONISBY'S VENGEANCE
PEREGRINE'S PROGRESS
SIR JOHN DERING
THE LORING MYSTERY
THE HIGH ADVENTURE
THE QUEST OF YOUTH
GYFFORD OF WEARE
THE SHADOW
EPICS OF THE FANCY
ANOTHER DAY
OVER THE HILLS
THE JADE OF DESTINY
CHARMIAN, LADY VIBART
THE WAY BEYOND
WINDS OF FORTUNE
JOHN O' THE GREEN
A PAGEANT OF VICTORY
THE CROOKED FURROW
A BOOK FOR JANE
THE LONELY ROAD
THE HAPPY HARVEST
A NEW BOOK FOR JANE
A MATTER OF BUSINESS
ADAM PENFEATHER, BUCCANEER
MURDER BY NAIL
THE KING LIVETH
THE " PIPING TIMES "
HERITAGE PERILOUS
MY LORD OF WRYBOURNE
THE FOOL BELOVED
THE NINTH EARL
THE GLAD SUMMER

Waif of the River

by

Jeffery Farnol

This reprinted edition published by

DIPLOMA PRESS LTD.

40 Broadway, London, SW1

Published in this edition 1974.
First published by SAMPSON LOW
in 1952

MADE AND PRINTED IN GREAT BRITAIN BY
WILLMER BROTHERS LIMITED, BIRKENHEAD

To

HERBERT TAYLOR
The oft-proven friend
of
his grateful
JEFFERY FARNOL

CONTENTS

Waif of the River

CHAPTER I

Flotsam

NIGHT on the river with mist of wind-driven rain and
two dim shapes up to their knees in slimy ooze, crouching
above their prey : this dreadful thing that rolled sluggish on
the lapping tide of Old Father Thames, whose broad bosom
has borne many such piteous burdens out and away from
misery and shame of life to a comfort and joy everlasting—
let us hope.

" A woman, eh, Si ? "

" Ay, a woman."

" Ain't dead yet, is she ? "

" No, but soon, Job, soon—give 'er time."

" Well, sooner the better ; us gets more for dead uns
than live uns. So she's agoin' to be a dead un when us
hauls 'er ashore. We can't wait all night in this cursed rain,
so in with 'er, Si ; souse 'er, boot 'er under, or lemme——"

" No, Job, no ! Kind natur' must do it for us, not you or
me ! For wot natur' does nobody can't 'old ag'in' us, and
the law can't touch us——"

" But, blast it, Si, oo's to know ? "

" Me conscience, Job, for one thing, and you for another !
And me conscience is a oncommon sensitive article, aye, as
spry and active as Jarsper Shrig, curse 'im ! So be patient,
Job, and let natur'—ah, wot's yonder ? "

" Eh—oo—where ? "

" I—I dunno ; footsteps mebbe ! Somewheres be'ind
us i' the perishin' dark—the wharf yonder ! "

"Gammon! Oo'd be yerabouts on sich a night 'cept the likes o' we? 'Twas trick o' the wind—or your cursed conscience! Wot of our 'found-drowned' now? Ain't she a goner yet?"

"No, Job, no. Y'see, 'er 'ead's got jammed above tide some'ow, and she's face up. But tide's arisin' pretty fast. So ha' patience."

"Not me! Shove 'er under, I tell ye! If you won't, I will. So make way and I'll tread 'er down 'till——"

Something whizzed viciously from the darkness behind them, and, smitten by a hail of unseen, painful blows, they screamed, cursed, floundered and scuttered away, whimpering like the vicious though craven animals they were.

Then their invisible assailant, dropping heavy stick, stooped to grope in that horror of darkness and slime until he felt—hair, long, matted tresses that twined and clung about his fingers, his wrists, his arms, so that for a sickening moment they seemed all over and about him, drawing his shuddering body down and down to the mud, the water and this awful thing that lay almost buried in the sucking ooze. . . . Ensued a period of fierce and desperate effort, brawn and muscle against swirling tide-race and hungry slime. Struggling to his feet at last, he turned and bore his awful burden up and away. Across muddy foreshore he stumbled, up crumbling steps, along a narrow causeway that his feet trod with the assurance of familiarity, and so to a dark court and thence to a spacious inn-yard lit by a beaming lantern and glow of red-curtained windows. And now this yard echoed to his loud though breathless hail:

"Waterman, ahoy! Ho, Tom . . . George . . . stand by to . . . bear a hand here."

At this summons a door was flung wide, letting forth a gush of warmth and rosy light, the while two voices bellowed together and in hearty welcome:

a voice gently, yet in tone so assured that instinctively he nodded and answered:

" Yes, Aunt Rosamond, I suppose so."

Now to him came this small though dominant lady, who, despite years and white hair, seemed young by reason of her quick, graceful movements and was made lovely by her large, gentle eyes and tender curve of smiling lips.

" My dear," said she, both hands outstretched to him, " you are gladly welcome."

" And well I know it, my lady of comfort!" he replied, taking off his sodden hat. " But pray don't touch me yet. I'm all slimy mud from the river and that—that frightful thing——"

" The poor, poor creature!" sighed Lady Rosamond, stooping above the settle. " So many are brought to me from the river and so often too late, but . . . tonight . . . I believe . . . Oh, Jemima, hurry! Bustle, girls, bustle, for here is a spark of life!" So saying, Lady Rosamond knelt beside the dripping, awful thing that lay a shapeless, featureless horror from which Robin shrank apalled as he watched his aunt's quick, deft hands begin their labour of mercy.

" Jemima . . . hot water . . . sponge."

" Here, m' lady."

" Scissors, Lucy!"

" Here, ma'am!"

" Helen, is the bath ready?"

" Oh yes, my lady."

" Well, now may the kind God bless our efforts!"

" And you, my wonderful Aunt!" said Robin fervently.

" Go away, Robin, and change those wet clothes. Off with you—I'm going to strip her. Now, girls!"

CHAPTER III

Tells of Old Friends

HAVING washed and changed his miry garments in that small, snug bedchamber long dedicated to his use and called for some unknown reason " Luff ", Robin descended to the spacious taproom, there to be welcomed by Sergeant George and Bo'sun Tom, and, moreover, saluted by a mouth-watering fragrance, the luscious emanation of cloves, lemon-peel and something else, cunningly blended in a large bowl set exactly in the middle of a small, polished table.

" Mr. Robin, sir," quoth the sergeant, smoothing his short, trim whiskers.

" Sir and messmate," said the bo'sun, fingering his shaven chin, " seeing as how your visits aboard is not so frequent since you took up farming them sheep o' yourn, and sich ree-markable black sheep——"

" True enough, Tom, though some are beginning to show a little greyish here and there, and one or two even a spot or so of white."

" Yet a crew o' reg'lar bloody-minded pirates, sir——"

" Cut-throats and jailbirds all ! " added the sergeant.

" Precisely, George. And yet maybe John and I shall change 'em into the men they ought to be someday—some of them, perhaps. But," enquired Robin, glancing round upon the many empty chairs and benches, " have we no company tonight ? "

" Not a soul, sir ! " replied the sergeant.

" Y'see, Master Robin," the bo'sun explained, " if you'd brought a ' dead un ' aboard us tonight as they gen'rally are

6

'twould ha' been business as usual. But yours was a ' live un ', consequently her ladyship our commodore is now aworking on and apraying 'eaven's 'ard for this ' live un ' to so remain, and, sich so being, our orders is ' silence all ', wherefore we're aflying the ' no entry ' signal."

" This is a new idea, Tom. There was no such order when I lived here."

" No, sir, 'twere institooted better nor a month ago along of a poor young lass as come ashore and was brought aboard us still alive and there was your lady aunt workin' and prayin' over her like she's adoing now with your woman."

" Not ' my woman ', Tom ! Good gad, she's nothing to me ! "

" Very good, sir ; 'twere only a way o' speakin'. How-ever, that's the position, when into the tap here come three sailormen, furriners all, and starts a fight, whereupon George and me and Cap'n Si runs 'em aboard and heaves 'em out, prompt——"

" Which," added George, " caused some bit o' com-motion, sir."

" Ay ! " nodded the bo'sun. " Consequently to us comes Jemima in tears to call us brutes and savages and tell us as how the poor lass wakes from death to life, but, hearing the din, gives a moan and ex-pires."

" Tom means as she dies o' fright, Master Robin," the sergeant explained.

" Therefore," continued the bo'sun, " this here noo order of ' no entry ' ! "

" But now, Master Robin, sir," quoth Sergeant George, " my comrade Tom and self begs as you'll sit atwixt us, this being a occasion——"

" Likewise a festive-all ! " said the bo'sun, setting a rummer of steaming fragrance into Robin's ready grasp. " So do us proud, sir, by sniffin', sippin' and swallerin'

this here as can't be ekalled except p'raps by Jarsper Shrig's
' one and only ', and as therefore be worthy to drink present
j'y and future happiness to Sir Oliver and his lady Clia, as
be our lady, too—and—their first ! "

" Ah ! " exclaimed young Robin, sighing mournfully.
" You mean their—their new baby."

" A boy, sir ; a son, and a nine-pounder ! " said the
sergeant.

" Belay, messmate ! " exclaimed the bo'sun. " You talk o'
this blessed infant as if 'e was a gun, a fo'c'sle carronade,
George ! Howsever, sir, we are now charged for to drink
long life and happiness to S'Oliver's noo little son and heir,
God bless him and them ! " So Robin, stifling another sigh,
honoured this toast.

"Lord ! " exclaimed Bo'sun Tom, setting down his empty
glass. " It do seem only yesterday as my lady being then our
little Miss Clia, were akissin' and acuddlin' her dolls, and
now—doing the same with a real, live baby, her own flesh
and blood——"

" Ar, and bones ! " added Sergeant George, refilling the
glasses.

" Bones ? " exclaimed the bo'sun, " Avast now, George ;
you're off course. Babbies noo-born don't have no bones,
same being no more than jelly——"

" Gristle, Tom, gristle ! "

" Well, jelly or gristle, here's hoping he may prove now
and hereafter a blessing to his ekally blessed mamma——"

" Mother, Tom ! Why not ' mother ' ? "

" Because, messmate, anyone can have a mother ; the
Quality always and ever has mammas. For d'ye see, when I
was sarving aboard the old *Belly Sarious*, seventy-four,
Cap'n Sir Willyam Wills, his lady presented him with a son,
which noos comes by packet as we cruised off Too Long
waiting for the mounseers to come out if they dared. So
the crew is drummed to quarters and we tumbled up

ely, hoping as the Johnny Crapaws was out at last. Instead, we was issued with a double go o' grog to drink j'y to
the noo infant and happiness to—now mark this, George—
happiness to that infant's ma-ma! And wot d'ye say to that
now?"

"Why, Tom, I says as how, Tom, when I was in the
Peninsula, Battle o' Vittoria, my colonel takes a musket ball
in the leg and down he goes flat as a flounder. But myself
chancing at hand and being pretty strong in them days, up I
picks him and along with him to the surgeon, who, being
pretty busy, keeps me to ass-ist. Scarcely is the colonel
bandaged and strapped than the post arrives and an orderly
brings him a letter which, having read, up he struggles b'
means o' me and says he, ' Corporal, it's a boy,' says he, then
off they carries him and back goes I to help beat the Frogs,
which we surely did! That night after roll-call, up limps our
colonel, and, ' men,' says he, ' I'm proud to command you,
so that means an extry ration o' rum. I'm gladly proud o'
the regiment,' says he, ' so that means another! But I'm
happy to inform you I am now a father who hopes someday
to be as proud of his son, and this means another. So
tonight the regiment will drink all joy and health to '—now
hearkee, Tom—' to my little son's mother!'—mother,
Tom; and mind you, comrade, our colonel was—an
earl!"

"Mother or mamma, George, a oncommonly shipshape
infant 'e is, so far as I could ob-sarve."

"Though smaller," said the sergeant; " ar, smaller than
expected!"

"Lord love ye, messmate! How big do your expectations
run?"

"Well, Tom, say an inch or so each way."

"George, how many noo-born infants have you fell in
with?"

"Not so many, Tom, but——"

" Then, messmate, belay your jaw-tackle and let me t
you as he's a right tight little craft and the breathing image
of his papa."

" Though pinker, Tom! Ar, 'tis a remarkable pink
infant ! "

" All infants is pink, messmate, as lobsters—'tis natur'."

" So," enquired Robin, gazing mournfully at his rummer,
though it brimmed anew, " you've seen—her baby ? "

" Ay, sir, we drove down to Abbeymead along of our
lady Rosamond last week and saw the noo arrival."

" And how was—she, Tom ? "

" Sir, the infant is a he ! "

" He means his mother, comrade."

" His ma-ma, sir, and our lady Clia is marvellous well and
happy, Master Robin, and axed when you, sir, was agoing
to bear away for sight of 'em. Sir Oliver ex-pects you, so he
said."

" Yes," sighed Robin, " I should have ridden down to
Abbeymead days ago—only that I've been kept pretty busy
of late with those lambs of mine."

" Lambs, sir ? Egad, wolves I'd call 'em, for raveenious
beasts they are—to a man ! Scally-waggy roofians all and
jailbirds aplenty, I'll lay—eh, Master Robin ? "

" Right you are, Bo'sun ! " answered Robin, eyes kindling
and powerful shoulders squaring themselves. " Thieves,
rogues and rascals they were and would be yet but for Black
John and myself. But we are teaching them better things by
rule of fist ; we out-brute the brutes. We are welding them
into a sort of brotherhood, a kind of ragamuffin fellowship.
These are the animals John and I are rearing on our
farm."

" Ay, Master Robin, but how do these yere baa-lambs
o' yourn when your eye ain't on 'em and those fists o' yourn
not handy ? "

" Fairish, Tom, fairish ! Only two cases of petty larceny

last week, fourteen of foul language and nine of drunkenness, which is not so bad, considering."

" And how many, sir——"

" Thirty-seven regulars, Tom, but sometimes we feed and sleep as many as a hundred-odd. Ah, we could have ten times as many if only we had room, for our farm, or club, is becoming famous and attracts more of 'em every week. Also we are self-supporting—or very nearly ; and clear of debt—almost ! We find 'em work for meals and lodging, rough-carpentry, tinsmiths, chairs to mend, knives to grind and what not, and b' George we've an oldish cove, a watchmaker by profession but cracksman by trade who can turn his hand to anything. . . ."

Thus they talked, yet alert and ready all three for any summons from that great kitchen where four devoted women wrought waging desperate battle with that dark angel whose name is Death.

So the hours dragged their weary length, the night wore away, and yet no sign. Midnight struck . . . then one o'clock . . . then two. Bo'sun Tom, blinking drowsily, bestirred himself to shake Sergeant George, who had snored. Robin was yawning till his eyes watered. And all were yearning for bed, when they roused to the sudden opening of the door and Jemima's voice, strained and hoarse with weariness :

" Master Robin, your lady aunt waits you in Salamander."

" Rightho, Jemima dear," he answered sleepily as he rose. " How's that frightful thing, that wretched woman, now ? "

" Pretty well, sir—and a dreadful time we've had wi' her. But my lady'll tell ee."

So forthwith Robin came to that small, cosy, triangular chamber called, now as of yore and for no remembered reason, Salamander, and here found Lady Rosamond leaning back wearily in cushioned elbow-chair, who, smiling wanly, beckoned him beside her, saying :

"Robin, I think and hope your poor waif is going to live and—I am wondering——"

"So am I, Aunt, at your small marvellous self, as I always have done and always shall ! For this little, gentle, immensely potent aunt of mine is the absolute incomparable, and—well—there is only one you ! "

"Dear boy," she murmured with weary sigh though smile gentle as her voice, "never mind me, at least for the present, and let me tell you of this very strange young woman."

"My dear Aunt, please, no. Instead tell me of—her—I mean Clia, of course. Is she well, and so on ? I mean, has she recovered and—well—is she pretty well ? "

"Oh yes, quite ! But now of this other, this young creature Old Father Thames bore to your arms, Robin, and I wonder why ? This woman you saved tonight, don't you wish to hear about her ? "

"Not a word ! " said he, shaking his curly head. "Women don't interest me now and never will again—never, since Clia was—not for me. Besides, I don't like horrors and dodge all such."

"But, Robin, this is a very beautiful young creature, dangerously so ! "

"Well, I don't like danger either—if it's feminine."

"And this unfortunate is superlatively feminine, my dear ; and besides beauty of face and perfection of form, she is evidently a person of breeding and refinement, judging by her speech."

"She is able to speak then, and so soon, Aunt ? "

"Yes, Robin, though not coherently. She raved quite terribly about some man, or men, and of the river, the cold, dark water. I fear hers will be a dreadfully sordid story, if it is ever told."

"Yet you think she is a lady ? "

"I am quite sure of it. For, besides her speech her

clothes and linen are of the very finest quality ; and besides these again, there is this most lovely and precious thing ! " Here, opening her hand, Lady Rosamond showed a scintillating glory that flamed in the candlelight.

" Eh—diamonds ! " exclaimed Robin. " And, by George, what magnificent ones ! A broach, Aunt ? "

" No, the half of a buckle ; the other part must have been wrenched away, because her dress, a silk robe, has been torn most brutally."

" Ha, robbery ? "

" Yes, or worse, my dear. So it would seem your miserable waif is——"

" Not mine, Aunt ; no no ! To me she is an abiding horror."

" My poor waif then, silly boy, judging by the splendour of this broken trinket, is not merely a person of condition but of wealth also. "

" Oh well, enough of her, Aunt, I beg. Instead do pray tell me all about your last visit to—to Clia."

" Not until you tell me why you have never been near Abbeymead since her baby was born."

" I wrote instead, my dear."

" Yes, I read it, the briefest of notes, Robin, and rather worse spelt than usual ! "

" I was never much of a hand at letter-writing, especially to Clia."

" Are you suggesting you still love her ? "

" And always must and shall, Aunt—not being a changeable sort of a fellow. Yes, I shall adore her forever, to the end of—well—everything," he replied mournfully.

" My poor, dear, nonsensical boy ! " she murmured, viewing his gloomy countenance with wise and loving glance. " But why in the world did you write and tell Oliver of this ? "

" Because I thought it right to be open and honest with him, confound him ! "

" It has troubled him greatly, Robin."

" Good ! Glad of it ! I meant it should ! Did he tell Clia ? "

" Oh no ; he merely read your letter to her."

" Ha ! Did it trouble her, too ? "

" Not in the least. She called you a silly boy and kissed her Oliver."

" Did she, by heaven ! "

" By heaven she did, Robin, fervently ! And she was perfectly right. You are indeed the very silliest of boys ; but then, of course, you are also the very dearest."

" However," he sighed, " I am faithful by nature ; there will never be any other woman for me, never ! Love's a tomfoolery and I'm done with it for evermore ! Yes, I shall live and die without it, b'gad ! "

" And you are not twenty-four yet, are you, Robin dear ? "

" No, but very nearly. Quite aged enough to know the blasting bitterness of grievous and irreparable loss and eternal grief for—for what could—yes and would have been mine."

" ' Blasting bitterness ! ' " she repeated gently, but with a dimple peeping beside her shapely mouth.

" Yes, b' George ! " he exclaimed fervently and quite unaware of this dimple, of course. " And to be perennially haunted by the carking phantom of the happiness that dawned but to fade, the joy that fled, leaving desolation behind ! "

" My poor, darling boy ! " she sighed, yet with the dimple more in evidence.

" Yes, Aunt, the perfection of bliss that could, would and should have been mine but for—old Noll ! And he old enough to be her father ! "

" Not quite, my dear."

" Oh well," sighed Robin dejectedly, " for me henceforth must be the path of loneliness and confounded solitude ! Yes, instead of wife and children, or even a single baby, I must be content with old John and my deuced black sheep."

" Yes, my dear," said Lady Rosamond, reaching to touch his bowed head. " And it is a truly noble work you are doing, you and your faithful Black John ! For, Robin, whoever has comforted one grieving soul or lifted one fellow creature from despair has not lived in vain. And I'm proud of you, my dear one, because it seems you and John are working miracles among the most abandoned and desperate characters. I'm constantly hearing of your work from my own poor folk, the wives, sisters and mothers of your— black sheep. Even Mr. Shrig bears out their testimony."

" Good old Jasper ! He hasn't been our way lately, which is just as well, for my sheep panic at sight of him, having had professional dealings with him at one time or another." Here the grandfather clock in an adjacent corner, having wheezed like the very old gentleman he was, struck an unexpectedly musical chime.

" Three o'clock already ! " exclaimed Lady Rosamond. " My gracious ! You should have been asleep hours ago, Robin, so off with you."

" The same to you, my lady ! " he retorted, rising to his splendid height. " So I'll light your ladyship's bedroom candle and kiss your ladyship good night at once, my lady ; you shall to your downy couch forthwith ! "

" Downy fiddlestick, boy ! There can be no sleep for me while that ill-used girl lies so near death. Jemima and Lucy are taking the first watch and I shall doze here waiting for my waif to wake to consciousness and life or sink into the everlasting sleep. And I am wondering which would be best for her and—others ! Yes, I'm troubled with a quite unwonted and very strange doubt—which, were I a nervous person, would be apprehension and—yes—fear."

" Yet you say she is a lady and beautiful ? "

" Yes."

" Is she dark or fair, Aunt ? "

" Dark, my dear. Oh, dark as the old river itself at midnight ! "

" As expected, Aunt ! And dark women repel me, because I have always adored fair women ; I mean Clia, of course—red-gold ! I remember the first time I saw her hair—and I then a half-starved little misery ; I thought she was an angel and I've worshipped her ever since."

" Her or her hair, Robin ? "

" Both, Aunt, as you know right well."

" Yes, my dear, but what I should like to know is—why did our Old Father Thames bear this midnight lady to your very arms, Robin ? "

" Chance, Aunt dear ; merest chance."

" I wonder ! " she murmured, looking up at him with troubled gaze. " For, my dear boy, since making my home here beside our old Thames I have come to regard it as a river—no, the River of Destiny—somehow concerned with each one of us. Which sounds absurdly fanciful, I suppose ? "

" No," said Robin gravely, " not to me, because I have always loved Father Thames and looked upon him as a live old thing, who, being so very old, is therefore infinitely wise and—understanding."

" Yes, Robin, because, though immortal, he is so very human—a thing of good and evil, of life and death, pure at his source from the hand of God and glad with youth, deepening as he flows past village and town, growing darker and saddened by experience of human grief, darker yet and fouler with the sin and needless suffering of this great city, yet flowing on—to be purified at last and made glad again in the merciful immensity of God's ocean. . . .

Dear me, how I prose ! And all because you and Thames betwixt you bring me this strange, darkly beautiful creature to whom life may be a blessing or curse to herself and others. And consequently I'm wondering who and which and——"

Here came a rapping on the door and Jemima's sleepy voice saying :

" Oh, my lady, she be awake at last and conscious——"

Up started Lady Rosamond and sped away, leaving Robin to sink into the elbow-chair and presently fall asleep. He awoke at a touch, to see the maid Lucy beside him and the new-risen sun making a glory at the narrow casement.

" Eh ? Oh, what now, m' dear ? " he murmured drowsily.

" Your aunt, sir, do bid you to her this moment."

Yawning, he arose and followed Lucy obediently to a certain door that stood ajar ; here he paused to enquire sleepily :

" What's this ? Where are you taking me ? "

" La, sir," answered Lucy, simpering, " to see your lovely lady, for sure."

" But I have no lady, and want none."

" Oh, Master Robin, I mean the lady as you brought us in your arms last night, then so muddy and horrorsome but now so lovely ! Your aunt bids you take a peep at her."

" Eh, a peep at——? No thanks, Lucy ; I prefer to remember her merely as an armful o' filth. So tell Aunt I'm off to my black sheep and bid her good morning for me ; say I'll see her again as soon as I've visited my lady Cli—the folk at Abbeymead."

But at this moment from beyond this partly open door his aunt's voice arrested him, for in it was a note of command :

" Robin, I want you ! Come in, do ! "

So, perforce, he entered this room, then halted suddenly ; he was aware of Lady Rosamond seated beside the bed, but all he saw was a face, a pallid oval framed in lustrous black hair and lit by eyes vividly blue such as he had never seen ; a beautiful face—marred all at once by hate, black brows close-knit above eyes that glared, shapely lips back-drawn from gleaming teeth hard-shut, a slender hand tight-clenched lifted against him as in menace. All this Robin saw ere, with swift, wild gesture this face turned and hid itself in the pillow.

" Lord love me ! " he whispered, and, backing out of the chamber, closed the door as against something evil.

" Lucy," said he softly, " you can tell Aunt I've seen— the devil ! Yes, b'gad, the evil eye or some such ; an infernal brimstone witch—and I'm off ! "

" But, oh, Master Robin, wi' no breakfast ? "

" By heavens, no ! Not with that—that creature any- where about." So saying, he hastened to the taproom for his hat, and thence sped out and away into the sweet, cool freshness of this early summer morning.

CHAPTER IV

Gives Some Description of Robin's " Black Sheep "

HARD BESIDE the river, on ground that was a dusty waste in dry weather and muddy swamp in wet, stood that conglomerate structure of wharf, barn, warehouse, stable and ancient gabled cottage, which Robin, with the aid of his sturdy and faithful Black John, had made a haven for human wreckage.

On this particular early summer morning, fresh and aglow from their usual swim, they stood side by side, Robin and John, shaving by means of a somewhat inadequate mirror in a smallish upper chamber that had once been a hayloft. They were stripped to the waist, Robin all supple power above and below, Black John six foot six of massive strength, which, together with ferocious joy of personal combat, had in his unregenerate days made him notorious as " The Thames-side Terror ".[1]

But now, as they stood thus peacefully occupied, he paused to wipe his razor carefully and say :

" Mr. Robin, I never see you in the buff, them shoulders and arms o' yours, but I'm minded how Jessamy Todd says as how if ever you hit a man with all your might and in the proper place that man'll go down and never come up again because he'll be stone dead."

" Which," answered Robin, razor arrested, " is a dev'lish disturbing thought, John, and cannot be right, because I hit you once and with all my strength, old fellow."

" But not in the right place, Master Robin ; yet down I went fast asleep till they soused me wi' a bucket o' water."

---

[1] See *The Happy Harvest*.

19

" Yes, that was a grand fight, John, and it turned you into a grander friend ; no man ever had a better ! And this reminds me of another good friend, John ; you've seen him here pretty often lately—old Rags and Bones."

" If you mean young Viscount Ragworth, sir——"

" That's the cove ; and he's not so young, six months or so my senior. However, he's so taken with this farm, this club of ours, that he wants to join and has sent me a hundred as subscription."

" Eh, a hundred pound, Master Robin ? "

" Which will be no end useful, John, of course, though the question is : can we accept him, considering he is not exactly homeless and destitute. To be sure we might enrol him as a broken-down rag-and-bone merchant, eh, John ? "

" Well, sir, I——"

" Hold hard, old fellow ! Since we are friends and partners, why the devil do you still persist in sir-ing and mister-ing me ? "

" Because, sir, you are one o' the Quality, a gentleman born, and I am only——"

" You," said Robin, wiping his razor in turn and not at all carefully, " are far better born than I, because, as a matter of fact, I—oh, damme, I'm only a sort of sham, an imitation of what a true gentleman should be ! For I was a London gutter-snipe, John, a nameless brat born most probably in some thieves' den or vile rookery, of unknown parentage, a ragged little half-starved misery steeped in filth and vice, a small savage and too-eager fighter even then ! I might have become a thief or worse and ended my evil days in prison, or more likely on the gallows, but for Sir Oliver Dale,[1] old Noll, though he was Mr. Dale then ; but he rescued me, John, took me to his care, had me educated—treated me as his son, God bless him ! And now

[1] See *The Crooked Furrow.*

the question is, what am I, John, and what am I going to be ?"

And with his dark, pensive gaze down-bent towards the river below their open casement, John replied :

" Sir, you are and ever will be the man you seem, and the gentleman Sir Oliver hoped for ; and so if I ' sir ' you now and then, Master Robin, 'tis because I so believe you and always shall, sir——"

At this moment came a sharp rap on the door, which, at Robin's bidding, opened to admit a smart-looking man remarkably stiff in the back and square of shoulder, who, saluting smartly like the guardsman he had been, said in a voice of military officialdom :

" Sir, beg to report James Darcey for re-fusing to wash and William Sawkins for ab-usive language, very ob-scene, sir."

" Ha ! " exclaimed Robin, struggling into his shirt. " I'll attend to 'em presently, Sergeant Bob. How many for breakfast this morning ? "

" Thirty-seven, sir."

" But damme, Bob, you know we can seat a hundred and two at a pinch ! "

" Yessir ! But this being Toosday, only thirty-seven could pay their tuppence. Tom Wilks and me was compelled to turn t'others away, rules being rules, sir."

" Then we must alter the rule—poor devils—and make our charge a penny or nothing ; and yet I don't want to pauperise them. Oh well, go and call 'em to ' attention ', Sergeant ; I'll be down in a minute or so. Ah hell ! " he exclaimed as the sergeant departed. " I hate to turn any poor damn wretch away without bite or sup."

" But," said John, " you—we can't feed all the hungry in London, sir."

" We could in time, by degrees, old fellow, turn about,

by rotation—maybe. At least we could have a dev-lish good try."

" Well, so we do. And, Master Robin, I'm all against lowering our charges, because a man likes to pay his way ; a rogue don't. And 'tis men we want."

" True enough, John, though 'tis want that often makes rogues ! Ay, starvation is a great breeder of crime." So saying, Robin donned snowy neckerchief and somewhat hard-used coat, then descended narrow, precipitous stair to a spacious chamber (once the lofty storehouse for ocean-born goods), where now the thirty-seven derelicts stood marshalled for his inspection, men these of every sort and condition, but all of them more or less brutalised by suffering and hardship.

Now as Robin surveyed these lost ones, these his black sheep, looking for some spark of good beneath the too-apparent evil, there stole to them a most delectable aroma, growing ever stronger, the delicious fragrance of freshly brewed coffee and frying bacon, whereto noses were lifted, nostrils quivered and mouths watered.

Then Robin spoke :

" James Darcey, step out here ! "

A heavy-shouldered ruffian lurched forward, growling :

" Wot's up, Gov'nor ? "

" Did you refuse to wash ? "

" Ay, Gov'nor, I did ! And for why ? says you. Becos, says I, for sake o' me perishin' precious 'ealth, I says, seein' as 'ow too much washin' don't soot me consti-tootion ! And, wot's more, I washed yesterday, me face and me 'ands, I did, Bible oath, Gov ! "

" James Darcey, are you hungry ? "

" Starvin', Gov'nor ! Me pore innards is all empty as so many perishin' drums——"

" Get washed, or not a bite do you have. Sausages, James, with bacon and——"

"Bacon, Gov; soss—cor strike a light. I'll wash me all over—or pretty nigh."

"Then go and do it."

"Ay ay, sir—wi' all me beatin' 'eart!"

"And plenty of soap, James!"

"Soap it is, Gov'nor!" And away shambled the grimy one forthwith.

"William Sawkins, step forward!"

A lean, scowling ferocity obeyed.

"You, Sawkins, are accused of using foul language."

"Well, wot of it?"

"You don't eat a morsel until you've sponged out that vile mouth of yours!"

"No bleed'n fear, you blood——"

"Ducking squad, fall in!" said Robin, whereat rose joyous cries of: "Ay ay, sir! Righto, Gov'nor! Come on —you!" And even then, the rebellious one was writhing in the ungentle grip of four grinning fellows.

"Off with him!" Robin commanded. "Scrub his mouth out thoroughly, and if he resists douse him in water-butt number three."

But now it was, and even as Robin spoke, that the great outer door behind him opened softly and upon the threshold stood one at mere sight of whom all other men were suddenly hushed and still. A shortish, powerfully built person this, very neatly dressed from crown of wide-eaved hat to well-polished top-boots, a man before whose bright, roving glance lean bodies seemed to cower and shrink, faces were averted, shaggy heads bowed or were back-thrown defiantly while nervous feet shuffled. Robin, looking round to know the cause of all this, exclaimed, glad-voiced:

"Shrig! Jasper, old fellow, you're heartily welcome. Come in, man, come in. Though—ha—what the deuce? Which of my lambs are you after this time?"

B

Crossing both sinewy hands on that formidable knobbed stick of his which was so very like a bludgeon, Mr. Shrig of Bow Street answered :

" Nary a vun, Master Robin, no ! I have took the pleasure of paying you a sociable wisit, sir."

" Good man ! " said Robin as they shook hands. " Breakfast is nearly ready. Tom Piper's hard at it in the kitchen yonder. Can't you smell it ? "

" Ar ! " sighed Mr. Shrig, tilting his short, pugnacious nose to this appetising fragrance. " Nosegays can't compare nor yet the spices of Arry Beer."

" Sausages, Jasper, with bacon and possibly an egg or so ! You know Sergeant Flint, of course—now Sergeant Bob, the tables ! "

At the sergeant's bellowed command rose a joyful clamour where thirty-seven hungry fellows forthwith placed long planks upon trestles, and at the sergeant's second bellow fell into rank again. Then Robin led their visitor into a smallish, cosy chamber (once a stable), where breakfast things were being set forth upon snowy cloth by Black John, whom Mr. Shrig greeted like the old friends they were. And presently, seated at this hospitable board, they ate and drank with appetites hearty as their long-time friendship.

" By the way," said Robin as he performed with the coffee-pot, " I believe I have—yes, finally settled on a name for our club at last. What do you both think of ' The Gamecock's Roost ' ? "

" Prime ! " quoth John with emphatic nod.

" Couldn't be better," answered Mr. Shrig, " seeing as how these here gamecocks is up to all manner o' games lawful and t'otherwise."

" Soho ! " chuckled Robin. " However, I'll paint it for our sign in good, bold capitals, Jasper, which will indeed be ' a deed ', a ' capital act ', eh, old fellow ? And this reminds me to ask how goes crime nowadays ? "

" Vich," sighed Mr. Shrig above half-emptied coffee-cup, " I can't complain seeing as highway robbery is fairly bobbish, petty larceny going strong, robbery vith wiolence ditto, but murder has fell away to nothing, or werry nearly. Though a few days ago summat occurred as suggested Windictiveness vith a werry large Wee and my hopes is rose according."

" Not your hopes of murder, surely, Jasper ? "

" My hopes, Master Robin, of windicating the possible murderee by clapping my daddles on the murder-er and bringing same to judgment and justice, as in dooty bound."

" Meaning the gallows, eh, Jasper ? "

" And talking of your lady Aunt Rosamond——"

" Good, great heavens ! What on earth——"

" She give me a letter for you, Master Robin, con-sarning the young fee-male party, name unknown, as you saved from a mud and vatery grave eight nights ago."

" Well, what of her, Jasper ? "

" Said young party has flew the coop, hopped the perch and wanished com-plete ! And talking of your lady aunt's letter, same I here and now dooly deliver." And reaching his hat from beneath the table, Mr. Shrig drew thence the missive in question. Uttering a word of thanks, Robin unfolded it and read :

" MY DEAR NEPHEW,

" The still unknown and very beautiful creature whom our Old Father Thames bore to your arms has vanished, leaving the note I enclose which could have been written only by a young and sensitive lady, in fine a gentlewoman. Jemima informs me how this unfortunate lady overheard you describe her as ' an armful of filth', and later I, and perhaps she, heard your too-loudly expressed detestation of black hair. I am loath to think this has anything to do with her very sudden departure and yet . . . However, I hope and pray she is now safe in the loving care of friends. Please, my dear boy, return her note by Mr. Shrig and know me always your devoted loving aunt,

"ROSAMOND."

He now read the enclosure, these words written in bold, flowing characters:

"DEAREST AND GENTLEST OF LADIES,

"Because in these few days you have taught me to love you, I rid you of my troublous presence lest I bring sorrow and peril upon you, but I am and shall ever remain your loving, truly grateful,

"WAIF OF THE RIVER.

"Because I have no money, please accept the jewelled trifle I leave for the benefit of your many poor ones."

"Not bad news of Lady Rosamond, I hope?" enquired John in sudden anxiety, struck by Robin's grave expression.

"No, old fellow. Oh no. Aunt is very well, but, as Jasper says, the young woman I dragged from the mud t'other night has bolted, and I'm wondering why."

"For a werry good reason, Master Robin."

"Oh? What, pray?"

"Sorrer and peril as by her wrote down."

"Then you've seen this letter, Jasper?"

"Your lady aunt give me same to pee-roose."

"Well, what do you think is meant by 'sorrow and peril'?"

"Master Robin, ekker alone responds—so fur——"

"Confound your echo, Jasper. I'm asking what you think——"

"Boats, sir; I'm thinking o' boats."

" Now what the devil——"

" Two on 'em, sir, Bill Bartrum's and another as Bill found adrift upstream not long ago, a werry nice boat vith nobody and nothing in same except a lady's silver-buckled shoe, a splash or so o' blood and summat else as Bill had missed, vich was bad luck for Bill but fort'nate for the law— this here ! " And from the right-hand pocket of his red waistcoat Mr. Shrig extracted a screw of paper. Very deliberately he opened this and laid upon the table the half of a gold clasp ablaze with splendour of diamonds.

" Good Lord ! " exclaimed Robin, gazing down at this precious thing. " Jasper, I've seen this before—yes, by jove, Aunt Rosamond found it on that young woman's muddy clothes.

" Not this, sir, no. The part as your lady aunt found is this." And from the left-hand pocket of his waistcoat Mr. Shrig drew another screw of paper, saying : " Lo behold half o' this here as is a gold buckle, the property, I pre-soom, o' the lady as lost her shoe, her gore and p'raps now her life, vich lady, Master Robin, is that same young fee-male party you described as a ' armful o' filth '."

" Well, so she was, all loathsome with slime, though somehow you make my words sound worse than I thought, damme ! "

" And where," enquired John, " did you find the part as Bill Bartrum missed ? "

" It had fell and hid itself werry artfully, John, abaft the sternmost stringer."

" It must be worth a rare lot o' money, Jasper."

" Ar, a fortun', John ! From vich I de-dooce as how Master Robin's armful o' filth must be a lady o' the Quality and young person o' terry-mendous po-sessions."

" Jasper, why harp upon that careless too-hasty remark of mine which I——"

" Talking o' harps, Mr. Robin, said young lady may be

per-forming on one in Kingdom Come at this i-dentical minute werry soulfully as her body, reposing in the buzzim of Old Pa Thames, floats peacefully downstream——"

"Now damn it all, Jasper, what evidence have you for such curst suggestion?"

"Not a scrinch, sir, neether tittle nor jot! But—if a person cuts and runs, it argufies per-soot and fear o' bodily harm, Master Robin; death sir, the capital act. And this young party has fled! So there y' are, though here she ain't, being now, alive or dead, in parts unknown."

"Which sounds dev'lish dismal, Jasper!"

"Howsever, Master Robin, your sassingers and bacon, not to mention coffee and eggs, has gone to the spot and been dooly appreciated by your old friend J. S., who begs to ex-press gratitood for same."

"And who is heartily welcome at any time, eh, John?"

"Ever and always is our united sentiments, Jasper."

And presently, having repocketed the glittering halves of that resplendent clasp, and tucked the brief note sub-scribed "Waif of the River" into his famous hat, Mr. Shrig crowned himself therewith, shook hands, and departed. City-wards he went, and at leisured pace beside the ever-busy river, this crystal road, this watery highway athrong with craft and ships of every sort, size and rig, past busy wharves where other ships lay moored wherein and whereby men of every sort and kind wrought and laboured; on past gloomy warehouses and grimy buildings, until in dingy corner remote from this tumultuous bustle and fury of traffic he beheld a man seated pensive upon a rusty bollard, a man entirely unremarkable except for a pair of hay-like drooping whiskers of the kind familiarly known as "weepers". As Mr. Shrig approached, this man arose with a certain lithe nimbleness, whereupon ensured the follow-ing murmurous conversation:

MR. SHRIG: Anything to report, Dan'l?

DAN'L: Only one man, a infant and a woman; nothing in our line, so fur, Jarsper.

MR. SHRIG: But—an ooman, Dan'l. Have you dooly inspected same?

DAN'L: I have so, and therefore pro-nounce as she ain't our con-sern, being a sight too old.

MR. SHRIG: Is my young Midget out along o' Bill Bartrum?

DAN'L: Ay, below bridge, but coming up along on the flood. But, Jarsper, where about d'you expect our young party to come ashore?

MR. SHRIG: I dunno as I do, Dan'l. I b'lieve and hope as our labour is all in wain.

DAN'L: Then why search the river for her?

MR. SHRIG: Because I promised our lady Rosamond so to do for three days, to soothe said lady's anxious mind.

DAN'L: And this'll be the third day, Jarsper.

MR. SHRIG: Ar! And you knowing the places where Old Thames gen'rally rolls his wictims ashore, you'll wisit them places turn about till the ebb and thereafter report to me at the 'Vaterman'.

DAN'L: Very good, Jarsper.

MR. SHRIG: And if any wictim favours you by showing up, let's hope as 'twon't be our perticklar young femmy-nine. Though, from information lately received, I know as there's a gen'leman—a reg'lar bang-up nob—making enquiries along-shore for a expected young lady-like corpse, vich fine gen'leman I am now agoing to meet.

Having said which, Mr. Shrig nodded, turned and went ambling back, slow of foot; but never had his roving glance been quicker or more keenly alert.

CHAPTER V

Introducing the Woman

MEANWHILE, that mysterious power called Destiny, Fate or merely Chance was about to begin the transformation of two characters, altering the course of their lives, changing their thoughts, aspirations and hopes for the future, and all this by means of Old Father Thames, two oars skilfully plied and a misused lump of chalk ; the particulars of which, after brief and needed description, shall be related forthwith, as follows :

Before this structural oddment henceforth to be known as the Gamecock's Roost, and well above high-water mark, was a small court enclosed by a woefully battered marble balustrade pierced midway by a stately arch, beneath which was a roomy platform whence a flight of stone steps descended to the river—once the water stairs of some noble mansion long since demolished and forgotten. But these age-worn relics of a splendid past still preserved a wistful beauty all their own, more especially the stairs, worn and hollowed here and there by the feet of many generations, and thus wise in experience of life, of joy, sorrow, fear and tragedy ; indeed, a very fateful stairway.

And it was above these stairs of destiny, in the shadow of this stately arch, that Robin stood, six feet of splendid young manhood, a lump of chalk in that terrible right fist of his, with which, upon a board propped at convenient angle, he was inscribing this legend and in his own original manner, thus :

THE GAIM COCKES REWST

He was viewing this effort rather dubiously, when he was startled by a voice, harsh though feminine, exclaiming:
" Aho ! "

Glancing swiftly thitherward, he beheld almost within reach the narrow stern of a light boat or skiff inscribed with the letters B. E. T., a pair of roughshod feet, slender ankles, shapeless petticoat and a face framed in black though lustrous hair, an oval face lit by eyes vividly blue beneath brows knit in a frown, above a nose delicately arched, and this again above a somewhat wide though shapely full-lipped mouth, which lips now parted to demand in the same harsh tone :

" Young man, wot d'ye think you're adoing of ? "

After momentary pause he answered :

" Young woman, I am about to paint this sign."

" Then rub it out, young man, and spell it right—and proper ! "

" Oh ? " he enquired, eyeing his handiwork more doubtfully than before. " What's wrong with it ? "

" Everything except the ' The '."

" B'gad ! " he axclaimed ruefully. " I was thinking it lookéd a trifle odd. I never was a great hand at spelling."

" Then you ought to be, considering the size o' you ! "

" What in the world has my size to do with it ? "

" Plenty ! And then, besides, there's your hair, your awful 'air ! "

" Eh ? What's the matter with it ? "

" Pink as a carrot and all pretty little quiffs and curls like a baby's——"

" Oho ! " he chuckled. " What of your own tangled mane ? "

" Well—what ? " she demanded, leaning across her oars to frown up at him again.

" Black as a barrel of tar or sooty chimney ! "

" So you don't like black hair, eh, young man ? "

" I prefer a—sunnier colour."

" Red, I s'pose, like your own baby curls—yah ! Now you're flushin'—pink as a noo-born babby ! "

" And—and you," stuttered Robin, flushing more hotly, " you are a—an extremely vulgar young woman, coarse as your shoes and petticoats. The best thing about you is your boat. And these letters on the stern B. E. T., do they spell your name ? "

" S'pose they do ? "

" It would be a misfit and doesn't suit you."

" Oh, and why not ? "

" Because it is a common name ; and though you appear so offensively common, I think you are the most uncommon longshore lass on Thames-side."

" Ho ? And in spite o' my 'mane o' tangled 'air'? S'pose you tell my why."

" Your ankles don't match your shoes, your hands are too white, you carry that black head too proudly high and sometimes forget to drop your aitches."

"Anything more ? "

" Yes, in spite of your coarse stockings and rough petti-coats, I notice——"

" That'll do, young man ! That'll—do ! I don't want none o' your impidence nor shameless talk——"

" Good lord—no ! Nothing was farther from my thoughts. I was simply going to observe——"

" Then don't ! You've observed quite enough of me."

" Oh no ! The more I see of you, the more there is to see, because——"

" My gracious ! Young man, whatever are you asaying of ? Don't think because I'm only me and rows a boat I'm to be took liberties with by the likes o' you or——"

" Now, damme," exclaimed Robin indignantly, " what sort of fellow do you take me for ? "

" I don't take you ! " she retorted instantly, with flash of white teeth. " I wouldn't take you at any price ; no, not if you was to offer yourself on your bended knees—with your pretty baby curls ! "

" Your black mane will be snowy white before I do, and even then I shouldn't, of course."

" Young man, who is she ? "

" Who is who ? "

" Her as you was in love with—last time ? "

" She is the first and will be the last ! " said Robin with youthful fervour. " For me there can never be any other."

" Jilted you, did she, young man ? "

" Certainly not ! She chose to marry a—a better man, and her choice is mine."

" That's wot you say, but I knows better."

" What, pray ? "

" She couldn't abide your pretty golden hair, and no wonder, no more can I ; so why don't you get your 'at and hide it ? "

" It's quite evident you are trying to annoy me, and I'm wondering why ? Not that it matters in the least. Whatever you do or say cannot affect me, my poor girl."

" I'm not your girl."

" No, of course not ! I merely——"

" So don't think as I ever would be your girl."

" Heaven forbid ! No no, the idea appals me."

" I wouldn't look at you ! "

" But you do ; you're staring at me now, and—by George, I never saw eyes so blue or more——"

" More what ? " she demanded.

And after brief pause, Robin answered :

" Beautiful."

Here the eyes in question instantly veiled themselves beneath lashes black as her hair, and after another brief pause she exclaimed :

" Yah—gammon ! "

Robin winced like a startled horse, gazed into the eyes that were looking up at him again, and frowned because of the mocking smile that curved her ruddy lips.

" Diss-gussting ! " he hissed angrily.

" What is ? "

" Such words from—such a mouth ! "

" However, my mouth does to eat with, like my eyes do to see with."

" Oh well," he sighed with hopeless gesture, " I should not have expected anything better of you, in spite of your hands and ankles, since you are indeed precisely what you are."

" Ah, and wot am I ? "

" A much too handsome, very ill-mannered, extremely offensive, hatefully vulgar, perfectly disgusting young female."

The black lashes widened to a blue-eyed glare, the delicate nostrils dilated, rounded bosom surged to fierce, deep-drawn breath ; then, instead of the expected furious tirade, she laughed, saying thereafter breathlessly :

" Yes . . . yes, that's me . . . that's me to a ' T '. So now, young man, I'll tell you, besides all this, I'm——"

" Who is in authority here ? "

The voice uttering these words, though not over-loud, was so imperious in tone that Robin turned to behold the speaker—in which moment was the sudden splash and beat of oars, and, glancing back, he beheld the boatwoman rowing with a sort of desperate fury and yet so skilfully that the light skiff turning in its own length, vanished behind a barge moored nearby. . . . And now it was that Robin, though familiar by sight with all sorts and conditions of men, beheld at last one such as he had never seen.

CHAPTER VI

Introduces a Remarkable Stranger

A FLAXEN-HAIRED, well-tailored Hercules tall as Black John, or very nearly, and of dominating presence, whose face, clean-shaven and bold of outline, was made the more remarkable by steely blue eyes shadowed by thick, black brows in startling contrast to his luxuriant blond hair and neatly trimmed side whiskers. Such was this strange visitor who, with no word or gesture of salutation, strode to the balustrade to scowl down at the river, apparently heedless of all else until Robin, scowling also, exclaimed:

" Well now, damme, but you're a cool customer ! What the devil can your high mightiness want hereabouts ? "

Without troubling to so much as turn his head, the stranger replied :

" Life ! I come seeking life instead of death, to embrace the beloved living instead of mourning the hallowed dead."

" And why here of all places ? "

" Because of all places here is one of many fouled by the tide of this accursed river."

" I resent your adjectives, sir. Thames is a glory and has been a blessing from time immemorial."

" And I repeat, it is accursed and the most damnable of all rivers if its murderous tide has stifled and borne from me the beloved whom I would have made my adored wife."

" If so," said Robin, still addressing his odd visitor's broad back, " you have my condolences—though your ' if ' implies a doubt."

35

" A dreadful doubt ! " sighed the stranger, shaking his fair head mournfully. " And it is to resolve this doubt and know the truth, good or ill, that I come seeking alongside this damned Thames—this insatiate, flesh-devouring monster ! Have you seen or heard of any woman's body being washed ashore hereabout ? "

" Oh yes, far too many, but none lately."

" When was the last ? "

" Seven or eight nights ago."

" Ah, that would be about the time and could be my beloved one ! Did you see her ? Can you describe her—what she was like ? "

" An armful o' filth ! " quoth Mr. Shrig, for this was the moment he thought proper to become visible. And now lifting knobbed stick to hat-brim in grave salutation, he said very solemnly :

" Sir, a fee-male body came ashore below bridge this werry i-dentical morning."

Throwing up his long arms, the stranger reeled back as from an unseen blow and leant against the balustrade, head drooping, as if this blow had been mortal, or almost."

" Dead ! " he gasped. " So . . . she is . . . dead ? "

" Sir," replied Mr. Shrig, his roving glance suddenly fixed and very keen, " no poor creeter could be deader ! Y'see, she ain't all there ; her left foot, or, as you might say, her toddler, is clean gone and ditto her left arm's missing from below the elber, but——"

" Must I be nauseated by these abominable details ? "

" Yessir, you must—for her head, or, as you might say, her tibby, don't show so damaged as you might expect, by reason of her long, thick, grey hair."

" Grey ? " The pitifully drooping form straightened suddenly ; the black brows twitched to a frown above eyes more steel-like than ever ; the too-full lips parted to demand angrily : " D'you tell me her hair is—grey ? "

" As any badger, sir."

" Then what the devil d'you mean by tricking me ? "

" Eh ? Tricking you, sir ? How so ? "

" By causing me to believe this grey-haired miserable old wretch was the dearly beloved I am hoping to find——"

" Dead, sir ? " enquired Mr. Shrig blandly, and never had his expression been milder or more benign.

" What are you daring to suggest ? "

" Only as them as Old Fayther Thames lays ashore is generally werry dead, sir ; their sorrers and pains all forgot e-ternally—I hope ! "

" Ha, now suppose you inform me precisely who and what you are ! "

" A redbreast, sir ; Shrig b' name, chief o' the Bow Street Office."

Here once again this strangest of arrogant strangers behaved unexpectedly, for with sudden, compelling gesture he seized Mr. Shrig's hand in immensely powerful grip, wrung it hard, shook it heartily, freed it as suddenly and said with the utmost finality :

" Now by all that's lucky you are the very fellow I require ! So, Jasper Shrig, serve me you shall ! "

" Sir," murmured Mr. Shrig, cherishing his crushed fingers, " all I responds is ar, so soon as you tell me the how, the wherefore and the when."

" And, my good fellow, your service shall be duly requited : the recovery or discovery of my beloved lost one. To the which end I will unfold my woeful tale, open my grievous heart to you——"

" Then," said Robin abruptly, " he'd better do it in the parlour, Jasper."

" Parlour indeed ? My good Shrig, who is this graceless young man ? "

" Sir, you—if you'll trouble to look, you'll behold Mr. Robin Dale, Ess-quire."

Here and for the first time the stranger turned to survey Robin, and even as they confronted one another antagonism was born. Then the stranger bowed with ironic flourish of his hat, Robin merely nodded, and Mr. Shrig spoke: " Mr. Robin, sir, the vord being ' parlour ', let's go."

CHAPTER VII

In which Count Hugo Explains

THIS PARLOUR, once four loose-boxes and still faintly redolent of horses, was now a place of orderly comfort, thanks to Black John's assiduous care. Against one wall stood a well-filled bookcase, another was tastefully festooned with boxing-gloves or muffles, above and around crossed single-sticks and masks, with in the middle a pair of duelling or small-swords, their narrow, triangular blades glittering evilly. Against a third wall hung fishing-rods and tackle with a pair of splendid sporting guns, while in a corner stood the desk whereat Robin was wont to transact such business as was necessary.

Upon this desk the stranger laid his modish hat and gold-mounted cane and, selecting the most comfortable of the easy chairs, commanded his hearers' attention with wide-armed, imperious gesture, saying :

" Now, my very good fellows, you must know that I am Hugo St. John Despard, Count of the Holy Roman Empire and——"

" Whoa, sir ! " quoth Mr. Shrig. " I must ax you to hold hard till I'm ready to take you down in my little reader." Here he plucked forth a somewhat battered pocket-book much as if it had been a weapon of offence. " Therefore, Mr. Robin, by your kind leave, I'll use this here desk o' yourn."

" Certainly, Jasper. Perhaps the Count will oblige by removing his impedimenta ! Your stick and hat, sir."

Shrugging those mighty shoulders of his, Count Hugo complied. Then, opening his note-book, Mr. Shrig said :

" Now, Mr. Count sir, I——"

" No no, Shrig, you will call me simply ' Count ', a title seldom heard in England, but I have lived much abroad in Spain, Italy and India, where at one time I commanded the Chundra Irregular Horse."

" And werry nice, too ! " murmured Mr. Shrig, busied with moistened pencil. " Present occipation, sir ? "

" You may write me down a philosopher, a seeker of Truth."

" Better and better, sir, for so am I. And Truth, being such a remarkable slippery customer, may need a precious lot o' seeking ! Now your res-i-dence, sir, or place of a-bode ? "

" Framling Manor, beside the Thames."

" Ar, about ten miles upstream, a werry old place vith a tower, dungeons and a flibbertyjibbet or ghost."

" Ah, you know the place, it seems ? "

" I did, sir, years ago, b' reason o' said ghostly wisitant."

" But surely you, a hard-headed law officer, don't believe in such nonsense."

" Sir, you'd be ass-tounded how werry much I can believe, so now I'll ax you con-sarning your wanished dear one : her age, condition, complexion, vith distinguishing marks if any, birth or othervise."

" Ha ! " exclaimed Sir Hugo, leaning back in his chair. " The vital subject at last, so attend now and hear me ! The lady in question—lady, mark you, for her father was a baronet of long and distinguished ancestry—is the elder of two sisters, my beloved and legal ward Lady Aramanthea Meredith, and——"

" Ara—— " Mr. Shrig's busy pencil faltered. " Sir," he sighed. " I must ax you to spell same."

" You may write her down as ' Thea '. She is aged twenty-two and the exact opposite of Rosemary, her gentle, golden-haired sister, being tall, dark as a gipsy and as lawless——"

" Twenty-two," muttered Mr. Shrig, writing busily, " of marriageable age and heiress to much property, a great fortun' and——"

" I did not say so ! "

" No more you did, sir."

" Then how dare you presume to set down such statement ? "

" From con-cloosions drawed, sir."

" From what, man, what ? "

" Obserwation, sir. Now as regards her wanishing act——"

" What grounds have you for assuming her to be an heiress ? "

" Count Hugo sir, ekko alone responds. So whose elder daughter is she ? "

" Of my deeply lamented friend Colonel Sir Richard Meredith, who received a wound at Waterloo from which eventually he died, leaving his two motherless daughters to my devoted care, making me, in fact, their sole and legal guardian."

" And now, sir, the why-for and how of her wanishing and specially her reason for same ? "

" Because I repeat, and grieve to so affirm, she is of a most wilful and headstrong nature, defiant of all authority, no matter how gentle."

" Meaning your authority, sir ? "

" Mine or any. She is a born rebel."

" Vich brings us to the how she took vings, and spite o' your loving care, and flew——"

" She seized the opportunity while I was from home. She and her sister Rosemary stole down to the boathouse meaning to row off together heaven only knows where and had actually launched the boat. Thea was already in it when my poor brother Claude caught them and attempted to prevent their folly, when Thea, like the fiery, tameless creature she is, felled him with an oar, then, crying out she would return later for Rosemary, rowed away, leaving my devoted, most unhappy brother weltering in his blood. This was eight days ago, since when her fate is an ever-deepening and more tormenting mystery, for nothing has been heard of her since she rowed out into this accursed river.

" Leaving aforesaid brother Claude wallering in his gore, but all alive and kicking—I hope."

" He is alive, thank God ! But my harassing thought and dread is—that Thea, believing she had murdered him, may have committed suicide to escape the frightful consequences."

" Or, Count Hugo, sir, she may have been overset and drownded by accident."

" Not at all likely, for she is an expert oarswoman and swims like a mermaid."

" Vich same," mused Mr. Shrig, " being a lady-like fish, can't be expected to drown ! Consequently at this i-dentical moment she may be as lively as your brother Claude, sir. And therefore her sister Rosemary can't and don't inherit sister Thea's immense po-ssessions till body is found, dooly i-dentified and death o' same proved. Though death may be presumed after seven years or thereabouts, I believe, which is enough to try the patience of any man, ah—even poor Job in the Bible vith all his boils, not to mention his——"

" Shrig, what the devil are you twaddling about ? Such meaningless farrago, such confoundedly wordy non-sensical ineptitude ! If you don't perform far better than you talk I shall have small use for you and expect less than nothing of you ! The men I employ must be sharp and the tools I use must be keen—ha yes, by God, and the weapons I handle shall always be—deadly! "

Here Count Hugo rose, seeming to fill the room with his extremely large and most dominating presence.

" But," said he, taking up hat and cane, " man Shrig and company, remember this : for any news of my beloved though murderous virago you shall be well rewarded, indeed paid lavishly, so—do your best ! "

Then, with no word or gesture of farewell, Count Hugo St. John Despard strode out and away like the supremely assured superman he was.

" Well, Jasper," said Robin, when their masterful visitor's heavy footsteps had died away, " what think you of the gentleman ? "

Mr. Shrig made a final note in his " little reader ", beamed down at it and answered :

" A bird o' price, Master Robin ; a werry rare specimen indeed and to be treated according."

" How say you, John ? "

" He'd be a toughish customer to tackle—even for you or me."

" Yes," said Robin, his shapely mouth curving to grim smile, " so much so that I should enjoy tackling him. And between you and me, John, I've a premonition that I shall soon or late, and, old fellow, it will certainly be a ' go ', or so I hope. And now, Jasper and John, how the deuce d'you spell ' gamecock ' ? "

CHAPTER VIII

Of Two Friends

ROBIN was looking about for the best and most conspicuous place in which to affix his newly painted sign, when from a narrow by-street nearby that long ago had been a bowery lane but whose trees and hedges had been ousted by grimy bricks and mortar, rose sound of approaching hoofs with a cheery voice hailing:

" Tantivvy, tally-ho, yoicks, hark forrard! Robin, Robert the Devil? Oh, Dev, where are you?" And into the courtyard pranced a horse bestridden by a slim young gentleman beautifully turned out from jaunty hat to glittering boots and spurs, a rider elegant as his steed and as highbred, whose pleasant, nearly handsome face was adorned by a pair of whiskers so small, fluffy and pale as to be almost invisible. Such, briefly, was Viscount Ragworth, only son and heir to that somewhat formidable nobleman, my lord the Earl of Storringdean.

" Oho, Robin, where the——?"

" Hal-lo, old Rags and Bones! It's good to see you! But what brings you hereabout so unexpectedly?"

" Clia's infant, of course, the new baby. Didn't we arrange to ride over and pay our united respects to parents and—the offspring?"

" Did we, damme?"

" Demme if we didn't, old boy! So jump into your riding toggery and let's be off. I'll lend you a hand if John'll come and hold my horse."

" Another, eh, Rags?"

" Yes; what do you think of him? I had him only

44

two——" Here the animal in question attempted to stand on his head, and, being checked in masterly fashion, reared in protest, and, checked again, snorted, capered, shivered and finally subsided. "Two days," the Viscount continued serenely. "How d'you like him, old fellah?"

"I don't!"

"Eh, you don't? Why the dooce not?"

"Because he isn't a horse."

"Oh? Well, what is he?"

"A tempest on hoofs."

"Ha, by jove, the very thing! I've been ditched for a suitable name and you've hit it first shot! 'The Tempest' he shall be! Oh, John, Black John, show a leg——"

"Here, my lord."

"And in prime condition as usual, eh, John! I'll shake hands if you'll favour me by holding my Tempest; he's feeling his oats, a trifle fresh and playful this morning."

"Playful?" repeated Robin. "He's a menace!"

"No more so than your Cannonball! However, cut off now and get ready; make the best of yourself for Clia's lovely sake, not to mention Sir Oliver." To the which purpose indoors went Robin forthwith, while the Viscount and John strolled to and fro with Tempest, which highly sensitive creature, soothed and gentled by Black John's voice and touch, had become the most docile of creatures—to his owner's profound admiration.

"Marvellous!" exclaimed the Viscount. "Look at him now, meek and mild as a confounded lamb! You've a wonderful way with all animals, John, especially horses and dogs! Can't think how or why! Must be sheer magic. Can you explain it?"

"P'raps because I'm fond of 'em, sir."

"So am I, and so is Robin, but we haven't your power over 'em. Yes, demme, all creatures seem to acknowledge your mastery."

"Except women!" sighed John, shaking his black head mournfully. "And most especially one, my lord, as you know."

"Meaning Jemima."

"No other, my lord, and never will be. Y'see, she still thinks of me as 'The Terror' and hardly looks my way, though no sucking dove could be softer nor yet milder than I am when we meet. Yet it don't seem to serve; she hardly troubles to notice me."

"Then why not terrify her till she does?"

"Terrify . . . Jemima?"

"Certainly; gently, of course! A little terror properly used, John, would at least attract her notice. By the way, how's the farm doing?"

"Prime, my lord! We can sleep a hundred and two at a pinch. But Master Robin has turned us into a club to be called the Gamecock's Roost."

"And, b'jingo, that's prime, too! Couldn't be bettered!"

"And your hundred pound, my lord, did a power o' good and was truly and gratefully appreciated."

"Well, there's more when wanted, John old boy. Grand idea—sleep the homeless, feed the hungry and so on! Whenever funds are short, let me know; Dev's a bit shy that way, so you must keep me informed, John."

"Yessir. And I've often wondered, my lord, why you sometimes call him 'Dev'?"

"Short for Robert the Devil, John, because he was, especially when we were younger, fight, swim, row, shoot, climb—anything and anybody, for ever daring Old Nick. And talking of the Devil, here he is!"

Thus presently these two young men, but old friends, astride their horses Cannonball and Tempest, set forth on this ride which was to prove momentous to both and fateful for one.

CHAPTER IX

Tells of Babies and a Fateful Meeting

WITH THE roar of London behind them and the open road before, away they went at full gallop, neck and neck, across Blackheath, but gradually the Viscount's lighter weight told and he was two lengths ahead when he checked for the long ascent of Shooters Hill, saying :

"You'll never make a jockey, old fellah, too much beef and bone."

"But not an ounce of fat, damme ! However," said Robin as their horses ambled up the hill, "we've taken some of the devil out of them, and your Tempest is a bit blown."

"And your Cannonball sweats ! "

"Naturally ! But tell me, Rags, what do you know about babies ? "

"Plenty, old boy ! You see, my cousin Ursula has one, so has my head groom's wife, and they're so much of a muchness it would be impossible to tell 'em apart."

"Have you seen Clia's infant ? "

"Not yet, but it'll be precisely like all the others, of course, and just as unexpected."

"Eh ? What do you mean ? "

"All babies lack restraint, old fellah, consequently they're safest at a distance and far best when fast asleep."

"Safest ? You mean—— ? "

"Exactly ! They're apt to damp one's enthusiasm and what not, and I know because my cousin Ursula persists in insisting that I hold hers every time and——"

" Good lord ! Were you ever—caught ? "

" Caught ? Ah, I see what you mean ! Only once ; ever since, I handed it back in time. And, Dev, babies take a lot of holding, I can tell you ! F'instance, you must never let their heads wobble or roll, and you must hold them either backwards, face up, or front-side down, a fairly intricate business, because they're apt to squirm ; remember this, old boy, if Clia insists on you holding hers, as she will."

" No—d'you really think she may ? "

" Bound to, old boy. All mothers always do ! "

" However, I shall refuse to touch it ! "

" D'ye think she'll let you refuse ? My poor ass, she'll have it in your arms before you know it. All you have to do is to keep a fairly tight hold, say ' Beautiful ' and pass it back as soon as possible."

" Now, damme, but I'm half-minded to turn back."

" Not so, old boy. Remember what the Bible says about the fellah with a plough—no turning back. And as for Clia's baby——"

" That's just it ! The idea that Clia's is precisely like the general run of infants—well—shocks me rather."

" Oh ? Ah ? Why ? "

" Because from what I have been able to observe by a not too close inspection ordinary babies are as bald, toothless and wrinkled as very aged worn-out folk instead of extremely young and new, and anything but beautiful. D'you agree ? "

" I do, old boy. And, what's more, they emit strange sounds, squeaks and what not ; they howl like bandogs or screech like small fiends ! Ursula's is always at it one way or another."

" All things considered, Rags, it seems that infants are unpleasant necessities ! You were, I was, and others must and will be, or nothing whatever could be. We were—babies ! An extremely repulsive thought, Rags."

" True, my dear fellah, and hence one best not to con-
template or harp upon, so let's change the dooced subject."

" Right you are, Rags ! Now listen to this ! " And forthwith Robin told of the Superman and the Vanished
Heiress with such particularity of detail that almost before
his story was ended they came in sight of that long-familiar
cosy inn called the Wheatsheaf.[1]

" Ale ! " sighed Robin, urging Cannonball to speedy
canter.

" Pint tankards ! " said the Viscount, urging Tempest
to a gallop.

Thus very soon they had clattered into the fragrant
stable-yard and were calling lustily for,

" Sam ! "

" Susan ! "

And forth came husband and wife to greet them ; Susan
all smiles and buxom as ever, Sam's hair a little greyer than
of yore, still stiff as usual, his eyes as round beneath those
thick brows still raised wistfully as if asking the question
that was never answered.

" How are you, Sam, old fellah ? "

" Right well, I b'lieve, m' lord."

" And you, Susan, my dear ? "

" The same, Master Robin, and that glad for to see ee,
and my lord, too ; 'tes like old times, that 'tes ! And by
good hap I've a lovely capon, stuffed aturning on the jack
at this minute, wi' apple-pie to follow and clotted cream."

" A capon ! " sighed Robin.

" Apple-pie ! " murmured the Viscount.

" So, my dearies," said she with the loving familiarity
of years, " if ee can wait——"

" We can ! " said Robin.

" We will ! " affirmed the Viscount.

" My Sam shall bring your ale t' ye in the garden."

[1] See *The Crooked Furrow*.

So thither went they to quench their thirst right nobly and breathe an air redolent of the blended sweetness of flower, herb and ripening fruit.

" Lord love us, Rags ! " exclaimed Robin, glancing up and around with shining eyes. " God bless our English countryside ! "

" And such fellahs as Sam to make it bloom like this garden—the yeomen and bowmen, Crécy and Agincourt, not to mention Trafalgar and Waterloo, and thereby the peace and security of such lovely places as this."

" By jingo, old Rags and Bones, some day you'll be an orator, and, what's more, a real statesman ! And you're right. The yeomen of England, sons of the soil and men of the sword to glorify and guard it, yes, and die for it. B'gad, I'm growing eloquent, too—so let's drink to 'em, the yeomen of England ! "

" Old fellow," said Robin, after they had drunk this toast and very solemnly, " how long is it since you saw Clia ? "

" Six months."

" Same here ; of course, we saw her together and I thought her more beautiful than ever."

" And lovelier, Robin ! She will always be—the One, eh, old boy ? "

" Ever and always, Rags ! We are both one-woman men."

" Precisely, Dev ; utterly, eternally, unitedly devoted ! "

" If," sighed Robin, setting down his nearly empty tankard, " it hadn't been for old Noll—who knows ? "

" Ah, who ? " sighed the Viscount.

" She might have chosen one of us, Rags."

" Not a doubt of it—and most probably you, Robin."

" Though very possibly you, my dear old Rags and Bones ; yes, most possibly it might have been you ! "

" Ah ! " murmured the Viscount, gazing down sadly into

his depleted tankard. " The ' might-have-been '—dooced pathetic phrase that ! "

" Heart-rending, Rags ! We both loved and lost ! "

" And were equally blighted, old boy ! Yes, and must ever remain so ! "

" Too infernally true ! " nodded Robin, beginning to scowl. " And all—all by reason of old Oliver ! Had he been anyone else I should have challenged his right, called him out and done my best to shoot the fellow, old fellow."

" Certainly. Like a dog, old boy."

" However, since he is old Noll, we must make the best of it, grin and bear it, Rags ! "

" Bite the bullet, old boy. Though Clia's infant will be the only baby in my life ! "

" Mine, too ! " quoth Robin. Here together they sighed again heavily, together raised their tankards, but in the act of drinking paused, as from the road came a sound of rapidly approaching hoofs and wheels, suddenly checked, and thereafter a clamour of voices and a woman's plaintive cry rising to a scream. . . .

Down went the two tankards, up started the two friends, and were half-way across the garden, when towards them sped a woman, her dainty frills and furbelows uplifted to aid the nimble action of extremely shapely limbs suddenly hidden as, reaching out appealing hands, she gasped :

" Gentlemen—oh—don't let them—drag me back ! "

" Not we ! " said Robin, taking the nearest hand.

" Never ! " said the Viscount, clasping the other in both his own. " Over our dead bodies and what not. Let them come and try."

" Oh, they will, they will. And Claude . . . Claude can be so terrible. . . . They're coming ! "

" Good ! " said Robin, smiling. " Pray step into the arbour and leave Mr. Claude and company to us ! " Turning hastily to do so, she tripped and might have fallen, but with the leap of an antelope the Viscount reached and caught her in his arms, and for a moment her bonneted head lay pillowed on his breast ; for a moment only, but . . . for one at least never was moment more fateful. A look, a sigh, and then :

" Phyllinda ! " cried a commanding voice, and into this hitherto peaceful garden stormed three dark-complexioned fellows in livery led by one a slim, young, too-exquisitely dainty person, yet the very embodiment of Authority (with a capital A), who, beholding the two, halted to survey each from head to foot with a very evident truculence.

" Aha ! " exclaimed Robin, squaring his shoulders. " Spanish brigands, eh, Rags ? "

" No, Italian banditti, old fellah. As for Sir Superbus, this intrusive gentleman, turned out like a buck from top to toe, he should be English, though."

The gentleman in question bowed graciously, but the airy gesture of his riding-whip was a menace and the flourish of his hat a challenge as he said :

" You, sirs, will forgive this intrusion——"

" But we do—not ! " said Robin aggressively. " No, sir. We resent it so much that we demand and insist on your instant departure."

The gentleman smiled, bowed again, and said :

" With the utmost pleasure, though not, oh, most certainly not, until my mission is perfectly accomplished."

" Your mission being what, pray ? "

" To escort this misguided young lady back home. Phyllinda, you hear me ! No more of this folly ! "

" Phyllinda ? " said Robin, as if pondering the name.

" I strongly object to be kept waiting, as you know, Phyllinda ! So take my arm and let us go—at once ! Come, do not force me to compel you."

" And who," Robin demanded offensively, " the devil are you to order or compel this lady ? "

" Her legal guardian's brother, sir ! I am Claude St. John Despard, and, what's more, I——"

" No ! " said Robin bluntly. " We want no more of you. Personally I object to you strongly. Your appearance, your air, your manners and your presence offends me and is evidently even more obnoxious to this terrified lady."

" So ? " exclaimed Mr. Despard. " Then, sir, I warn you——"

" On the contrary, Mr. Despard, I warn you that I am this lady's humbly devoted servant and will not suffer her to be molested."

" Indeed ! " Mr. Despard smiled at his whip, glanced from this to his three silent watchful men, glanced at grim-smiling Robin, at the placid-seeming Viscount, smiled and enquired :

" Such highly unselfish devotion is most chivalrous, of course, and very affecting, but means—precisely what ? "

" That Mistress Phyllinda, distressed by your outrageous pursuit, has sought the protection of my friend and myself."

" But I," said Mr. Despard, " inform and warn you she is an absconding ward who has fled her home and the care of her legal guardian."

" Yes, yes, I have ! " she cried bitterly. " And shall I tell these gentlemen why ? Must I describe your odious persecution of me—your ceaseless hateful——"

" Silence ! " cried Mr. Despard, with graceful though threatening gesture.

" Sir," said the Viscount, confronting him, grim as smiling Robin but far more deadly, " ' persecution ' is a most detestable word ; its infliction demands condign punishment. Say at twelve paces with the necessary tools, favour me by accepting my card and——"

" Certainly not, sir ! I've wasted time enough already.
. . . This damned feminine hysteria ! Phyllinda, do you
return home with me of your own free will or——"

" No ! " she panted, retreating farther into the arbour.
" No—no——"

" Avanti ! " cried Mr. Despard and raised his whip,
whereat the threatening four advanced against the devoted
two.

" Now for it, Rags ! " cried Robin, leaping to snatch up
the nearest of their empty tankards. " Your whip, my fist
and a quart pot, shoulder to shoulder ! "

" The thin red line, old boy ! Steady the Buffs ! Aim
low, strike hard and——"

" 'Old ! " roared a voice. And there, close in the attackers'
rear, stood Sam with his famous brass bell-mouthed
blunderbuss levelled. " 'Old ! " he bellowed. " All o' you
furrineers 'old 'ard ! Stand and don't ee move or I b'leeve
most of ee'll get peppered very 'ot, seein' as 'ow I be loaded
wi' buck-shot, bits o' glass and a bent nail or so, which if
I pull trigger might come a bit sharp like, I b'leeve. So I'll
ax ee all to git out o' my gardin ' ! "

Startled by Sam's sudden roar and dismayed by the yawning muzzle of his levelled weapon, the invaders retreated
sullenly to the road ; only Mr. Despard remained to nod and
smile at them, saying :

" Rejoice and triumph now while you can ! If you can,
laugh, gentlemen, laugh ! Ah, but rest perfectly assured this
is merely the beginning ! What is to be shall prove no laughing matter for any of you. And, Phyllinda, for whatever
evil the future may bring—as it shall—you and your folly
are to blame. So laugh you now and be merry, for tomorrow
—ah, tomorrow ? " Then Mr. Despard saluted them with
an ironic bow, leaving Sam, blunderbuss at shoulder,
staring after him very wistfully, until out from a certain
window came his wife's buxom head to demand :

" Sam, whatever be ee doing wi' that nasty thing ? "

" Nothing, m' dear," he replied, with mournful shake of his head, " and I don't b'leeve I ever shall, though so wishful for to try a shot."

" Fie—don't ee talk so vicious, Sam ! Come you indoors this moment and put that murdersome thing away and help me shell they peas."

CHAPTER X

In Which the Lady Explains

THEY WERE in the arbour, and Robin sat as though enthralled, for she had taken off her shady bonnet, and thus he beheld hair of the exact and only proper colour, that is to say, richly yellow as ripe corn, silky, lustrous, Clia-like; while the Viscount gazed in awed rapture at a face of singular beauty made lovely also by its inherent gentleness. Furthermore he was aware of a form whose shapeliness her high-waisted robe displayed with her every graceful movement. . . .

Such (and all too briefly) was she who, throned in beauty, between these two friends, parted them one from another and, alas, in more senses than one, as, glancing from the Viscount to Robin and back again, she enquired very shyly :

"Please may I know who . . . to whom I am so . . . so deeply indebted and so truly grateful ? "

"Well," answered Robin, laughing a little ruefully, "I think our united gratitude is due to Sam——"

"And his blunderbuss ! " added the Viscount.

"However," said Robin, "I take pleasure to present my friend, and your other humble servant, Mortimer Randolf Deverill, Viscount Ragworth, known to his intimates as 'Rags and Bones' or merely 'Rags'."

"Precisely ! " said the Viscount, bowing. "And it is my pleasure to present Mr. Robert Dale, commonly known as 'Robin' or merely 'Rob'."

"And I," said she, glancing at Robin again but gazing at the Viscount, "I—in whose defence you—you were both willing to shed your blood, I am Rosemary Phyllinda Meredith, called by—by those who love me, 'Linda' or simply 'Phyl'; and because in this short time you have proved such good, kind friends, I would have you call me just plain 'Phyl'."

"Impossible!" said the Viscount instantly.

"Quite!" said Robin.

"Oh? Pray—why?"

"Because," answered Robin, "you never could be."

"Plain!" said the Viscount.

At this, and for the first time, she laughed, then shook her head, saying:

"I suppose I should inform you why I ran away."

"There is no need!" said Robin.

"Not the least!" added the Viscount.

"Oh, but I ought to, I should like to, so I will—if you will allow me to. May I?"

"Of course!" answered Robin.

"I shall be honoured!" said the Viscount.

"Well then, I—I fled my detested guardian Count Hugo because I was afraid he would terrify me into—marriage with his even more detestable brother Claude, who—oh, who——"

"Is no fit husband for such as you!" said Robin.

"Not to be thought of!" added the Viscount.

"Oh, but he compelled me to think of it daily, hourly, ever since we left Italy, and I have always been afraid of him, and lately even more so! You see, I am not a heroine; not a bit brave like my sister Thea, who is never afraid, not even of Claude! She is as valiant as our noble father who fought and died for our dear England——"

"Then all honour to him!" said Robin.

"Amen!" the Viscount responded.

"And because my sister is so fearless she planned our escape and fought Claude off with the oar and rowed away along the dark river to London. I should be with her now if only I could be more like her and not such a dreadful, silly coward as I am ! "

"And pray," enquired the Viscount gently, "where should you have sought refuge ? "

"With our dear father's old friend, the Duchess of Camberhurst."

"And, by jingo," exclaimed Robin, "from all accounts you could never find a more powerful champion, eh, Rags ? You know her grace, don't you ? "

"Yes, she is my father's age-long friend also."

"And a regular fire-eating, formidable old lady, eh, old Rags and Bones ? "

"The Guards at Waterloo, m' dear fellah, the Light Brigade in the Peninsular, the pick of Nelson's fighting crews at Trafalgar, mix 'em up, boil 'em down, and you have—Her Grace of Camberhurst ! "

"She sounds rather—awful ! " sighed Phyllinda.

"She does," smiled the Viscount reassuringly, "and she is, but only when necessary. But do you not know her, Miss Phyllinda ? "

"No, and neither does Thea. Oh, how I wish we did. All we do know is that she is now in London—a place called Saint James's Square. And this is why I am becoming so terribly, terribly anxious, because if Thea ever arrived there safely, why—oh, why have I had no word, no news of her all these days ? Why ? "

"The question is," said Robin, instinctively changing the subject, "what of yourself ? "

"I don't know," she sighed, with hopeless gesture. "I drove this far in the phaeton, but Claude has taken it and with all my money and other things in it, so here I am penniless and destitute."

"That need cause you no least anxiety," said the Viscount, "so please don't worry on that account. Our present and most pressing concern is——"

"Dinner, gen'lemen!" quoth Sam, peering in at them and touching an imaginary hat-brim. "Dinner be ready, sirs, I b'leeve, leastways so my Soosan do tell—a chicken stuffed, wi' green peas noo-picked and——"

"Joy!" exclaimed Robin, taking Phyllinda's right hand.

"Rapture!" murmured the Viscount, taking her left, though very diffidently.

"Wi' apple-pie t' foller, sirs, I b'leeve, not t' mention cream clotted and——"

CHAPTER XI

Tells how the Sweet Spirit of Friendship was Ousted by the Demon called Rivalry

THE CHICKEN (stuffed) with all that followed had become a happy memory; Phyllinda had retired to prepare for the road, with Susan's motherly aid; and the two friends sat neither looking at the other and in a pensive silence nowise induced by the late chicken nor even its memory.

" Yes ! " said Robin at last.

" What ? " enquired the Viscount.

" She is an amazingly beautiful creature ! "

" Yes ! " said the Viscount.

" Though, of course, her eyes are quite wrong ! "

" Eh ? Wrong ? Now what the devil —— ? "

" I mean they're the wrong colour to go with her glorious hair. With such splendour they should be blue instead of brown—if they are brown."

" Violet ! " said the Viscount.

" Well, with such hair her eyes should —— "

" No ! With such eyes any hair would be perfect ! "

" However, I fail to see what possible objection you can have to my escorting her to Clia's tender care—to Abbeymead."

" It's perfectly obvious, m' dear fellah. We, you and I, are committing a serious felony, crime and what not."

" Are we, b'jingo ? And how so ? "

" By abducting a young lady from her home and legal guardian and she still an infant in the eyes of the law."

" Ha ! Well, what has this to do with Abbeymead ? "

" The fact that Abbeymead is the home of your governor,

Sir Oliver Dale, who is a magistrate and, as you know, a rare stickler for law and order, duty for duty's sake and so on——"

" Very well, then why object to my escorting her to Aunt Rosamond for the time being ? "

" Because the ' Waterman ' is no fit place——"

" Not fit ? Now what the devil——"

" It being in the very worst part of the riverside squalor. And, what's more, Lady Rosamond, God bless her, has work and anxieties enough already, and——"

" And why," demanded Robin, leaning across the table to frown, " should you drive with her to your governor at Storringdean ? "

" Sam will drive her there in his gig ; I shall ride Tempest——"

" Don't palter, man ! Why should I permit you to carry her off to Storringdean ? "

" Again it's all perfectly obvious," said the Viscount, flicking a breadcrumb from his shirt-frill. " Storringdean is nearer London ; my father, as I've told you, is friendly with the Duchess ; and consequently Miss Phyllinda will——"

" Have the pleasure of your company, eh, Ragworth ? Is that your game ? Is it ? "

" ' Game ' ? " enquired the Viscount, glancing up at angry Robin beneath raised brows.

" Game, yes ! You know, you understand what I meant, damme ! "

" No ! " murmured the Viscount. " Damn you, I refuse to understand ! "

" Then, b'gad, I'll tell you plainly as I can. You would ride off with Beauty and leave Friendship in the lurch. You'll make your confounded hay in the infernal sunshine and leave me in the mire, the very Slough of Despond ! You love her already and——"

" Yes, I do."

" Well, so do I, most truly—sincerely and for only the second time in my life."

" Same here ! " murmured the Viscount.

" Well now, seeing this is so, my life's happiness being at stake, I shall fight for it—to my last breath."

" Again, same here ! "

" Consequently, Ragworth, I will not permit you to go—gallivanting off with her to Storringdean, London, and the Lord knows where, making your cursed sheep's-eyes at her and urging your suit behind my back. I say you shall not ! Now do I make myself clear ? "

The Viscount nodded, saying :

" Too plainly, very coarsely and without warrant. For I'm no such headlong wooer or hasty amorist as yourself and should scorn to take advantage of any man."

" Tush and the devil, Ragworth ! There's that foul saying that ' all's fair in love and war '——"

" Yes, it is an adage very foul, Dale ! So vile and un-sportsmanlike, indeed, that it is beneath the conception of such as myself—if only for my father's sake and most honourable name."

" Very fine ! " sneered Robin. " But even you, despite the noble earl your father, your ancestry, blue-blood and all the rest of it, even you, my lord Viscount, are only human, she is beautiful and——"

" Stop ! "

The Viscount's tone was not loud, his brow quite un-ruffled, but in voice and look was that which checked Robin's outburst and caused him to open those grey eyes of his rather wider than usual, though his frown grew the blacker as the Viscount continued.

" I have allowed you to say more than I would take from any other man alive, and therefore I suggest you change the subject or quit my company, for I will endure no more of your clumsy insults ! "

Up started Robin so violently that over went his chair with a resounding crash.

"Ragworth," said he thickly, "damme but I'm minded to throw you out of the window!"

"Then," said the Viscount, with slight though eloquently contemptuous gesture, "I suggest you change your mind, for both our sakes. If you are determined to force a quarrel, do so, but at least—like a gentleman or as much so as you find possible."

Robin crouched and clenched his fists; the Viscount sighed and took up the empty wine bottle. But at this moment the door, which had been ajar, swung wide to show Phyllinda cloaked and bonneted; and once again she glanced at handsome stalwart Robin, but gazed at the slender Viscount. Then, before she could speak, in at the open lattice came Sam's bristly head to announce:

"Me and my gig be awaiting, m' lord!"

"So am I!" said Phyllinda, and, taking his hand, she led him where Robin stood gazing blankly at nothing in particular, to whom she now proffered her hand, saying and very tenderly:

"Dear Mr. Dale, I want to thank you, so won't you please bid us farewell?"

So Robin took this small, appealing hand in both his own, raising it to his lips, then, uttering no word, strode out into the sunny garden. . . . And presently, seated in the shady arbour, he heard Susan call a cheery goodbye and thereafter the crack of Sam's whip, then the sound of hoofs and wheels growing ever fainter with distance till all around him was silence except for the drowsy hum of insects, sleepy twitter of sparrows and the plaintive song of a blackbird.

So in this same arbour, where years ago another man as youthful had sat[1] feeling just as hopeless, as solitary and

[1] See *The Crooked Furrow*.

desolate, but in no such evil temper, here now gloomed young Robin.

Insects hummed, birds twittered, day mellowed to evening, while Robin sighed and scowled, until came Susan at last to enquire with motherly solicitude :

" Why, Master Robin, my dearie, whatever be wrong with ee to look so sadly fearsome ? "

" Fearsome ? Do I, Sue ? "

" Ay and so murder-like as my Sam's nasty blunderbush ! What be troubling of ee ? Come now," said she, stroking his close-cut auburn curls, " tell thy Soosan as have loved ee since ever ee were a boy, is she thy grief, yon lovesome young lady ? "

" Ah, Susan," he groaned, " she is the only other woman I could have loved and—she's gone ! Again—yes, again it seems love is not for me. Ha, and all because of Ragworth, damn him ! "

" Hush now, and fie, Master Robin ; that be no way to talk——"

" I tell you he's been making confounded sheep's-eyes at her ever since she appeared—she, the only other woman— and Ragworth ! He and she are together now and I—alone, left in the lurch as usual ! Why the devil should others win and I always lose ? There's a curse on me, it seems."

" Whatever do ee mean ? A curse ? Such wicked non-sense ! Come now indoors wi me, my dearie. I be agoing to brew tea, so come thy ways now ! Tea be good for most ills, 'specially curses, so come along o' Soosan."

So it was in glow of late sunset that Robin mounted his horse, eager to be gone, but, seeing how Susan stared up at him with an almost dreadful anxiety, he checked his restive animal to enquire :

" What is it, my dear ? "

" You ! " she replied, clasping her hands. " 'Tes you, Master Robin. Changed you be and—changing ! "

" Well, all earthly things must change, Susan, and I'm confoundedly earthly. There's nothing heavenly about me ; there never was."

" Oh, but yes, my dearie ! There was times years ago, afore you growed so big and strong, when you could show like a very angel o' God, wi' your golden curls and them lovely eyes ! Ah, but now—you'm changed ! "

" More like a devil nowadays, eh, Sue ? "

" I never say so, Master Robin."

" But your eyes did, Susan, and they are telling me so at this moment. Oh well, angel or devil, I shall always love you, Susan, for those boyhood days that seem so far and long ago. You with your dear motherly ways and Sam with his blunderbuss. D'you remember the day he let me fire it, bless his heart, and how you boxed his ears ? "

" Ay, dearie, I mind the day, and so I did sure-ly, though not very hard."

" D'you still—pray for me, Susan ? "

" And always shall, Master Rob ! "

" Well, that's a comfort, considering."

" What, my dearie ? "

" How very uncertain life is."

" Whatever do ee mean now ? "

" One of us, Sue, may be fated to die, and I hope to God it will be myself, my fairly useless self."

" No—no ! " she cried, lifting her hands as if in prayer. " You be too young to die ; you that be so hale and strong, how could ee die ? "

" By a stroke most likely—and suddenly, I hope ! Ha, now damme what a pitiful fool am I to trouble you with such confounded nonsense. Forgive it, my dear ; forgive it and forget." Then, stooping from his saddle, he kissed her as he had not done since boyhood days, then rode away through the sunset that was so very like blood.

CHAPTER XII

Tells how Robin Became " A Man Possessed "

IN OLDEN days, when life was simple, it was believed that folk could be possessed of devils, spirits good and bad, whereby they were empowered for high achievement or compelled to the commission of sin against God and their fellows, and all without their own volition.

Be this how it may, certain it is that as Robin fared Londonwards through the ever-deepening shadows he rode not alone, for with him at either ear crouched two spirits of evil, and the name of one was Jealousy and of the other Hate. And now by these unseen though very potent devils he was harassed and tormented as many a poor soul has been in the past and will be in the future, alas! For these spirits of wickedness, though unseen and never heard by happier mortals, can to the doomed be very eloquent, and it was thus they now urged and tormented Robin :

JEALOUSY : He is with her now, looking into her eyes, kissing her perhaps ; she may even be in his arms, or—he in hers.

HATE : While you ride in loneliness, a man forlorn and desolate—because of him. Well then, punish him. Strike him down! All women love and admire the conqueror! Strike him down!

JEALOUSY : The longer you allow them together the shorter will be your chance and the surer your loss. For him her kisses, her lovely self ; for you solitude and desolation.

HATE : So, haste, make haste to smite him down!

Be his master, spare his life, but lay him low and she
shall yet be yours.

JEALOUSY : Yes, yes, make haste! The longer you
permit his wooing, the less your chance of winning.

HATE : Hurl him from between you and your dear
desire. Away with him for life or death, and your
conquering arms shall assuredly clasp her as your own
—your wife. So up and at him! Smite him down!

Plagued thus and harassed almost to distraction, Robin
came at last to the Gamecock's Roost, and there, having
groomed and stabled his beloved Cannonball, strode
indoors to meet John's hearty greeting with a perfunctory
nod and, refusing supper, sat at his desk in the corner,
snuffed candles, trimmed quill and began to scrawl the
message whereto his evil spirits urged and compelled him
—thus :

" To Viscount Ragworth.

" MY LORD,
" The words uttered by you at our last meeting leeve
me no rekorse but to demand another and with the
neccessary implyments, sords or pistoles to suit yourself,
and there can be no better plaice than the cortyard
here. And I suggest sharps as steel makes less noys and
shall do our bisness hansomly and with less chance of
interfearance. My ernest hope is to be done speedily,
tomorrow or soon as possible.
                              " Yours, etc.,
                                   " ROBERT DALE."

Having scanned this ill-spelt, devil-inspired screed, and
added a comma here and there, he sanded, wafered and
sealed it (while Jealousy chuckled and Hate laughed), then
he summoned Sergeant George to bear it at once to the

Viscount's lodgings in Jermyn Street with orders to await an answer, or, if the Viscount was in the country, that it must be sent on to him immediately.

This wickedness accomplished, forth went Robin to pace the courtyard restlessly, to think of Phyllinda and watch the moon come up in ever-waxing splendour, by whose gentle magic, hideous bricks and mortar, grime and squalor were all transformed to things of beauty and the old river a scintillant mystery ; but even now his twin devils haunted him until indoors he strode and up to bed, there, for a wonder, to be blessed almost at once by deep, refreshing, dreamless slumber.

CHAPTER XIII

Lady of Thames

IT WAS early morning and glad with sunlight, wherefore Old Father Thames in his gayest mood was singing his age-old song of joy and grief, hope and despair, life and death, as he has done from time immemorial. . . . Thus on rolled the river, its broad bosom all asparkle with this early sunshine amid which glory, storm-battered ships, homing from afar, rode in a splendid tranquillity.

Into this radiant morning stepped Robin, who, having no mind for company or breakfast, launched the lightest of his three boats and rowed away upstream. And thus, after some while, instead of grimy brick and mortar, was open country green and lush where cattle browsed, larks carolled and a voice cried :

" Watto, young man ! "

Glancing over his shoulder, he beheld her whom he knew as Bet seated in her skiff with idle oars.

" Aho ! " she exclaimed, as he drew level. " And a precious dismal, damn-y'-eyes young man y' look ! Wot's matter ? Was y' drunk last night ? "

" Drunkenness isn't a pastime of mine so far, but thanks for the idea ; maybe I'll have a go at it and——"

" That's fool's talk ! For though I don't like your goldi-locks, your eyes is good, clear and bright 'stead o' bleary and bloodshot. And your face ain't so bad as some ; it ain't blotched and bloated—yet."

" Ha, so, my Lady of Thames, you find my phiz not so bad as faces go ? Well, neither is yours, in spite of your black mane."

" It ain't a mane ; 'tis fine and soft as silk."

" I've only your word for it."

" But you've got things in your face wot look like eyes, so use 'em."

" Come a little nearer and I will." With deft stroke of oar she urged her light craft so close that he might have touched her—almost.

" Well ? " she demanded.

" Very ! " he answered. " And if you'll come just a little nearer I——"

" Oh no, not me ! And keep your distance, young man, or——" She paused, as towards them came a boat rowed by two stalwart young fellows in smart uniforms, each of whom grinned and saluted her as they swept by.

"And them," said she, glancing askance at Robin, "them's officers o' the noo River Patrol. One's Sergeant Fallon and t'other's Sergeant Batson."

" Ha ! " quoth Robin, frowning. " They're friends of yours, it seems ? "

" Well, they ain't my enemies, and, wot's more, they know my uncle."

" So you have an uncle ? "

" Why shouldn't I 'ave an uncle ? Him and me lives together——"

" Where ? "

" Never you mind ! "

" And is he a man of the river ? "

" No, he was a soldier and fought at Waterloo, which is more than you ever did—with your golden curls ! "

" No, I wasn't there," Robin admitted, his head drooping. " I ought to have been a soldier ; fighting is about all I'm good for, it seems ! A soldier ? And that's another idea, Bet."

" Young man, I never told you my name was Bet."

" No, your boat did."

" Well, don't go makin' so free wi' your ' Bets '."

" Certainly not."

" And you told me ' Bet ' was a very common name."

" Yes, so it is—and so it isn't. It all depends on who bears it—Queen Elizabeth, for instance—so, proud Lady of the River, may I call you ' Bet ' ? "

" Oh—if you like."

" Then, Bet, what do you propose to do this fine morning ? "

" I'm agoing to row two mile or so upstream for to buy milk an' butter an' eggs."

" Then may I go with you ? "

" Don't say ' my pretty maid ' like the silly old song."

" I wasn't going to. Besides, you're not pretty ! "

" Oh, ain't I, ' kind sir, she said ' ? "

" No, you're too handsome ever to be pretty."

" In spite o' my black 'air ? "

" Yes. Now what about those eggs and things ? "

" Can y' row ? "

" Sometimes I almost fancy I can ! "

" Then let's see ! " In went her oars with a strong, smooth sweep, and away shot the light skiff to show the letters B.E.T. upon its narrow transom ; then after her went Robin, pulling a longer stroke to draw level. But when after some while he glanced over his shoulder the letters B.E.T. had drawn even farther ahead. Robin frowned, squared his powerful shoulders, lengthened his stroke and rowed harder, counted twenty, glanced round, and there, far ahead as ever, those letters seemed to mock and defy him. Robin scowled and quickening his stroke, rowed with all his strength and every part of him. And thus when he drew level with her at last, she lay on her oars to laugh and jeer at him, though very breathlessly :

" Oh my—I've made ye—sweat—young—man—and

your baby curls—all wet and—curlier and—more baby-like than ever! So don't frown so man-like and—bad-tempered!"

"I'm not—in the least—bad tempered," he retorted pantingly.

"Then try to—smile if—you can."

"I can and will—when I—feel inclined."

"Do you ever?"

"Now and then."

"But oftener 'then' than 'now'—eh, young man?"

"My name is Robin, as I told you"

"Oh, did ye? I must ha' forgot."

"Then pray remember to call me so instead of 'young man'."

"Well now, as we've both got our breath back, let's go on more easy-like."

So in went oars and forward they rowed slowly side by side and near as possible. And each time that he glanced at her (which was very often) it was to find her gazing at him with eyes that met his unwavering and with look of impish mockery.

"Aho!" she exclaimed suddenly. "I don't think you're a bit like a robin Robin. Robins whistle and sing so pretty and you don't do nothing but frown that fretful as I dunno wot! And the sun so bright and the water so sparkly an' all! Wot's matter wi' you? Is it a pain in your inside or only love?"

Robin scowled again at radiant sky and water, then sighed deeply and shook his head at her, saying:

"Ah, Bet, don't mock me, for indeed I have recently suffered a loss and bitter disappointment!"

"A woman, eh, Robin?"

"Yes, of course."

"Not like me, I s'pose, poor and common and wi' black 'air?"

" No, her hair is like a—a glory of sun on ripe corn ; a golden splendour, Bet ! "

" And is she very beautiful ? "

" Yes—oh, very ! And her name is lovely as herself."

" Nothing so low and common as Bet, I s'pose, eh ? "

" No, nothing at all like it. Hers is a name that sings ! "

" Lorks ! 'Ow can any name sing ? "

" Hers can and does. It sings in my ears now and always will ! Listen, Bet—what do you think of Phyllinda as a name ? "

Bet evidently thought so well of it that her oars faltered suddenly, but all she said, and again quite breathlessly, was :

" Oh ! "

" Don't you think that is a truly beautiful name, a small sweet song in itself ? "

" Yes—oh yes. But you've lost her, did y' say ? Not—dead ? "

" Oh no, she's very much alive, thank God, and now should be safe in the care of a very great lady. Ah, but there's another fellow in love with her, damn him—and he's extremely rich, Bet, a man of title and I'm neither."

" Ah, then poor you ! "

" Yes, I'm a miserable, confoundedly mournful dog, doomed to failure in love, always fated to lose what I most desire ! Bet, I'm accursed ! "

" Yet you look very strong and healthy."

" Yes, I am," he admitted dejectedly. " Yes, physically I'm well enough, but mentally I'm a—a confounded, shattered wreck and going to pieces—fast ! "

Here she ceased rowing to shake her handsome head at him and ejaculate :

" Lorks ! " And thereafter : " Gammon ! "

Whereat he also ceased rowing to say reproachfully :

" If you have no sympathy, for pity's sake do—not spit such detestable words at me."

To which she retorted :

" Though I'm no beautiful lady, I ain't so common as to spit—even at you ! "

" Ah, Bet," he sighed reproachfully, " you're worse than merely common ; you're hard-hearted and cruel."

" Then why don't you leave me ? "

" Because I enjoy your ungracious company and I'll be shot if I know why—and, b'gad, I probably shall be."

" Wot shall y' be ? "

" Shot, Bet."

" Oh ? Why and who by ? "

" Never you mind, and no matter. Shall we go on ? "

" No, we're there."

" Where ? "

" At Brent's Farm, silly, b'ind them trees. So 'ere's where I land and say goodbye."

And, turning her skiff very dexterously, she ran its sharp bow ashore. Robin did the same, at which she frowned and demanded :

" Didn't I say goodbye ? "

" You did, but I did not. So with your kind permission I'll wait for you."

" You ain't got my permission," said she, taking up a large market basket and stepping ashore.

" However, I'll wait—no, I'll go along and carry your basket."

" I've a good mind to bang you with it ! "

" Well," he laughed, " bang away, bewitching Bet, but be warned ! "

" Wot of, I'd like to know ? "

" A kiss for every bang, Bet."

" Oh ? And wot about your golden lady ? "

" Yes—by George, I was forgetting ! Which is re-markably odd ! Besides, she isn't mine and probably never will be."

" Well, I ain't for the likes o' you to kiss—not me ; I ain't that sort ! "

" No, of course not ! I never imagined you were."

" Then beg me pardon."

" Most ungracious Lady of the River, I crave your pardon for daring to shock your modesty by daring to suggest I might kiss those most tempting lips."

" I ain't agoing to pardon you ! " she cried, and so angrily that he stared in surprise.

" But, my dear girl, I was merely joking——"

" And that's why ! Kisses ain't jokes, not to me they ain't, and never will be, and I should hate to be kissed by the likes o' you. I think I hate you more than I thought."

" Then for heaven's sake don't ! There's more than enough hate in the world as it is, and I'm feeling pretty low, so won't you try to like me, Bet, just a little ? "

" Oh, get back into your boat and row off—do ! "

" Ho—no ! " he retorted mockingly. " If you ain't for the likes o' me to kiss, I ain't for the likes o' you to order about, not me—lorks no ! And as for you not liking to be kissed, I says ' gammon '——"

At this, she threw her basket at him, which he caught, set down and then she was in his arms, was lifted high, kissed and set down again, and all in as many moments and to his own amazement.

" Well ? " he demanded, stung by her scornful look. " Well ? "

" No—evil ! " she answered, quick breathing. " Evil, in your hateful strength, your hateful face, your hateful voice and all your hateful self ! "

" And, bewitching Bet, you're forgetting to drop your aitches and making a ridiculous fuss about nothing."

" Oh, give me my basket, noble gentleman ! "

Mutely he obeyed ; and with it upon her shapely arm,

away she went, and walking very gracefully (he thought), despite her clumsy shoes.

Now being alone, Robin turned to gaze down at the river, his constant and well-loved companion, which he now addressed thus :

" Well, there you are, Old Thing, uncommonly bright this morning and busy as ever, while here have I been making a complete fool of myself, kissing a girl I don't love and never could ! On the mouth, too ! And, though she's the wrong girl, I found kissing her so—so extraordinarily delicious that, damme, it quite astounds me ! As you know, Old Thing, I've never been a kisser, even in those happy days when I believed Clia loved and meant to marry me— no, not even then ; and ever since I've kept free of women for her sake and my own, being really and truly a one-woman fellow. And yet, only a few minutes ago I was kissing this black-haired female and—enjoying it, which perfectly shocks and confounds me. To be sure she's handsome and not so vulgar and uneducated as she tries to appear. I wonder why? But I don't like her type, and consequently the question is, why on earth did I enjoy kissing her so much that by all that's wonderful I should like to——" A wild scream, hushed cruelly to strangled gasp, banished his ruminations and set him running so speedily that very soon he beheld a great powerful fellow, who bore his desperately struggling victim towards a certain gloomy stable.

Robin leapt, seized the ravisher's thick hair, jerked his head back and, grasping his throat, choked him until he released his prey, then :

" Turn ! " snarled Robin. " Turn, and—fight ! " Uttering a beast-like, inarticulate cry, the fellow obeyed, and, confident of his oft-proved strength, rushed in to butt and smash, great head lowered, long arms whirling, fists to smite, fingers to clutch and rend. . . .

Laughing happily, Robin checked him with punishing left, straightened him up with powerful upper-cut and staggered him with hard-driving right.

So began this battle between murderous Ferocity and skilled Brutality; for instead of ending this hideous business speedily as he might have done, Robin fought only to inflict as much pain and disfigurement as possible. Thus murderous Ferocity bellowed and spent his strength vainly while skilled Brutality laughed, drawing blood with almost every unerring blow, until Ferocity, battered and half-blind, tottering and helpless, was smitten headlong at last, to lie with great arms wide-flung and gasping mouth agape in a face that was now a horror of blood.

But even then Robin would have stirred this groaning thing of helplessness with his foot, but two arms were out-stretched above this now pitiful wretch, two brown and shapely hands outspread on Robin's broad chest, held him at bay, and, looking up at him with those vivid blue eyes of hers, Bet cried :

" Ah, don't ! You are cruel—cruel ! You've done too much and you enjoyed doing it. Yes, you—enjoyed hurting him so terribly ! "

" I did indeed ! " said Robin, staring at her in a kind of joyous wonder. " But, by jingo, Bet——"

" Oh, horrible ! " she panted. " I believe you would have—killed him."

" Not quite, though such as he are nicer dead ! But, oh, Bet——"

" You, what are you staring at ? "

" You—your black mane ! " And indeed her hair, now a tumbled glory, was cascading below her rounded hips in lustrous splendour.

" What about it ? "

" Amazing ! I never thought black hair could be so— so——"

" So what ? "

" Becoming ! And so surprisingly long and silky."

" Well, I told you it was."

" So you did. But, as I say, I never thought——"

" You don't do much thinking, do you ? "

" Now and then. But I shall always think of your hair as it is now—all about you like a shining cloak ! I suppose very few women have such hair." Here, gazing at Robin, she began to wind it up, while he watched, and both of them perfectly oblivious to the battered wreck of Ferocity at their feet.

" No," murmured Robin, " I never saw such hair, or——"

" And you don't like black hair, do you ? "

" No, no, I don't, of course. But yours looks so very silky. May I touch it—once ? "

" Not with those terrible hands—they're all blood ! "

" Only my left. I must have cut it on the fellow's tusks."

" Then you'd better let me tend to it ! "

" A lovely idea ; but how ? "

" The pump yonder and your hank'chief if you 'ave a clean one."

" Of course I have ! so come, prithee, beautiful be-witching Bet, bathe, bind and bandage your bravo's bleed-ing bruises blessing him by your beneficent——" But here Ferocity, tamed now to whining meekness, ventured to stir and groan. Thus, reminded of his presence, Robin menaced him with ready foot, whereat Bet leapt again to his defence, saying :

" Let him be ! You've nearly killed him as it is, and, after all, the horrid beast only tried to do what you did."

" No, Bet, I merely kissed you, but thanks to me he didn't even do that. So you ought to be as grateful to me as I am, and later on bestow on me the kiss I saved."

" You're lots too free wi' your kisses ! "

" Not I, Betty. No, indeed ; quite the reverse. That's what I find so confoundedly odd. I have usually shunned women. I've no society graces, and I'm certainly no lady's man, and yet——"

" Oh goodness, here comes the farmer's wife, Mrs. Brent ! Whatever will she think ? " exclaimed Bet, as towards them sped a small, neat, bright-eyed woman flourishing a long toasting-fork, whom Robin saluted, saying :

" Mrs. Brent, ma'am, I'm afraid I've spoilt one of your men for the time being. He looks pretty bad, but——"

" Which I therefore says ' Glory be and likewise halle-lujah ' ! " quoth the little woman, gesturing at the fallen man with her toasting-fork as if she yearned to stick it into him. " For, oh, sir, this great two-legged beast, this pest'lent brute, has plagued and afflicted us these ten days. He come seeking work, but work he won't and go he won't, only yesterday he beat my poor Tom and his rheumatics so bad, beat him black and blue, and Tom be alaying abed in conse-quence. But now, thanks to you, here lays the murdering brute as done it, and nice and bloody, glory be again ! And him so fierce, so big and strong us dassent get rid of him and all our men afeard to tackle him. This be why I'm so joyful as he lays now ableeding, and very truly grateful to you, young sir, for so doing."

" My dear Mrs. Brent," said Robin heartily, " it was a pleasure."

" Then, sir, if you'll do yourself a bit more pleasure and kick him into the river, leastways drive him off our farm and bid him never come back, you'll do me and my poor Tom a power o' good and we'll be mighty thankful."

" You," said Robin, stirring the fallen with his toe, " you hear ? "

" Yes, I got ears, but——"

" You've also got legs, so get up and use 'em."

" Not me ; I'm a dyin' man ! "

" Mrs. Brent, pray lend me your toasting-fork."

The " dying man " scrambled to his feet with surprising nimbleness, saying in voice between whine and groan :

" I'll drop dead afore I've gone 'arf a mile."

" Excellent ! " said Robin. " Walk off and do it."

" Can't I even wash me bleedin' face ? ".

" Certainly, in the river. Take a header and wallow yourself cleaner, or, better still, drown yourself. Now off with you and don't come back or you'll certainly get really hurt."

And so, evil of look and gesture, beaten Ferocity shambled away.

" The Lord be thanked ! " sighed Mrs. Brent, the toasting-fork clasped between piously folded hands. " Not forgetting you, sir. My, but you must be turble strong to beat that great Jabez ; so beautiful, 'twas like a miracle ! However did ye do it ? "

" Easily, because he didn't know how and I do. To fight is about my one and only accomplishment."

" And it ain't one to take pride in ! " said Bet. " So don't go boasting about it——"

" And don't you talk so silly ! " quoth Mrs. Brent. " If he hadn't fought and saved ye from yon two-legged beast, you'd be crying your eyes out, I rackon, yes, and ready to kill yourself for shame. So, Miss Tracy, you be grateful, and if you ever pray, mention this gentleman in your prayers. And so, sir, because of all you've done for us, I should like to know your name, if you'll be so kind ? "

" I'm Robin Dale, ma'am, nobody in particular, and what I did was a——" Here, with sly glance at Bet, he continued, " To be of service to you, Mrs. Brent, was a real pleasure."

" Well now, Mr. Dale, sir, if you and your sweetheart would like a cup o' coffee——? "

" I should indeed, ma'am—but she is not my sweet-heart."

" Ah, meaning as she's your wife ? "

" Not me ! " exclaimed Bet with fervour. " Wife to—'im ? Not likely ! "

" Oh, then I beg your pardon."

" Granted, ma'am. But y' see, he ain't my taste—them goldilocks—lorks, no ! But if 'e wants a cup o' your coffee, ma'am, I'll take one, too, and thank you kindly, though first I think 'e'd better wash 'is 'ands. Look at 'em ! "

" Oh dear me ! You're hurt, sir. Your poor hands are all blood——"

" Most of it his, ma'am. So I'd be glad if Miss Tracy will pump on them."

" No no ; in the kitchen, a bowl and warm water. Come ! " said Mrs. Brent, wafting them housewards with her toasting-fork and so into a spacious kitchen fragrant with the mingled odours of coffee, frizzling ham rashers and the great bunches of herbs pendant from the rafters. And when Bet had washed his stained hand and bruised knuckles (and very tenderly, thought Robin) :

" Now," said Mrs. Brent, "since you're here, you must taste of our home-cured bacon with an egg or so ! " And she commanded the services of her two trim maids with eloquent gestures of her toasting-fork. " And now, if you'll please escuse me, I'll take my poor Tom his breakfast and tell him how you've drove away that great brute, bleeding like a stuck pig and spattering blood with every step, hal—ee—loo—yah ! "

Thus presently seated at a small table in a corner of this extremely neat and fragrant kitchen, Robin and his now silent companion began their breakfast ; and as this un-expected most delicious meal progressed, he was quick to notice how delicately she ate and with what natural address she plied knife and fork, until, catching his watchful glance, she gobbled and clattered, whereat he smiled, and she made a face at him. Thus Robin, for the time at least, forgot his devils, for what thing of evil might breathe the same air as this daughter of the river? Surely none!

And after some while, back came little Mrs. Brent, her eyes brighter than ever, to say with a joyous lilt in her voice:

"Oh, Mr. Dale, sir, when I told my Tom of your noble doing ag'n that terrible Jabez beast, he were so mighty joyful that he forgot his bruises, almost, and wanted to come down and shake your hand, sir, for gratitood, ay, and would have, too, if I hadn't drove him back with my toasting-fork. And so, sir, he hopes you'll come again and give him the chance when he's better. And, says we, any time as you and your lady feels inclined, us will be proud and happy to make you welcome. And for you, my dearie miss, anything as you want today, butter and eggs and milk, is our gift for sake of your dear, grand preserver."

And so, with the well-laden basket between them, down went they to the sun-kissed river, and, pausing side by side, gazed on this glittering, crystal highway and both mute until:

"Oh!" she exclaimed impulsively. "Oh, the glory of it! How I love our dear Old Father Thames!"

"So do I!" said Robin. "And I always shall! Often lately when I can't sleep, I've dressed and gone down to him for comfort, to look at him, so dark and mysterious, and listen to his never-ending song, and sometimes he talks to me—as he is doing now."

"Oh? Wot's 'e a saying of?"

"He says: 'Friend Robin, tell the young woman beside you, to be her truest self and stop pretending to be what she is not, never was, nor ever can be.'"

"Do 'e say anything about me 'orrid black 'air or your goldilocks?"

" Not a word ! "

" Then gimme me basket and I'll go."

" Not until you ask for it properly—and answer a question." She frowned, then her ruddy lips curved to a smile and, bobbing a rustic curtsy, finger crooked beneath dimpled chin, she said demurely :

" Oh, please, Mr. Dale sir, will ee be so kind to give me my basket ? And now, sir, what be your question ? " And with gesture unconsciously appealing, Robin said :

" May I kiss the lips I saved from brutality ? "

" No," she answered, shrinking from those bruised hands outstretched so appealingly. " No, sir, you may—not ! "

Turning from her to the river, he sighed :

" Oh, Father Thames, dear Old Thing, when I am gone and she is alone and lonely as I must always be, it seems, remind her of this moment and of me."

" But why d'ye want to kiss me ? "

" Because, oddly enough, you have become very dear to me. I can't tell you how and I don't know why, but so it is."

" And so it ain't ! " she retorted angrily. " I won't be your ' dear ' neether ' oddly ' nor ' strangely ', because you don't—— Oh, gimme my basket. I'll go afore you insult me any more."

" Now, damme, how—— ? "

" Don't swear ! "

" Well, but how—— ? Oh, Bet, how can you think I ever would insult you ? I meant no more than——"

" Yes," she cried, " you meant so little that you mean less to me, less than nothing ! The man who kisses me must love me and—— Oh, what damned nonsense ! " she exclaimed furiously.

" Fie, Bet ! " he chuckled. " It seems you can swear, too, like any trooper or modish fine lady."

" And all—all because of you ! " she panted. " And you know why."

" But I don't ! It isn't as if I had actually dared to kiss you, which I never shall, of course, without your positive consent, approval, wish, approbation and desire. But this I do know—the man who loves you will be either the happiest fellow or most miserable dog alive ! Well, my Lady Spitfire, here's your basket—take it. No, I'll put it aboard for you. See, the tide's on the ebb and will take us down handsomely."

" Thankee, Mr. Robin sir, but I be wishful to go alone."

" However, my shyly rustical Bet, we'll go together. I should like to meet your soldier uncle."

" 'Spose 'e don't like meeting you ? "

" I'll risk it. Eh, what are you staring at so fearfully ? "

" Look ! " she whispered. " Is that a man spying on us from the bushes yonder ? "

" I'll see ! " quoth Robin, and away he strode, indignant and aggressive. But after some while, his search proving vain, back he came, to find she had launched her skiff and, seated therein, was flourishing an oar at him triumphantly.

" Yours ! " she laughed. "I took it while you were looking for the man who wasn't there ! You shall have it back when next—if ever we meet again. So now—good morning and goodbye, Mr. Robin—sir ! " Then away she rowed, and, the tide being with her, was very soon out of sight, leaving Robin to fume and scowl, until, seeing the humour of it, he grinned, though a little ruefully, launched his boat and, setting his solitary oar astern, went downstream at his leisure. And now, the day being so warm, the sun so gladly bright and the river so glorious, Robin began to whistle that merry old song " Come lasses and lads " which Father Thames must have heard many a time in bygone days. So Robin whistled not merely because of the radiant world around him as the fact that beside him, in

fancy, was that daughter of Thames whom he knew as
" Bet ". With him she made fast the boat at the ancient
waterstairs ; beside him she crossed sunny courtyard ; but
indoors, alas, she was not. Instead, there met him the
demoniac two—whose names are Jealousy and Hate.

CHAPTER XIV

Which is Mercifully Short

IT WAS about this time that Robin's disposition changed for the worse; he developed a scowl, he became sullen and morose, especially of a morning, and more particularly this morning, as, having descended the narrow stair from his small, lofty bedroom, he demanded an answer to the usual and oft-repeated question; and:

"No, sir. No letter from the Viscount and no message," John replied, his face clouding. "But we've kept your breakfast hot, sir; kidneys, bacon and——"

"Then throw 'em away; I'm not hungry. Have Cannonball saddled; I'll go for a gallop." And presently, booted and spurred, gallop he did whenever the traffic allowed, and whither but to the Viscount's chambers in Jermyn Street.

"No, Mr. Robin," replied Old Henry, the Viscount's aged valet and an old acquaintance, "his lordship is still at Storringdean. . . . Oh yes, your missives were sent on to him at once. . . . No, sir, there is no message or reply for you as yet. . . . Good morning, Mr. Robin. . . ."

So back again at furious pace goes Robin, so harassed and beset by his devils that he is greatly minded to seek the Viscount at Storringdean, but, knowing the futility of this, takes a country ride instead, but, fast though he rides, he cannot shake off the unseen demoniac two. . . . Night comes and, jaded and weary, he clatters into the courtyard, grooms and stables Cannonball, and, avoiding Black John and all others, goes supperless to bed.

But now tormented by his two devils beyond hope of sleep, he starts up from his tumbled couch and, dressing hastily, goes down, candle in hand, to crouch at his desk ; and here, goaded by Jealousy and prompted by Hate, scrawls these lines :

"To Viscount Ragworth.

"MY LORD,

"Since you have left my letters unansered, I now denownce you as a cowardly polltroon and theirfor instead of nobler weppon, shall seek you with a dogwhip and thrash you when and where met, for the craven cur you are, at the first oppertunity. So take heed and beware of—

"ROBERT DALE."

Having addressed, wafered and sealed this message of evil intent, he scribbled this note :

"DEAR JOHN,

"I have gone rowing. If not back before breakfast, have this letter carried ammediately to the Viscount's lodging, Jermyn Street.

"ROBIN."

Then forth he went into a night of stars and a rising moon.

CHAPTER XV

A Midnight Interlude

IT WAS midnight and the great city's roar muted to a drowsy hum as, spare oar on shoulder, Robin descended the ancient waterstairs, stepped aboard his boat, cast loose and pulled out into the tideway which as yet was a glooming mystery except for the fugitive beam of some lantern, the riding lights of ships, anchored and moored, or the faint reflected twinkle of stars. But as he rowed slowly upstream, all about him were vague sounds, ashore and afloat, distant voices that sang or shouted, muffled voices that laughed or growled, but loudest, most insistent and clearest of all, was the familiar voice of his life-long companion, Old Father Thames : a voice of throaty gurgles, kindly chuckles, murmurs and sly whispers, a voice of many intonations, and immensely wise with the knowledge of life the wonder and tragedy of it, and death the profound mystery and eternal hope of it ; a voice to match Robin's every mood and therefore one he loved.

" Hallo, Robin. Ware your starboard oar ! Whither away at this time o' night, you ass, when you should be abed and asleep as she is ? You know who. You're thinking of her now as you have done so often lately. And why ? You don't know and the more fool you—a fool now as always ! "

" Yes, Old Thing," answered Robin, keeping a wary eye for obstacles around and before him. " Yes, the longer I live the more I know what a damn useless fool I am."

" Good, boy ! To be aware of folly is the beginning of

wisdom ! And, my Rob-fool, you may not live very long, your life cut short by the very evil of you, so make the most of every moment."

" I am. This is why I have come to you, Old Thing, as I used to do."

" When you were a homeless, starving brat, eh, Robin, you found some meed of comfort along o' me, boy. And what of you since then, what ? "

" Dear Old Father Thames, you know how I've tried to make the best of myself for old Noll's sake, bless him, and you know what a curst disappointment I was and am— school, college and university ; golden opportunities all wasted on me, my only gift brute strength, my only attainment knowing how and where to hit a man."

" Well, Rob my boy, that's something in a world of violence."

" Thanks for that small comfort, Old Thing ! But you know I shall never be a true-blue gentleman, the complete aristocrat like Noll and Ragworth, Vibart, Devenham and the marquis and the rest of 'em. You know what I truly am because you fathered me when I was a wretched little mudlark playing beside you hereabouts and how often you refused to drown me—I wonder why ? "

" I saved you, Robin, because in you is a spark of greatness."

" In me, Old Thing ? Oh no, impossible."

" In you, oh yes ! Hold your tongue and listen to your Aged Dad ! In you, Robin, burns a spark, very dim at present, but which if cherished as it should be, shall blaze to noble purpose someday or other."

" ' Someday ', my dear Aged Dad, is the day that never dawns ! "

" Someday or other, my puppy-blind young fool Robin, shall certainly come, so prepare yourself therefor."

" How, old friend ? Tell me how ? "

"First by getting rid of your pets Jealousy and Hate, your cherished devils."

"I don't cherish 'em."

"Then kick 'em back to the hell whence they came! Second, by retracting your very damnable dogwhip letter. Third, by saying boldly to your ill-used friend, 'Rags, for old times' sake, forgive this poor fool named Robin'."

"I can't, I couldn't—not I—quite impossible—no, damme——"

"Then, my poor Rob, damned you will be, and all because you are afraid!"

"Eh—me? I—afraid? Absurd! Preposterous! You know I fear no man."

"Yes, dolt and chucklehead, one man!"

"Well, name him."

"Robert Dale! He is Robin Goodfellow's worst and most dangerous enemy. Brutal Robert the fighting bully, the two-fisted tyrant, disgusts and terrifies Robin the gentle man! So until Robin Goodfellow thrashes Robert Dale or I drown him, there can be no hope that Robin Dale shall ever be the man he should and could be. Now put that in your fool's pipe and smoke it!"

"You know I never smoke; it's bad for the wind and——"

"Yah-boo, Rob-dolt, boo-yah! Don't dodge the question but heed me or go your own damned way, down —and down, deep on deep!"

"To what? Oh, Father Thames, to—what?"

"Misery and despair—till in the dark remorse smites you helpless! And then, my poor, blind, wilful son, call on me and, if not too late, I'll bear you up to a new and better life, to hope and—perhaps——"

It was at this moment that from the shadows astern a voice hailed, crying his name; and thinking he recognised this voice, Robin ceased rowing to gaze in the one direction with the full-orbed moon now very bright above him. Thus presently out from the looming darkness of wharf and warehouse, out into the radiant moonlight, a boat came gliding towards him and the voice hailed him again :

" Oho, Master Robin ! If that be you, stand by ! "

So, resting on his oars, he watched this boat, and as it drew level he saw it was rowed by a rough-seeming fellow, all hair and whisker, with Mr. Shrig seated aft, who saluted him with flourish of hat, saying :

" Here's luck to find ye so soon, Master Robin. I called at your Gamecock's Roost and John said as how you was off upstream."

" How the devil should he know ? Well, what d'you want with me, Jasper ? "

" Your company so fur as Locketts Wharf yonder."

" Why there, and at this time o' night ? "

" Because there's a landing-stage and a empty shed conwenient to the o-ccasion."

" What occasion ? What's to do ? "

" Master Robin, so soon as us are there I'll show you—ar, in a pig's visper ! "

" Who's that with you, Jasper, at the oars ? "

" Only Bill Bartrum. So let's get on. Easy now, Bill ! And, Master Robin, take good care not to foul us."

" No fear of that ; the moon's so very bright that I can see. Ah, now what the devil, Jasper ? What do I see—that line towing astern of you ? "

" A lady, sir ; a young fee-male party as come down on the ebb and is, by said line, being took up on the flood, sir."

" A lady ? Jasper, do you mean—a body ? "

" Not a, but the body, Mr. Robin, the remains o' that misfort'nate young miss as has been searched for so diligent o' late. For this here as we've got on the end of our line, this ' found drowned ', so fur as I've been able to ab-serve, is that same young lady as you took from Old Father Thames and carried to your lady aunt——"

" Good God ! I hope not."

" So do I, sir. Howsever, I'm now axing you to go along of us and do your best to i-dentify same, telling us if she's your young fee-male or no."

" But—oh, dammit—she's not mine ! I don't know her or anything about her."

" Yet your lady aunt tells me as how you saw her——"

" So I did, but only for a moment, and in bed. How on earth can you expect me to be able to identify that—that ghastly horror towing astern ? I can't and I won't attempt anything so loathsomely impossible ; no, damme, and that's final ! "

" Sir, what's towing yonder ain't so werry horrible, being nice and fresh. So, Master Robin, you as I've see grow from wexacious imp[1] into the proper man and fine gen'leman you are, let the woice o' friendship plead ! All I ax is as you'll take a peep and do your best for old friendship's sake. Come now ! "

" Oh hell ! " exclaimed Robin, dipping his oars. " The very idea sickens me. I detest anything of—this sort ! "

" Ditto here, sir ! But dooty so being, I swallers my feelings and acts according. Give way, Bill, and easy ! "

And now, as they rowed on again, Robin, despite himself, watched that grisly length of tow-line, saw how it drooped slackly one moment then tautened, straining to the weight of the thing it dragged rippling through the moon-bright water, a vague mass which, rising to the surface ever and anon, showed—was that white thing a clutching hand ?—and there again—was that pallid oval the glimmer of a face ?

Reaching Locketts Wharf at last, Robin landed and made fast his boat ; then, as Mr. Shrig and his man Bartrum

[1] See *The Crooked Furrow.*

began to haul in that line, he turned away. Presently he heard them behind him, treading heavily because of their burden.

" The lantern," said Mr. Shrig. " The lantern, Bill. The moon's wonderful bright and shows her werry nice and clear, but let's have the lantern, too ! Right, Bill, set it down there, close, closer—so ! Now, Mr. Robin, if you'll be so o-bliging as to turn and have a good look——"

Robin did so, and recoiled with gasp of disgust :

" Her face, Jasper, what—in heaven's name, what——? "

" Ar ! " murmured Mr. Shrig sadly. " Looks rayther as if she'd fouled summat in the tide-way ! To be sure, her chivvy, or, as you says, her face, ain't hardly all as it should ought to be, but there's enough to show as she's been young and werry handsome. Shove the lantern nearer, Bill ! Now, Mr. Robin, twig her eyes, or, as you might say, her ogles, blue or grey, and her eyelashes, black and thick. Now her hair so fine and remarkable long, black as charcoal. Her height, at a guess, five foot seven or eight. Lastly, these hands and silk petticuts, from vich and the rest of her so far as now appears, I dee-dooce she has been a lady o' condition. So now, Mr. Robin, the question I put to you is : do you see any likeness here to the young party as you took from the river ? "

" No—yes—oh, I—I don't know ! " stammered Robin, " There is a strong resemblance—but—I'm not sure, nor could I ever be. So, Jasper, for God's sake, cover—her up."

" Not yet, sir. Bill, set the light a bit nearer. Now, Mr. Robin, you saw her alive. Can you i-dentify her dead ? Come closer and look harder ! Because if you can and do recognise her, then I'm pretty sure you are now regarding the young miss as the Count is seeking so diligent and expects to find dead—as this here——"

" Ah ! " exclaimed Robin. " You mean the ' beloved ward ' he spoke of—the Lady Aramanthea Meredith ? "

"That werry same, sir. Vich raises the question : how comes it he should expect to find her a corpse ? So now stoop, Master Robin, stoop closer, and look your hardest, if you please."

"It doesn't please me, Jasper ! No, damme, it revolts and appals me ! I've told you all I can, so now I'm going and—nobody shall stay me."

Back to his boat sped Robin, and was in the act of casting off, when to him came Mr. Shrig to say :

"Talking o' kettles, Master Rob——"

"Kettles ?" repeated Robin in staring amazement. "Did you say ' kettles ' ? "

"Ar, a kettle ! Vich reminds me to remind you as a kettle calls for a teapot, and that again, for a frying-pan, not to mention a cup or so——"

"Jasper, what—what under heaven do you mean ? "

"Breakfast, Master Robin. Beside the river ! A fire o' sticks ! You ab'iling the kettle ; her afrying the bacon. And the birds avistling all around you. And the old river asinging to you of her. And you alistening and looking at her. And her alooking at and listening to the sizzling bacon——"

"Hold hard, Jasper ! What the devil are you driving at now ? Whom do you mean by ' her ' ? "

"Tallish, handsome, black hair, Mister Robin, and rows a boat bearing the letters B.E.T., sir."

"Oh ? Ah ? And what more do you know of her, pray ? "

"This and that, sir ; no more than I do—vich ain't ! "

"Jasper, old fellow, you talked of the voice of friendship, so now, if you know anything about her, for or against, good or bad, tell me, for our old friendship's sake."

"All as I knows of her is good, Master Rob—ar, and so is a rasher o' ham cut thick and done slow over a fire o' sticks. Burn my neck if I couldn't relish a rasher now !

Howsever, dooty forbids, and, being dooty, I must back to our 'found drowned' as con-sidering shoes, two, and never a buckle may prove to be a—ar—a ass-tonishment. So good night, Master Robin, and if you can wed them rashers to a egg or say a couple, so much the better, how says you?"

"That it's a mighty good idea, Jasper. Thanks, old friend, and good night."

Then homewards against the flowing tide rowed Robin, the night's horror banished and not so much by thought of ham-rashers as of her who with him might partake of them, that most vital, somewhat mysterious, decidedly handsome young "fee-male party" whom he knew as "Bet".

CHAPTER XVI

Concerning the Counsel of Old Father Thames and a Compact of Friendship according to Plato

HAVING shaved rather more carefully than usual and breakfasted with remarkable haste, Robin strode out into the sunshine, and, reaching the ancient waterstair, was about to descend to his boat, when to him John came hastening with a letter.

" Sir," said he with something very like apprehension in look and tone, " Viscount Ragworth's groom has just brought this, says there's no answer and has rid away again."

" Ha, at last ! " Robin exclaimed and, while John watched with troubled eyes, took this letter, broke the seal and read :

" To R. DALE, ESQR.

" SIR,

" Since I find you not only a nuisance but a swaggering bully and public menace, I shall do my best to end both by removing you from this sphere of activity for good and all, with the utmost dispatch. Three days hence at the time and place you name shall be our last meeting and final encounter, so be prepared.

" The weapons you prefer shall suffice.

" Yours, etc.,

" RAGWORTH."

" Sir ! " exclaimed John anxiously. " Oh, Mr. Robin, is all well atwixt you and my lord the Viscount ? "

"Perfectly!" Robin answered. Then, refolding the letter very precisely, he went down to his boat; though as he began to row upstream he glanced up at cloudless heaven and around him upon the familiar sights, and never-ending bustle, rather wistfully. Thus as he swung at the oars, listening to the musical ripple at the sharp prow of his boat, Old Father Thames (or his own conscience) began chiding him, thus:

THAMES.   Well, fool Robin, my poor wild boy, you've had your wicked way! Yes, you have provoked a good friend into fierce and implacable foe eager for your life's blood. For unless this sinful business is stopped he will certainly kill you.

ROBIN: Why be so sure of this? I'm as skilled with the "sharps" as Ragworth, anyday.

THAMES: Do you mean to kill him?

ROBIN: Certainly not! I meant to blood him a little, no more and——

THAMES: Ah, you meant to—then! But now you have so goaded him that he is determined to end you! Hence you must kill him or die.

ROBIN: I shall do my best to live, of course. But, if it must be, I—don't mind dying——

THAMES: Oh yes you do; ay, and will do more so. After this morning you'll yearn for life!

ROBIN: Old Thing, what do you mean?

THAMES: That a woman's beauty will make death the more horrible! And you know it.

ROBIN: Oh? What d'you suppose I know?

THAMES: After you've heard her voice again, looked into her eyes again, beheld again her beautifully hateful night-black hair, life will seem more precious than ever before.

ROBIN: Old boy, I tell you she is nothing to me—nor ever can be!

THAMES : Young, self-deluding dolt, you may thus fool your young self, but you can never deceive me. I'm far too old and man-wise. Though man has changed me somewhat, here and there, begrimed me with his labour, and fouled me with his sinning, yet he is much the same today as when he fronted the embattled might of Rome, hereabout. Humanity was and is purblind ; the Genus Homo, a creature of good and evil, angel and devil, but, when young as you, Robin, always and ever a self-deluding fool. So here you are, pulling at those oars with the sole purpose and hope of meeting Her again, and the more eagerly because you know now that with every tick of the clock old Death stalks nearer.

ROBIN : No—not necessarily, dammit !

THAMES : Yes, beyond all peradventure, my Robin. By your own evil you have summoned evil—to your own destruction. My present concern is—how to protect you from your damned self.

ROBIN : Dear Old Father Thames, why still bother with me ?

THAMES : Perhaps because you have become a habit, or because I think you may become worth while.

ROBIN : Call me a habit, Old Thing—and a pretty bad one, for I'm worth nobody's while. And if you are a true prophet——

THAMES : Fool boy, of course I am ! Therefore take heed and know this for very truth : except I compass some miracle, you have just three days of life. Yes, my poor, doomed wretch, you will be lying a bloody corpse three days hence, a helpless, useless, repulsive clod, your precious life thrown to waste by your own accursed folly.

ROBIN : Which sounds pretty devilish grim. But, old friend, if there is an after life—which is an extremely

big " if "—but if so, then, given another chance, I
may perhaps do a little better in the hereafter.

THAMES : But what of the here-and-now ? Life was
given for use to noblest purpose, and how constantly
you have misused your opportunities, been your own
curse, ay, and will be again if——

" Aho ! " At this odd though now gladly familiar cry,
Old Father Thames was instantly speechless and Robin's
gloom banished as, glancing over his shoulder, he beheld—
her.

The grime and noise of London were behind him, lost
in distance and out of mind ; before him flowed the river
between grassy banks shaded by trees, beyond which lay the
quiet beauty of this English countryside. Beauty was all
about him, but Robin was aware only of her who sat
leaning across her motionless oars, gazing at him so wistfully beneath her coronet of lustrous black hair, for she
wore no hat.

And after they had viewed each other thus dumbly
awhile, Robin said and with unwonted fervour :

" Oh, Bet, how glad I am to see you ! "

" Oh ? " she echoed. " And why so wonderful glad, I'd
like to know ? "

" Because," he replied impulsively, " the chances are
I shan't be able to see you at all in the future. I may have to
—go away."

" You mean from London—hereabouts ? "

" Yes."

" Far away ? "

" Too far ever to—return, Bet."

" Lorks ! " she exclaimed, though with face averted.

" Ah—don't ! " he cried, wincing. " For mercy's sake
no more, not now ! Don't pretend to be vulgar and common
when I know you are nothing of the kind ! Don't act with
me today ; there's really no need ! Who or what you were

doesn't matter; what you are does! So, for these last few days I beg you to be your best, your gentlest and kindest——"

"If you want me to make love with you, I——"

"No, no—I don't! In three days' time I—I must go——"

"And never return?"

"Most likely."

"You must be going a long way?"

"I am."

"And you think it will help you to pass these last days by making love to me——"

"No, I tell you, most certainly not! All I desire is the—the joy and comfort of your friendship, no more."

"And that's all?"

"That is all, absolutely."

"Are you sure?" she demanded, gazing at him, eye to eye. "Quite sure!"

"Positively certain," he answered, meeting her look with one as direct.

"Why are you so—positively certain?"

"Because I could never fall in love with you, Bet."

"Oh?" she murmured, gazing now on the sunny distance. "Couldn't you?"

"No, never." Here, to his indignant surprise, she laughed and, beginning to row, contrived to splash him.

"Ah, Bet," he sighed reproachfully, "how can you giggle at the idea of our being parted so soon, probably, and forever?"

"I did—not—giggle!" she retorted, as they rowed on slowly side by side. "I never do. I laughed most politely and—only at you. But now, because you are so mournfully urgent, I will endeavour to please your manship by doing my best to seem as ladylike as possible."

"Good! For this at least I am profoundly grateful. And

will you also kindly address me as ' Robin '? Will you—
please ? "

" If you wish, Robin—yes, Robin."

" My humble thanks, Bet. And now let's talk." So as
they progressed slowly, side by side, talk they did—thus :

SHE :   What about, Robin ? Robin ?

HE :   Yes, and of Bet—ourselves, of course.

SHE :   Very well, you begin.   Though first—Bet ought
to have a better name, one more suited to her suddenly exalted social rank. You christened me " Bet ",
for Elizabeth, I suppose. I suggest " Eliza " or
" Beth ".

HE :   No. I don't care for " Eliza ", and " Beth " sounds
confoundedly like " death ", so " Bet " or " Betty "
you shall remain. And what beside ? May I know
more about you. For instance, are you living with
your parents ?

SHE (*mournfully*) :   I am an orphan.

HE (*gently*) :   My poor child ! Yet this is a bond between
us, for so am I ! Have you any relations ?

SHE :   A sister.

HE :   Are you living with her ?

SHE :   No. Just at present she is in London. A—lady's
companion.

HE :   Since we are going to be the friends I hoped—for
this last few days—may I know where you live ?

SHE :   This depends.

HE :   On what, pray ?

SHE :   Well, this friendship you proffer is so very sudden
and overpowering.

HE :   But most truly sincere ; yes, and reverent ! So,
Bet, where do you live ?

SHE :   Why would you know ?

HE :   That I may find you when necessary.

SHE :   However can I be necessary to you ?

HE (*shaking head in bewildered manner*): That's the amazing thing, Bet! I don't know why; the astounding fact remains that you are. So, pray where do you live?

SHE: In a cottage beside Thames, the loveliest, dearest little place!

HE: However, that is no answer. Don't you, can't you —won't you trust me?

SHE: Ben might not; he is very suspicious and quite as sudden, yes, and fierce as you are.

HE: Ah, so you think I'm fierce, do you?

SHE: I think we should talk much better sitting still, under the trees yonder.

HE: A good idea!

Now as they approached the shady bank, they passed a man who sat fishing, a man this entirely unremarkable except for a pair of mournfully drooping, haylike whiskers, so entirely inconspicuous indeed that neither of them noticed this angler; also they happened to be looking at one another. Thus presently beneath the shade of these bending willows Robin demanded again:

" Can't you trust me? "

And glancing up at the dense leafage above them, she replied:

" I'm thinking of my Ben."

" Eh? " exclaimed Robin so vehemently that his boat rocked. " Now who—who the devil——"

" Hush! Don't be so sudden and fierce! And, goodness, how you scowl! "

ROBIN: Naturally, under the circumstance.

BET (*innocently*): What, pray?

ROBIN: Your Ben! Who is he?

BET (*demurely*): The man with whom I am living at present, and——

ROBIN (*shocked*): Well—now—damme——

BET (*rebukingly*) : And you've no cause to scowl and swear, too——

ROBIN : But you—you're telling me——

BET : Of my dear, faithful, grey-haired guardian-angel Ben.

ROBIN : Grey-haired ? An oldish fellow ?

BET : Oh, very ! He is quite sixty.

ROBIN (*calmed*) : Ah, I see ! And yet a ferocious customer, you tell me ; a fighting man, eh ?

BET : Oh, very.

ROBIN : Ha, good ! I like the sound of him.

BET : Though he has only one eye.

ROBIN : Oh, bad luck.

BET : But with that one he sees far more than most people do with two. And he is very tall and strong and brave as a lion and perfectly devoted to us.

ROBIN : Pray whom do you mean by " us " ?

BET : My sister and myself. And now since I have told you all about myself, suppose you tell me everything about yourself, especially where and why you are taking this long journey, so suddenly never to return, which sounds almost tragic.

ROBIN (*sighing*) : Circumstances, no—just one, make it more tragic than I thought possible.

BET : What circumstance ?

ROBIN : You ! Our new friendship. Which reminds me. You haven't told me all about yourself—what you are, where you have been, what you have done for a living, and so on. So will you honour me with your further confidence ?

BET : Yes, if you wish. I might tell you I am one who " has seen better days ". But don't think of me as a " decayed gentlewoman "—it sounds so shockingly like coffins and cemeteries and death, doesn't it ?

ROBIN (*with fervour*) : Yes, by jingo, it does !

Here, reminded of what so soon was to be, he glanced from the beauty of her face to the beauty of the river, earth and sky more wistfully than ever and stifled a sigh as :

BET (*continued*) :   Instead I might tell how I was a poor, forlorn governess who had—lost her situation, of course, through the fault of another, his vile wickedness and——

ROBIN (*in sudden dreadful apprehension*) :   And what, pray ? What ?

BET :   A pair of scissors.

ROBIN (*amazed*) :   Scissors ?

BET (*gazing up at the leafage above as if for inspiration*) : Yes—just a very ordinary—pair of scissors, though —— (*Here she contrives to shudder most realistically.*)

ROBIN (*his apprehension growing*) :   Though—what ?

BET (*with shudder more violent*) :   Though—these scissors were—imbrued with a villain's blood——

ROBIN (*aghast and greatly agitated*) :   Good God ! Blood ? How ? Why ? Whose ?

BET (*clasping hands*) :   I might tell you how the pampered son of the house developed such a frantic passion for —black hair, that at last——

ROBIN (*breathless and dreadfully expectant*) :   Yes—yes, tell me—all !

BET (*dramatically*) :   At last, upon a moonlit night, and she—very lightly garbed—he stole to her room and, creeping upon her, like the vile creature he was—oh, then——

ROBIN (*wildly*) :   Yes—ha, damn him—yes——?

BET :   He found her—alone, of course, and utterly defenceless—almost.

ROBIN :   Good merciful heaven ! How—how then ? Why, almost ? Ah, you mean——?

BET :   The scissors ! For in that dread moment of loneliness, shame and despair she found them ; she caught them up, and, armed with these and—her immaculate virtue, she arose, she smote and—laid the infamous wretch bleeding at her feet.

ROBIN (*immensely relieved*): Mag-nificent! Stu-pendous! Oh, glorious woman! Did you kill the foul beast?

BET (*self-conscious and somewhat dismayed*): Of course not—a mere scratch.

ROBIN (*enthusiastically*): No matter, you splendid Bet, it was a truly heroical effort. No wonder you fled to hide—the protection of our good Old Father Thames! This quite explains the mystery of you.

BET (*demurely*): Yes, I thought and hoped it might. So now you shall explain just why you are to take this long journey.

ROBIN (*glancing up at the leafage for inspiration in his turn*): Certainly. I am compelled by—an accursed fate! Though there is a hope that I may not—have to— go.

BET: A hope? Ah, then you don't wish to go?

ROBIN (*with the utmost fervour*): Most decidedly—not! The mere idea becomes more hatefully detestable every time I look at you.

BET (*with swift side-glance at him*): Oh! Well, I become increasingly glad of my detested black hair!

ROBIN: Oh? Why, pray?

BET: As some protection against your amorous advances.

ROBIN (*surprised and indignant*): Mine? But—oh great good heavens, what irritating nonsense——

BET (*serenely unheeding*): Because, were I an inexperienced, charmingly innocent bread-and-butter miss —which, alas, I am not—I should deem you were doing your best to make love to me at this moment.

" That's the worst of the feminine mind—always harping on the one confounded old theme!" he retorted. "For ever suspecting, seeing and hearing love where it isn't and never can be ! I protest again and most solemnly, my desire is simply and solely for your friendship, asking, expecting and wanting nothing more of you than merest sympathy and companionship."

" According to Plato ! " she added.

" Precisely ! " said Robin emphatically. " Well, is it a go, Bet ? I mean, will you honour and bless me with your friendship, if only for these few days ? If so, shake hands to prove it ; and as a pledge of your trust and so on—will you ? "

So for a moment their hands met : his large, powerful though unexpectedly gentle ; hers extremely vital and some-what hardened by the oar.

" And now," said she, " your extremely platonic friend demands to know why, if you take this journey, you can never return ? "

" Because," he replied, glancing askance at her intent face, " grim circumstance forbids."

" That is the merest evasion and tells me nothing. What is this circumstance, and is it so very grim ? "

" Nothing could be grimmer, Bet ! "

" Will you tell me just how and why ? Will you trust your friend although she's so new and platonic ? "

" With my life, if I could—but I can't, of course ; I wish to heaven I could ! As it is, all I can do is to—to beg you merely as a friend to make these last days as happy for me as possible. Will you ? "

" If I can ; but how ? "

" First by calling me ' Robin ' as often as possible, and secondly by having breakfast with me tomorrow, here beside our Father Thames, bless him ! "

" Oh, but—what an idea ! "

" Yes, splendid, isn't it ? I thought of it last night, and please don't say no. I'll bring all that's needful : food, kettle, teapot and so on—unless you prefer coffee. I'll bring both and meet you here tomorrow at—let's say five o'clock."

" Six would be much too early, Robin ! "

" Then we'll make it half-past five. Lord love you, what a meal we'll make of it ! "

" Platonically ! " she repeated.

" Of course ! Do for mercy's sake believe that I'm no confounded ogling philanderer ; and even if I were—you would never attract me, Bet. No, all I want is merely to look at you, to see and hear you often as possible in the last few days, to have you near me."

" I'm wondering," she murmured, " just how old Mr. Plato would regard that."

" Like the wise old owl he was, of course ! And you'll meet me here tomorrow at six o'clock ! "

" At six-thirty, Robin ! "

" Hurrah ! " he exclaimed. " Then all shall be revelry and joy ! "

" So early in the morning, Robin ? "

" Yes, and all day and every day, friend Bet—every one of these last three days, by your gracious kindness. However, I shall be here at six o'clock tomorrow morning."

" At six-thirty Robin ! "

So thus it was arranged.

CHAPTER XVII

Explains, Among other Matters, Why the Man Daniel Went Afishing

ROBIN, on his homeward course, was in sight of the Gamecock's Roost, when he became aware of a boat astern and bearing down on him, a fine, large craft impelled by four men in smart liveries and steered by Mr. Claude Despard who was lolling in the cushioned stern seat. But espying Robin, he forgot his languor and, sitting up, cried imperiously :

" Ha—you there, stop ! Mr. Dale, wait, I say ! " Robin merely scowled and lengthened his stroke, whereat Mr. Despard jerked his starboard tiller-line, swerving his heavier boat so suddenly that it was only with a powerful effort that Robin escaped being run down.

" What the devil are you about ? " he demanded furiously as the boats drew alongside.

" I told you to wait ! "

" And I tell you to go to the devil ! Now sheer off and be damned."

" Dear me ! " exclaimed Mr. Despard with gleam of white teeth. " Did I so alarm you ? Indeed, I meant no more, otherwise you would now be—in the river, struggling for life. As it is, I desire a word with you. I demand to know what you have done with my brother's ward, the Lady——"

" Then you can demand till you're black in the face and breathless ! So sheer off and——"

" Ah no, Mr. Dale, not yet ! Not until I have informed

you that you will be proceeded against for the crime of abduction. We shall invoke the law——"

" Invoke hell ! " snarled Robin and made to row on. Mr. Despard uttered a word in Italian, and one of his men struck at Robin with his oar. But, eluding this awkward weapon, Robin freed his own oar and thrust at Mr. Despard, who, rising at that moment, was hurled overboard and all was uproar and confusion. Robin laughed ; but seeing the four Italians did no more than shout and gesticulate, though it seemed their master could not swim, Robin cursed them heartily, drew in his oars, shed his coat and plunged in after the drowning man—only to be clutched by desperate hands, clasped by arms and legs that would have been the death of them both ; so, wrenching his right arm free, Robin smote Mr. Despard in the right and proper place. Thus and thereafter he contrived to urge the now limp body within reach of his still clamorous servants. Hardly had they dragged their still inanimate master to safety than one of them cried :

" Ah—you hit-a our milor, so now I hit-a you."

" No y' don't, y' damn furrin dog ! " cried a harsh voice, and Robin's would-be assailant was smitten aside by a dripping oar. Glancing up, he beheld first the hairy visage of Bill Bartrum and beyond this the square-jowled face of Mr. Shrig, who beckoned, saying :

" Aft to me, sir ; this here boat's easy for to capsize, so the vord is ' aft ', Mr. Robin." Thus presently over the stern, with Mr. Shrig's powerful assistance, Robin clambered safely aboard, then saw Mr. Despard's boat turn, with great splashing of oars, and speed away upstream whence it had come.

" So much—for him ! " said Robin between chattering teeth. " And now for—my boat."

" Ay, sir ! " said Bill Bartrum, plying his oars. " But oo's them furrin swine as tried to run y' down ? "

" Ar ! " quoth Mr. Shrig. " And the fine gen'leman as you poked overboard so werry neat and fished out again so proper after bestowing on same such a sweet and powerful bender as put him to bye-bye, for, by goles, you hit him pretty hard, Master Robin ! "

" Yes, Jasper, I—had to. The fool would have—drowned himself and—me, too ! Besides, he—deserved it ; yes, he—needed hitting."

" May I ax the reason for your wiciousness agin him and his agin you, sir ? "

" Because he is Viciousness personified, Jasper, a smiling too-dainty gentleman I do not like, and his name is Mr. Claude Despard."

" Blow—my—dicky ! " murmured Mr. Shrig, beaming. " So he's brother to our precious Count Hugo, is he ? Now may I ax again for the reason o' the trouble atwixt you and Mr. Claude ? " And when they had captured and made fast his boat astern, Robin, warmed by the exertion and basking gratefully in the hot sunshine, told of Rosemary Phyllinda Meredith, giving a vivid (and sighful) description of her surpassing beauty, the golden glory of her ; how she had fled to the protection of Viscount Ragworth and himself, how they had defied Mr. Despard and his men, and how these had been routed eventually by Sam the inkeeper's blunderbuss ; nor did Mr. Shrig's bright gaze rove or his shaven lips utter a word until this vivid recital was ended ; then :

" Ass-tonishing ! " said he. " Ar, dog bite me if it ain't ! And my lord the Wi-count takes her to his feyther the Earl o' Storringdean, eh ? "

" He did ! " said Robin, frowning.

" And the Earl of S. to the Duchess o' Camberhurst—in London ? "

" So I believe."

" The—Duchess ? A vonderful, small, great lady ! "

" D'you know her, Jasper ? "

" No, not—yet, sir, but I've heered of same, and so the Wi-count takes this werry lovely young miss from you, eh, sir ? "

" Yes ! " answered Robin, scowling blacker than before.

" Vich didn't please you nohow, p'raps ? "

" It did not ! "

" Consequently you and him had vords, p'raps ? "

" Yes, we did, Jasper."

" Vich led to blows, p'raps ? "

" Certainly not ! It would have been like hitting a baby, because old Rags—I mean Viscount Ragworth—is no match for me with naked mauleys ; he prefers more—more lethal weapons."

" Swords and pistols, p'raps ? "

" Oh, something of the kind."

" And you'd be ready to oblige him, p'raps ? "

Now here, meeting his shrewd questioner's keen side-glance, Robin made a great business of shivering with complaint of wet clothes, and, to change the subject, bade Bill row a little faster. Yet even so, as they drew in to the old waterstairs Mr. Shrig remarked sententiously :

" In this here poor old world, Mr. Robin, there's two troublesome things has caused more battling and bloodshed than anything else, and one's religion, and tother's voman ! And here y'are at your old river stairs. And werry handsome they be ! Folks knowed how to build beauty into stone, not to mention bricks and mortar, long ago. Good day for the present, sir. Get inside some dry clothes and outside a drop or so o' summat hot and spicy, leming-peel with a clove or two, and you can't ketch cold. Heave ahead, Bill ! "

And now as he was rowed upstream, Mr. Shrig became a profoundly thoughtful man, apparently quite oblivious to the busy life around him afloat and ashore, until all sight and sound of this traffic was far behind ; then never were his eyes brighter or his roving glances keener—questing every bush, every tree and thicket that crowned or shaded the adjacent river bank."

" Easy, Bill ! " he said at last.

" Easy it is, Jarsper."

" He should be hereabouts, I reckon."

" Ay, like enough, Jarsper, 'e's allus somewheers or other and shows up here or theer sudden-like, afore 'e's noticed."

" Ar ! " nodded Mr. Shrig. " Nobody in this here uni-werse'd ever notice him if it weren't for they viskers ! Frequent have I axed him to shave 'em off, but—all in wain. He refuses to part—ar, he clings to they viskers like they clings to him."

" And it aint," said Bill, shaking his own luxuriant adornments, " as if they was whiskers to be anyways proud on—no life nor sperrit about 'em, Jarsper ! "

" Being," Mr. Shrig explained, " viskers o' the kind known as ' veepers ', Bill. Howsever, he treasures 'em ; and, seeing as he ain't to be ekalled for speed, dash and daring, I puts up with 'em therefore. Pull inshore a bit, Bill. Now hold hard—I'll try for him here." And fixing his keen gaze on a certain bush, Mr. Shrig whistled, and in dulcet tone, the opening bars of that song the old River must have heard many a time when it and the world were younger, " The Leather Bottle " ; at the which signal, and from a thicket in totally different direction, a fishing-rod was flourished and the whiskers known as " weepers " appeared, together with their owner, of course.

" How goes it, Dan'l ? "

" Fairish, Jarsper. I caught a fish ! If you're agoing to land, here's a good place." So presently Mr. Shrig stepped nimbly ashore, and, bidding Bill wait, followed the whiskers through maze of thickets to a shady coppice, where rabbits frisked and birds piped. Mr. Shrig paused to enquire :

" Anything to report, Dan'l ? "

"Ay, as you expected, Jarsper, she's meeting him for breakfast hereabouts at ha'-past six! Though how you guessed as she would I can't imagine."

"It weren't hardly a guess, Dan'l. And at ha'-past six, are ye sure o' this?"

"Sartin sure! I fished near enough to hear 'em. Precious early for breakfast, eh, Jarsper?"

"Ar!" sighed Mr. Shrig. "Earlier than I bargained for —vich means as I must rise along o' the dewoted lark! Anything more, Dan'l?"

"Ay, she's living in a cottage nearby, with an oldish cove, tall, grey hair, very stiff in the back and only one eye, but looks a pretty tough customer. And she calls him 'Ben' and he calls her 'my lady'."

"So? Are ye sure o' this, too?"

"That I am; I've heered 'em! Presently I'll show you where and how."

"Then, by goles," exclaimed Mr. Shrig, beaming, "blow my dicky if I haven't hit the nail fair and square on the nob! It's domino me again and no mistake, Dan'l, and you can lay to it!"

"Jarsper, I don't twig!"

"Dan'l, I didn't hardly expect as you could—yet! But you shall, later on. Now show me so as I can get a peep at this here cottage."

Traversing this little wood and with scarcely a sound, Dan'l halted suddenly, parted the dense leafage, and Mr. Shrig beheld a deep-thatched cottage amid a very glory of flowers and throned beside a broad, still pool, a silent backwater that narrowed between bush-girt banks, where, thus unseen, it joined the mighty river.

"Well, there's the cottage," said Dan'l softly, "but from the river it ain't seen by reason of all them trees and thickets."

"And," quoth Mr. Shrig, turning away, "werry pretty, too; no place could be better."

" Well," enquired Dan'l as they retraced their steps, " what now, Jarsper ? Do I go on fishing and try to cop another ? "

" No, Dan'l. You're going along o' Jarsper to wisit a brace o' werry fine gen'lemen, upstream."

" Meaning them brothers, One and Two, Jarsper ? "

" They i-dentical."

" In the matter of the nooest ' found drowned ', Jarsper, black hair, silk petticuts—identification, eh ? "

" Ar."

" D'ye think as they'll claim her ? "

" If they don't, 'tis no loss to us, Dan'l ! Ar, but if they do—it means Count H.'s blunt in our pockets and—summat more."

" What more, Jarsper ? "

" Willainy, Dan'l."

CHAPTER XVIII

*Being Mostly of He and She, with Some Mention of the
Ubiquitous Mr. Shrig*

CLOCKS were striking the hour of five on this radiant
morning, and Robin, packing the breakfast hamper for this
their third meal together, was thinking (naturally enough)
of her with whom he would soon be sharing it . . . the
vivid blue of her steadfast eyes, the curve of her sensitive
lips, the inherent grace and dignity of her, with those quite
bewildering ch nges of mood from demure gravity to
inexplicable gaiety, now kindly gentle, now mocking and
aloof, tenderly feminine or hard and repelling, haughty fine
lady or illiterate vulgarian ; in a word, he was thinking of
Bet. And in a little while they would be sitting beside their
gipsy fire enjoying breakfast together for the third time !

Yes, this was the third and probably the last time he would
breakfast with her or anyone else !

Closing the hamper with a slam, he turned to gaze up at
that wall where, festooned by such innocuous weapons as
boxing gloves and single-sticks, hung those two silver-
hilted swords, their narrow, triangular blades glinting in the
early sunlight ; these splendidly wrought implements
especially designed for gentlemanly murder politely known
as duelling !

So Robin gazed up at these evil things beneath drawn
brows, since today, in a few brief hours, one or other of
them might be his death, and he " a bloody corpse, a
useless repulsive clod, a thing soon to be corrupt ". At this
dreadful prospect his six foot of youthful vitality quailed

instinctively—for the moment, then he laughed, not very convincingly, saying aloud :

" Oh well, what must be will be, and the sooner the better ! " Here he took up the hamper and with this comforting thought : that, anyhow, it was a glorious morning and She (with a capital S) would be meeting him as promised. Ah, but—suppose She failed him ? Here he set down the hamper again with a thud. If She did not come, then how on earth was he to pass the intervening hours between now and six o'clock this evening, when these accursed swords would be so busily at work ? Yet why suppose any such infernal nonsense ? Of course She'd meet him as she had each morning. Here he caught up the hamper, strode out into the heartening sunshine and was presently afloat.

But now, though rowing Her-wards, and despite glory of sun and river, Robin's brow was gloomy, miserably certain that he was rowing upstream for the last time. And so, for consolation, he questioned his age-long friend :

" Old Thing, good Old Father Thames, is it life or death for me today ? And I ask because, 'twixt you and me, I know now as I have always known and scorned to admit it, that I am no match at rapier play with old Rags. And, as you know, my Old One, when a man fights doubting himself that poor devil is beat already. So, old friend, what's it to be ? "

But for once, and in this hour of need, Father Thames made him answer none. Instead, a wherryman coming down on the ebb cursed him harshly for not keeping a better lookout ; whereupon Robin instantly retorted with curses as deep, as bitter, and far more fluent, after which he felt rather better and more himself. Thus as he pulled against the tide, leaving the mighty city behind, when instead of grimy bricks and mortar was the lush green spaciousness of the countryside, his gloom began to lift. At last, rounding a bend, he glanced over his shoulder and beheld the light skiff with the letters B.E.T. Ah, then ! His heart swelled with a gladness that banished dreadful gloom as though it had never been ; instead, was glory of sun, of life and the abounding joy of it. Yet when their boats were alongside all he said was :

" Morning, Bet ! I hope you're as hungry as I am."

And she replied :

" So hungry, Robin, that your sham fine lady, forgetting to nibble and sip daintly, will bite and bolt and gulp like the commonest of Bets, unless I take great care. What have we this morning, pray, sir ? "

" Gammon rashers, madam, cut thick ! "

" Oh, most noble gentleman, how truly and supremely delectable ! My lady's mouth waters, alas, at the mere thought ! And as for vulgar Bet, the avid creature would positively smack her lips but for my stern restraining influence ! " Here, with deft manage of sculls, she ran her skiff aground, sprang lightly ashore and stood with hands outstretched to aid him with the capacious hamper. And when he had secured the boats they each betook them to their usual tasks, he to collect dry twigs and sticks for their fire while she laid the cloth ; what time the old river nearby sang murmurous, never-ending song, whereto the birds above and around them piped in joyful chorus.

And surely no young man and woman more happily carefree than these twain, though to be sure he was less talkative than usual, and more than once she glanced at him curiously across the large frying-pan perched somewhat precariously upon the blazing fire.

" You are very silent this morning ! " said she at last.

" Yes, I was thinking."

" Of your journey ? "

" No, of you," he replied, settling the frying-pan more

securely; " of you and your tale of the scissors. Was it true ? "

" True ? " she repeated indignantly. " Of course it was perfectly true—in parts."

" Which parts ? "

" The worst ! "

" Then it's a great pity I wasn't beside you."

" Oh—indeed ? " she demanded, turning to front him, eye to eye.

" Yes, by heaven ! " he exclaimed, scowling at the ready fist he had raised. " Had I only been there——"

" I should probably have used my scissors on you, too ! " said she, jutting her dimpled chin at him. " All things considered——"

" Eh ? Oh ! Ah, I see what you mean. I was forgetting, you were in your night——"

" I was, as I told you ! So now don't remind me of the hateful vileness."

" Certainly not. Only, suppose you hadn't found the scissors——"

" I refuse to suppose anything so appalling ! Don't speak of it. Instead set the plates to warm. These glorious rashers are nearly done ; can't you hear them ? "

" Yes, they sputter and sing sweet as any bird, yes, b'gad, even as our grand old river here, my good old playmate, always my friend and lately my companion, bless him ! Twice he refused to drown me when I was a little impish brat."

" Oh ! " she exclaimed impulsively. " And he spared me too, Robin ! "

" Did he, Bet ? Did he ? Then bless him again, for this is another bond between us ; we both love the Old Thing, and with equally good reason ! But tell me when and how he spared your life and——"

" No, you shall tell me instead—how and why this bond

of his making must so soon be broken? Well?" she
enquired, for he had turned from her to gaze very wistfully
at the river. "Are you my friend, Robin?"

"Yes, most truly!"

"And you desire me to be your friend?"

"You know I do and merely as a friend, with no love
nonsense, and with all my heart."

"Then treat me as a friend; trust me, confide in me.
Will you?"

Again he hesitated, then, still avoiding her gaze, replied:
"Yes, yes, of course, so far as I may."

"Well now, tell your 'mere' friend who or what com-
pels you to this journey, why and when and where are you
going—never to return?"

"There's my difficulty, Bet, because this—this journey
may not happen; no one can possibly be sure until the
time arrives——"

"What time, Robin?"

"This evening about six o'clock."

"And if it—happens—why must you go?"

"I can only tell you—force of circumstances."

"Which is no answer, of course! So I ask where must
you go if go you must?"

"That is—the question!" said he, smiling rather grimly.
"For on my life, Bet, I'm not sure; I can only—hope!"

"And what is your hope, Robin?"

"That the climate may not be—too hot! And now
permit me to draw your ladyship's attention to our ham-
rashers which I venture to think are done to a turn."

"What a clumsy evasion! You are not a very clever
Robin, are you?"

"No, and I don't pretend to be, however, if——"

"And what a pitiful mockery is your offer of friendship!"

"Eh? A mockery? How so, pray?"

E

"So, Master Clumsy Robin, since you will not accept my friendship, I'll have none of yours."

"But I do accept your friendship."

"By evading my questions and refusing to trust me."

"But I do, I have ! Yes, I've answered you the best I'm able and——"

"Then your ability is so extremely limited that we will talk of something more mundane ; these rashers, for instance, require another ten minutes or so, and to beguile the time and change the subject again you may tell me of your love."

"My—love ? " he exclaimed, turning to gaze his astonishment. "But good lord, Bet, I thought we——"

"Yes, Robin, your love, the beautiful, lovely golden lady of your adoration. What of her ? "

Here he turned to gaze at the river again, and after a moment of gloomy thought answered—and with a sigh :

"She married—another ! "

"Poor Robin ! But I didn't mean that one. I was referring to your last whose name you told me was like a ' small sweet song '. Let me see, what was it ? "

"Phyllinda," he answered with another sigh.

"Well, what of her ? "

"She—prefers another."

"Oh, miserable you ! "

"Precisely ! " said he, nodding dejectedly. "She is the second and only woman I could have loved and who, as usual, is not for me ! I am left in the confounded lurch, as I always am and must be, it seems."

"Oh well, perhaps you may be more fortunate next time."

"There never will be a ' next time ', Bet ; no, never ! "

"Yes, Robin, there will be many, because you are such an—easy and frequent adorer, are you not ? "

"No, Bet ; no, indeed. I'm too deuced faithful by nature !

I am, I was and shall be again a one-woman fellow. So love is not for me. I'm done with the nonsense, and—so long as I'm permitted to live, all I desire is our friendship, Bet."

" I suggest you choose someone else, Robin."

" Not I ! None other would do, because in all this world is only one Bet."

" And she is going to eat, Robin—not Robin, of course, because he would be so horridly tough and indigestible. Please reach me the plates and let us eat together."

So they began breakfast and with proper enjoyment, making the utmost of every bite and sip until :

" Forgive this here in-troosian ! " said a voice so un-expectedly near that Robin, in the act of sipping, spilt his coffee and, starting round, beheld Mr. Shrig beaming at them, hat in one fist, knobbed stick in the other.

" Where on earth have you sprung from, Jasper ? " he demanded, frowning.

" Chancing, Mr. Robin, in this here wi-cinity, sir, I was drawed, or, as you might say, aloored, by two whiffs o' fragrance, first o' coffee and second o' frying bacon vich I see is ham, and following said whiffs—you now behold me. And a werry good morning to you."

" But what the deuce are you up to hereabouts, Jasper, and so early, too ? "

" Master Robin, since you ax so p'inted and seeing as you are you and I'm me, I'll answer you full and free— dooty, sir ! "

Here she whose blue eyes had been regarding Mr. Shrig so intently now smiled as if pleased, and said in her very sweetest voice :

" And, Robin, you are forgetting to introduce us. Pray do so."

To the which he replied and rather sullenly :

" Oh well, this is Mr. Jasper Shrig of Bow Street, a friend as old as Father Thames, or very nearly. Jasper, I honour you by making you known to—my Lady of the River, Mistress Bet Tracy."

"Mr. Shrig," said she, still smiling up at the face yet beaming down on her, "you are very welcome! And if you care to join us, pray sit down here beside me and share our breakfast; we have plenty, because Mr. Dale always brings so much too much."

"Ma'am," replied Mr. Shrig, with his bobbing bow, "gracious Lady o' Thames, seeing as how you're kindly beautiful as this here morn, I'll sit along o' you vith J.O.Y. j'y and share your meal vith all doo gratitood."

"But," Robin demurred, "what about a cup?"

"Sir," said Mr. Shrig meekly, "seeing as how I'm only me, I'll make do vith your sarcer."

And when they all three had enjoyed this excellent fare in a silence it deserved, Robin, aware of how often Mr. Shrig's roving glance strayed to the beautiful She who was seated so demurely between them, broke this beatific silence with a somewhat forced and hollow chuckle, saying:

"Aha, Bet, I'd better warn you. The man sitting beside you and so confoundedly near, who looks so meek and mild as if butter wouldn't melt in his mouth, though a gammon rasher can and has, this pleasant-seeming person is truly a being of blood and death in frightful shape!"

Now at this, gazing wide-eyed at the placid Mr. Shrig, She recoiled instinctively: whereat Robin nodded and continued:

"Oh yes, this mild-seeming fellow has hounded more miserable wretches to prison and the gallows and ferreted out more guilty secrets than any other law officer!"

"As in dooty bound, Lady o' Loveliness," sighed Mr. Shrig, saucer arrested at shaven lip.

Here she leaned towards him, saying:

"Then I am very glad to meet you, Mr. Shrig, because

I have a mystery I hope you can resolve for me, or help me to elucidate."

" Werry humbly at your sarvice, my Lady o' Light. You speaks and I does my best."

" Well then, Mr. Shrig, mine is a two-legged mystery who tells me that this evening at six o'clock or thereabout he will be compelled to make a journey to some place unknown because he has no idea where it is ! All he can tell me is that the climate of this unknown place may be very hot, and that it is so very far away that he can never return ! This is my mystery, Mr. Shrig, and there it sits at this moment, scowling at its breakfast ! Pray what do you think about it ? "

" Two and twenty years, Miss Bet, or thereabouts, I have thought about it off and on, and 'tis a mistree still—almost ! "

" Please, what does ' almost ' mean ? "

" Lady of Lovesomeness, it means ' werry nearly '."

Here Robin, glancing at his old friend keenly, demanded :

" What are you driving at now, Jasper ? "

And beaming on him, Mr. Shrig replied :

" Master Robin, sir, all as I can tell you is as how I never got my champers, or, as you might say, ' ivories ', into a more toothsome gammon rasher, vich reminds me of the misfort'nate miss, that lady o' yours who——"

" Now, damme, but I've told you repeatedly I have no lady——"

" Meaning," continued Mr. Shrig patiently, " the lady as you lugged out o' the mud of Thames and named your ' armful o' filth '——"

" Oh, curse and confound it ; why the devil must you be forever reminding me——"

" Because it seems she's that same young fee-male oo flew the coop, hopped the perch and wanished so complete, same being the Lady Arrymanthy Meredith as——"

" Well, you suspected as much weeks ago."

" Ar ! But here's summat as I didn't nohow suspect—
this here werry arternoon. Are you listening, Master Rob ? "

" Yes, of course I am, since I must. What about this
afternoon ? "

" This werry arternoon, sir, at three p.m., the Lady
Arrymanthy Meredith is being buried and——"

" Lord love us ! " exclaimed Robin in sudden anxiety.
" What is it, Bet ? " For, uttering a choking gasp, she had
covered her face with both hands, yet not before he had
glimpsed her expression of wide-eyed horror. " Bet—ha,
Bet, are you faint or something ? "

" No ! " she answered, and contrived to laugh, though
rather shakily. " I am—neither ' faint ' nor ' something '.
It was nothing, but if anything it was a very little thing, a
crumb that went the wrong way. And, anyway, it has gone
now, so, Mr. Shrig, do please go on with your story, it
promises to be quite delightfully gruesome and interesting."

" Jasper's stories generally are gruesome and perfectly
unfit for such peaceful bower as this and especially on such
glorious morning, so, Jasper, if you must talk, tell us of
something pleasanter than funerals and drowned bodies."

" Oh, was this poor lady drowned, Mr. Shrig ? "

" Ar ! Ma'am, nobody could ever be drownder ! "

" But how—when ? Dear Mr. Shrig, tell me about her.
Be a pet and tell everything you can." Mr. Shrig blinked,
beaming more radiantly than ever, as he answered :

" Lady o' Sunshine, they vords ' dear ' and ' pet ' are so
werry on-usual to me that they goes straight to my heart, or,
as you might say, my throbber, and vill sing there so long as
throb it do, therefore I now acts according."

" Well, pray do. Dear Mr. Shrig, go on with your tale—
no, first let me refill your cup—I mean saucer."

This done, Mr. Shrig sipped the fragrant beverage,
nodded and continued :

" Werry recently this drownded lady is took from the

river and nothing on or about her to tell oo she is, though werry richly dressed—silks and laces and—long tresses o' beautiful black hair—ar—as long and as black as your own, my dearie lady miss, and her face, too, though——" Here he paused to shake his head.

"Yes, well ? Oh, do pray go on ! "

"Her face were not all as it should have been ! Howsever, she is, in doo season, i-dentified by her guardian Count Hugo Despard and brother as their lost and wanished Lady Arrymanthy Meredith."

"You say they identified her in spite of her disfigurement ? "

"Ar, in spite of or because o' same, werry readily they did, and mourned over her most loud and affecting ! So the coroner and his jury having dooly sat on her, she is, this day, to be in-terred, a reglar bang-up funeral. So there's the end o' this stoopendiously rich heiress Lady Arrymanthy Meredith—or—is it ? "

"Have you any doubt of this ? If so—ah, Mr. Shrig, what do you mean ? "

"Nothing ! " said Robin. "He's simply trying to be confoundedly mysterious as usual, so enjoy your breakfast and never heed him, Bet."

"Dear Mr. Jasper," she persisted, "please tell me what you mean."

"I-dentity ! " he replied, keen glance roving from his pleading questioner to the murmurous river and back again. "In my experience o' humanity, good, bad and indifferent, though mostly bad, in my line o' dooty, I've knowed folks identify wrong, sometimes accidental and other times the rewerse, my Lady Bright."

"And you think—pray, what are you thinking, Mr. Shrig ? "

"At this moment I'm thinking as your two-legged mistree don't feel too friendly to me."

" And, begad, you're right ! " said Robin, frowning.
" For you, confound you, Jasper, have completely ruined
our breakfast ; hasn't he, Bet ? "

" No indeed ! " she answered. " So never you mind him,
dear Mr. Jasper ! I think you have been so very interesting
that I hope you will be—even more so—at another time,
will you ? " Here turning to meet her wistful look, Mr.
Shrig saluted her again with his awkward bobbing bow.

" Ma'am," he replied gravely, " Lady o' Thames, that I
promise, and p'raps you tell me a thing or two—if you can
trust me."

" Yes," said she gently, " I can, I do and shall be im-
measurably glad to trust you, Jasper Shrig ! " Then with
swift, impulsive gesture, reached her hand out towards him.
Mr. Shrig doffed his hat, placed it upon the grass beside
him and, taking this slender, sun-burnt hand in both his
own, gazed down at it as though it had been something
extremely rare and precious (as indeed it was, of course).

" So ho ! " exclaimed Robin mockingly. " Why not kiss
it and be done, Jasper ? " Here, and to Robin's indignant
surprise, Mr. Shrig bowed his head and very deliberately
kissed it for the truly precious object he deemed it.

" Well," exclaimed Robin, " now, damme, Bet, if——"

" Hush ! " said she, lifting this same hand against him
reprovingly. " Do—not—swear ! And now, Mr. Jasper,
what of our two-legged scowling mystery yonder, who is
compelled to make a journey this evening ? "

" At six o'clock ! " quoth Mr. Shrig.

" And," said she, " this a journey he knows not where
and of which he also knows nothing except——"

" That it's pretty hot ! " quoth Mr. Shrig.

" And," she continued, "from which he can never come
back ! What kind of place must that be, Mr. Jasper ? "

" I should say as said place is pretty fur off—ar, so werry
distant as can't be, and therefore ain't in this here wale o'

tears and tribulation. Vich so being, said journey must
be to another sphere."

"Yes," said she, " ' that bourne from which no traveller
returns ' ! So, dear Mr. Jasper, what can we do about it ? "

"The question is, Master Robin, what says yourself about
it ? "

"I say rubbish, Jasper ; a pack of tomfool nonsense ! So
let's get on with breakfast, for, let me tell you, Bet,
I——"

"Listen ! " said she as a distant church clock began to
chime the hour. "My gracious—eight ! " she exclaimed.
"How the time has flown ; and so must I. No, no, don't
try to stay me, Robin. And if you must take this—this
journey, I shall pray that—somewhere at some time you
will live to find content and happiness—maybe. Goodbye,
Mr. Shrig, I am so very glad to have met you and hope to do
again soon—and often. Also, I know you will do all you
can, yes—everything in your power to prevent evil ! "

"Lady o' Goodness," he replied, clasping the hand she
now proffered in farewell, "you can trust your werry dewoted J.S. to do all as in him lays, for yourself and—they as
you love, now and hereafter—amen ! "

Here, standing now between them, she turned first to Mr.
Shrig, saying :

"Now and hereafter, good friend, you will be a great
comfort to me ! " Then, glancing at gloomy Robin : " Meet
me here tomorrow morning at seven o'clock—if you are
able." And so, with Mr. Shrig's ready aid, she stepped into
her skiff, shipped her sculls and rowed speedily upstream
until a bend in the river hid her from their sight. Then Mr.
Shrig shook his head, saying very solemnly :

"And, Master Rob, that most lovelly She is agoing to
pray for you ! Vich under the circumstances is werry proper
and fort'nate for you—I hope ! And talking o' doo-els, d'you
expect to die stuck on a sword or blasted by a ball ? "

"Oh, the devil!" exclaimed Robin pettishly. "What d'you know of this damned business?"

"That 'tis werry damnable indeed, sir, for that at six this evening you'll kill the young Wi-count or him you or both each other."

"Nonsense, Jasper! I don't intend to kill old Rags; most certainly not, damme!"

"Then s'pose he kills you?"

"That's as may be, but fight him I must and shall!"

"May I ax your reason for sich on-reason?"

"Jasper, if I tell you, I'm pretty sure you could never possibly understand."

"Master Robin, you've knowed me and me you ever since you lived along o' this old river, a little, wicious Thames-side mudlark called 'Snod'; wherefore if any man ought for to know and understand you—I'm that man! Howsever, try me and let's see."

"Very well then, Jasper. I'm fighting because I don't want to fight. And I don't want to fight, except with fists, of course, because the idea of killing old Rags, or anyone else, shocks and disgusts me. I don't want to fight because the idea of being—run through—skewered on a sword-blade appals me! Yes, Jasper old friend, I'll confess to you, this so terrifies me that fight I must or be my own abiding shame. Now do you understand?"

"Ar!" replied Mr. Shrig with slow nod. "'Tis your own self as you're most afeard of, Master Robin!"

"Maybe yes—perhaps. And yet I don't know. For I'm so damnably afraid of—something or other, though, as you can testify, Jasper, I have never feared anything or anyone until quite recently! Which is devilish odd, yes, b'gad—it floors me completely, old fellow."

"And me, too!" quoth Mr. Shrig with another slow nod.

"Eh, you, too? Now what the deuce d'you mean by that?"

" They most beeootiful twinklers, or, as you might say,
ogles, apeep twixt their long, black lashes. That prideful,
little dellycate nose, they lips, scarlet as ripe cherries. That
woice. That shape ! That lovely all might floor any man—
ar, even toughish, oldish Jay Ess ! "

" Eh ? Why now, what the—if you are alluding to
Bet——"

" Ar ! None other ! And she called me her ' dear ' and
' pet '. Lord love her loveliness ! 'Tis the likes of her as
sweeten this here poor, old frowsty world ! And besides,
she's sharp as a packet o' needles ; that beeootiful head aint
stuffed wi' straw ! And if you get brains along o' sich
armful o' loveliness, ketch hold o' same werry firm and make
the most of it—'stead o' risking your precious life and that o'
your best friend for no——"

" Hold hard, Jasper, and listen to me ! " said Robin very
grimly, laying his powerful hands on Mr. Shrig's broad
shoulders. " Hearkee, Jasper ! Since it seems you and she
have contrived somehow or other to worm the news of this
damned duel from me, you will now promise on your
honour to be mum ; you'll not utter a word of it to anyone !
For, come what may, fight I must, for my own peace of
mind's sake ! So, give me your promise. Is it a go ? "

" Ar ! "

" Good ! Now bear a hand with these breakfast
things."

This done, and the hamper aboard his boat, Robin held
out his hand, saying :

" Step in, old fellow ; I'll row you as far as the Roost, or
farther if you wish."

" Thankee ! " said Mr. Shrig, shaking hands. " But it so
happens as my gig and Dan'l are waiting pretty near. So
now all as I can say is : goodbye, good luck ; may you live
long and die happy."

" Thanks, Jasper ; and whether I live long or short, I'm

grateful for your good wishes, old friend. And remember—
no talking ! "

But now whereas Robin pulled slowly downstream, Mr.
Shrig became imbued with a very fury of haste, striding so
rapidly that very soon he was perched beside the man Dan'l
in his high-wheeled gig, urging his fast horse to such pace
that Dan'l enquired :

" Why the hurry, Jarsper ? What now ? "

And touching his fleet animal with the whip, Mr. Shrig
replied :

" Life or death, Dan'l ! Soon as maybe you're agoing to
bear a letter to a noble lord, and you'll bear it right speedy,
for 'twill be a letter o' death or life ! "

CHAPTER XIX

Has the Virtue of Brevity

THE WHISKERS of my lord the Earl of Storringdean, those hirsute tell-tales and only betraying features, were just at present in a high state of agitation by reason of the three letters lying open before him. Firstly this :

" MY LORD AND DEAR FATHER,

" I deem it only right to inform you I go out today with my one-time best friend Robin Dale. I did my utmost to avoid this meeting because of past friendship. But his last letter, enclosed herewith, explains why I am compelled to this hateful business. But however it ends, pray know I shall comport myself as your son should, and, believe me, now as ever, to be

" Your very dutiful and loving son,

" RAGWORTH."

And the second letter, marked " enclosure ", thus :

" To Viscount Ragworth.

" MY LORD,

" Since you have left my letters unansered, I now denownce you as a cowardly polltroon and theirfor instead of nobler weppon, shall seek you with a dogwhip and thrash you when and where met, for the craven cur you are, at the first oppertunity. So take heed and beware of—

" ROBERT DALE."

And the third letter, thus :

" To the Earl of Storringdean.

" MY LORD,

" Jasper Shrig begs to inform you as your one and only
son and heir, this evening fights a duel with Mr. Robin
Dale ; place—the Gamecock's Roost by the river ;
time—six o'clock. J.S. therefore suggests as you duly
inform Sir Oliver Dale of same and with speed to prevent
this bloody business. J.S. suggests haste.

" Your ldshp's obedt. svt,

" JASPER SHRIG."

Having read these three effusions, my lord the Earl
quelled his whiskers and thereafter rang bells and issued
orders to such effect that some half-hour later, astride the
speediest horse in his stables, he was galloping up the
splendid avenue at Abbeymead, here to be welcomed
heartily by the stately Sir Oliver, who, so soon as he had
also read these letters, instantly forgot his stateliness and in
his turn rang bells and issued orders ; then, staying only
to explain and bid farewell to his lovely wife, hurried out
with the Earl where their horses awaited them.

So these two friends and neighbours mounted, and, side
by side, rode for London Town, slack of rein and ready of
spur, staying for nothing, up hill and down, since they rode
a race against the clock, a race against relentless Time and
the grim, dark angel of Death itself.

CHAPTER XX

Tells how Robert the Devil Triumphed

MEANWHILE, as the fateful hour approached, Robin busied himself to dust and furbish the two smallswords, wondering as he did so which of them was probably to be his death.

So engrossed was he that when the door behind him opened he started violently and, glancing round, beheld Black John gazing down at him beneath drawn brows.

" So, Master Robin," said he with a growl in his usually pleasant voice, " that's it, is it ? 'Tis as I've suspected and feared, you're agoing to fight the Viscount, him as was your friend—and with them cursed things, will ye ? "

Answered Robin lightly :

" At six o'clock, old fellow, in scarcely half an hour, and it should be a pretty good go—while it lasts. Now listen, John, and I'll tell you your part."

" My part, sir ? "

" Yes, you'll second me, of course, and——"

" No, Master Robin, this I will not ! I'll have no part in such damned wicked business ! That you as was such good friends and right gentlemen should use such murderous tools agin one another instead o' nature's proper weapons ain't English. 'Tis foreignly murderous and I'll have no hand in it ! "

" So you—you refuse to be my second, do you ? "

" Yes, sir, I do."

"You'll leave me in the lurch—just when I need you most, will you?"

"Sir—Master Robin, I couldn't bear to stand by and watch you as was such friends cut and stab each other to death with them damned swords!"

"Oh ah?" enquired Robin gentle-voiced but fierce of eye. "Then what the devil will you do?"

"I'll take a walk till it's all over, one way or t'other, and——"

"Then—walk!" said Robin, laying down the sword and clenching his fists. "Walk now and go on walking! Walk to the devil and don't come back! A man who could desert his friend at—at such a time is no friend o' mine, nor ever shall be."

"D'ye mean I—must leave you—for good?"

"Yes, for my good—and the sooner the better. Away with you!"

For a moment John hesitated, then, bowing his tall, black head, he turned, sighed deeply and strode away. . . . Long after the sound of his slow, heavy footfalls had died in the distance, Robin sat gazing down at the swords with troubled eyes, until with sudden gesture he caught them up, went out into the courtyard and laid them upon the marble balustrade, ready to hand. And here he leaned to gaze down into the water immediately below and once again propounded the question:

"Life or death, Old Thing?" And once again received no answer. Yet still he leaned there. He roused at last to the expected sound of approaching hoofs and wheels in that narrow, grimy street that had once been a bowery lane, and, glancing thitherward, presently beheld Viscount Ragworth escorted by three friends, one of whom now advanced, hat in hand, to bow and enquire:

"Mr. Robert Dale, I believe?"

"The same, sir."

"Mr. Dale, I am Captain Clare acting on behalf of my friend Viscount Ragworth. And first, sir, I beg to ask if there is any hope that this unhappy affair may be—accommodated between yourself and my principal?"

Robin glanced where the Viscount stood, head averted gazing at the river, and felt such sudden yearning for this his lifelong friend that, turning to the captain, he answered with the more abrupt finality:

"None, sir. None whatever!"

"Very well, Mr. Dale. Pray where are your seconds?"

"I have none and desire none."

"But we do, sir! In fact, Mr. Dale, I insist you provide yourself with seconds—if only to be witnesses of this lamentable affair."

"Captain Clare, I tell you again I want no one to second me. Here are four of you to witness what is to be; here are the tools; so pray let us get at it and be done."

"Mr. Dale, this is most irregular, and permit me to say your conduct is reprehensible and I positively refuse——"

"To the devil with your refusal, sir!" said Robin, unbuttoning coat and waistcoat. "Play your part, whatever that may be, but stand out of my way while I play mine. Stand off, I say, or, damme, I——"

Horse-hoofs, coming at furious gallop, a voice that cried his name, a commanding voice long familiar and well beloved; hoofs that rang nearer with clattering rush; foam-spattered horses reined to rearing halt; a tall, dusty figure striding towards him across the echoing courtyard. The voice again.

"Give me these accursed things!" And, snatching up the two swords, Sir Oliver Dale hurled them far out into the river and turned to front his adopted son.

"So much for your damnable purpose!"

"And, sir, damned foolish of you and dev-lish hard on

my Lord Viscount, for you thus compel us to use our fists, and I, of course, shall hammer the——"

" Be silent, Robin, and listen to me ! "

" Sir and revered Governor," he replied with ironic bow, " speak and to the point, I beg. Bless me with brevity."

" I am here, Robin, to save you from your most evil self and to learn if you are man enough to—ask pardon of Viscount Ragworth for your very atrocious letter."

Robin merely smiled and, folding his long arms, glanced slowly from face to face of the silent company, teeth agleam between parted lips but uttering no word. Therefore Sir Oliver, with gesture almost pleading, turned to the young Viscount.

" My lord," said he, " if you can be so great-hearted and magnanimous—to excuse and overlook such wanton affront for all our sakes and—especially mine, I beg you——"

" Oh, my dear Sir Oliver," cried the Viscount, " I have no will to this affair ; indeed, I hardly know what it is all about, and so—for your sake, sir——" With these words he stepped forward and, looking on Robin very wistfully, proffered his hand.

Now because Robin so yearned to take and clasp this hand, he hesitated ; and because of the many watching eyes, he struck this hand aside so violently that the Viscount staggered. Then Sir Oliver was between them, deathly pale, and so distraught that, for the moment, speech failed him. Then :

" My—my lord," said he, actually stammering, " Viscount Ragworth, pray accept my humblest apologies for this—this brutal fellow's most contemptible behaviour. As for you, Robert, before God I despair of you at last, for you have become my ever-growing shame ! Instead of the splendid man and gentleman I hoped for, you are——"

" A sow's ear, sir, and no silk purse, eh ? "

" You have forfeited my respect and are—killing my love."

" So ? " exclaimed Robin, clenching his fists. " Very well. Now stand aside or, damme, I——"

" No ! " retorted Sir Oliver, advancing. " No ! Away from me—off——" Then Robin struck, but in the moment of impact unclosed his fist ; yet, even so, Sir Oliver was hurled back so forcibly that he would have been in the river but for the balustrade. Speechless, he leaned there gazing at Robin, who, quailing beneath this look, yearned to beg forgiveness but was dumb. Thus for a space was no sound except the voice of Old Father Thames. When at last Sir Oliver spoke it was very deliberately and in voice hushed to a murmurous gentleness that made his words the more terrible :

" I think this is the bitterest moment of my life, for you have failed me ; you have destroyed my hope for and faith in you, and this is beyond any possibility of forgiveness. The wild, tameless nature of you, the inherent evil of you, shames us both and the name I gave you. It is this inbred savagery that may—bring you to the gallows, fouled with blood. So here and now I disown you. I forbid your presence at Abbeymead. Henceforth you are a stranger, because my Robin Goodfellow is dead and only Robert the Devil remains, and with me and mine is no place for such vile, such murderous, inhuman monster as Robert the Devil."

And now from Robin's back-drawn, pallid lips burst a shout of raucous laughter very evil to hear—then a rush of breathless mocking words :

" Aha, gallant gentlemen, blue-blooded aristocrats all, I now take pleasure to inform you how this right noble and —most virtuous gentleman, Sir Oliver Dale, murmuring in my ear, names me murderer-to-be and Robert the Devil ; well, damme if he isn't perfectly right—as usual, for so I am, yes, and, by all that's accursed, so I will be. Wait, sir; only wait and you shall hear of me. You shall learn how true is your prophecy. So now, this moment, I'll away to make it very fact! Gentlemen all, Robert the Devil bids you—au revoir, to our next merry meeting and then—to hell with you every one."

CHAPTER XXI

Concerning Robert the Devil

SO AWAY strode young Robin, apparently serene and perfectly assured as usual, but in that youthful mind of his was a very tempest of conflicting emotions : fury and regret, despair, and hope of vengeance, dismay, and an ever-growing remorse, though just at present dominating all was wounded pride. He had been made ridiculous, and, thus mortified, self-esteem became a clamorous torment. And so, to soothe this torture and to hush the small though persistent voice of conscience, he could think of nothing better than violence, ferocity of action, the wild joy of personal combat.

So came he to a certain ancient, villainous, riverside tavern built centuries ago by holy men in a more pious age to comfort the bodies and souls of distressed mariners, and called the Angel of Mercy. But through the ages, little by little, it had degenerated into a mere " boozing ken ", a place of iniquity, of robbery and murder, the haunt of pirates from the river and overseas. Today it was little better, being frequented by the most desperate characters ; a beetling, heavy-gabled structure, grim without and within, where strife was still frequent and bloody—which den of evil was still known as the Angel.

To this celestial haunt of roguery came Robin to throw wide the massive old door, crying :

" Aha, my ruffians and rascals ; here stands Robert the Devil, to drink and sport and fight with any that dare. Oho, landlord, fill every rogue's pot ! Who'll fight a round or so with Robert the Devil for ten shillings ? There's the money ! " And upon dingy, battered counter he tossed the gold coin, crying : " Come, who'll stand up to me for five minutes—or longer ? "

Hereupon, amid the swirling reek of tobacco smoke, burly forms lurched and swayed towards him. Eager faces ringed him in. Harsh voices cried gleefully :

" 'Tis a young buck as fancies hisself ! "

" Ah, a sportin' tippy ! "

" A fibbing, 'eavy-toddler, mates."

" Wants a fight, does 'e ? Gimme room and I'll smash 'im and put 'is lights aht ! "

" Me, too ! Blind me but I'll tear aht 'is liver and eat it for 'arf the money."

" Come on then," laughed Robin, setting his back to the nearest wall. " Have a try ; the more the merrier ! I'll take all comers as you will ! Fight's the word ! I'm Robert the Devil and want action, so come on—and fight your hardest ! "

And by ones and even twos, they came, fighting their best ; and by ones and twos went down or reeled away before the might and skill of those terrible fists, backed by the speed of dancing, leaping feet. And when, after some while, the thud of hard-driven accurate blows, the heavy shuffling tramp and lightsome trip of feet had subsided, Robin laughed again, a little breathlessly, saying :

" What, all done ? Then, landlord, fill every tankard again and drink my merry rogues all, drink to your playmate Robert the Devil ! "

And drink they did, with hoarse acclaim and rousing cheer for " The Devil ". So they quaffed and sang in roaring chorus, they capered and danced, treating Robin as one of themselves or hailing him as " The Guvnor ", until clocks were chiming the hour of midnight, and then, as if this had been a summons, in upon this wild company, towering above them all, strode Black John. Uttering no word, he took the slopping tankard from Robin's lax grasp and, setting mighty arm about him, led him out from riotous noise and heat, into the sweet cool night air. Here Robin halted to blink and say somewhat thickly :

" Eh ? John, old horse, my faithful John, I—I dreamt you'd d-deserted me, curst-fool of a dream. And, b'jingo, I was never so—so nearly drunk as I am now. And I don't like it—'s worse than I imagined ! Foxed 's the word, John, foxed—trifle unsteady on m' pins—so, never again, no or damme ! Diss-gussting ! Aha, but, John, old f'low, you're in—in shocking bad company ; you're on the cursed downward-path, m' poor old John, the path that leads to—to hell and damnation—with—Robert the Devil."

Thus home came Robin, and presently to bed, there to slumber heavily until the sun was high and the day so far spent that he knew She must have waited him in vain. This troubled him strangely ; also he cut himself shaving, and this angered him. Descending to a solitary breakfast, he enquired for Black John, only to learn he was still absent, and this made him woefully dejected and then so morose that none dared approach him.

CHAPTER XXII

In Which Mr. Shrig Advises

AND NOW, as the days passed, he left his sheep—the black
and the grey—quite untended, and, shunning all companionship, became a man apart, passing long hours on the river,
but ever and always—downstream.

Night after night he fought and rioted in tavern and
alehouse, up and down the river; and because he was as
ready with money as with fists Robert the Devil became
notorious and was hailed and acclaimed, feared, admired and
hated for the all-conquering champion he was, even as
Jessamy Todd, that Champion of England and unbeaten
master of the Ring, had foretold years ago.[1] As a matter of
course, he drank, but always ale and that sparingly, not from
any sense of virtue, but merely because he abominated
intoxication—especially in himself.

This morning he sat slouched on the old waterstairs,
elbow on knee and chin on fist, glowering dismally at the
river, feeling wretched as he looked, and this for several
divers reasons. He missed John; he had not dared to seek
Her. The vicious joy of combat was beginning to pall. He
yearned desperately for sight of Abbeymead, the once
loved home of his youth—for Clia, for Sir Oliver, dear old
Noll, his more than father whom he had struck. Abbeymead and all it stood for was now forbidden him—he was
outcast, and no wonder. Remembering that blow, he
bowed his head in very anguish of remorse. Also after a
wild night of furious combat, he had risen even later than

[1] See *The Happy Harvest*.

usual and eaten no breakfast. He was unshaved. His money was nearly all gone. And he had a black eye.

Thus he sat in a dreary world, filled with sullen rage against Circumstance, remorse for past conduct and bitter disgust of himself. . . .

It was now that Mr. Shrig made one of his sudden and totally unexpected appearances, saying cheerily :

" A werry fine morning, Master Robin ; I give you j'y of it——"

" Joy be damned ! " snarled Robin. " What the devil are you doing here ? "

" Looking at your damaged ogle, sir."

" My eye ? " said Robin, feeling it very tenderly. " I've had worse."

" Howsever, your poor peeper has certainly went into mourning, sir ; I never see a blacker. May I ax how ? "

" I got it last night—two pretty tough customers. I've been taking on all comers two at a time lately and very enjoyable it was—while it lasted, which was never long enough. Still, two of 'em last night certainly earned their fee ; this eye cost me a sovereign."

" So you pays 'em to fight you, eh ? "

" Well, of course ! The devil of it is, I'm getting confoundedly short of money. But what are you after hereabouts this morning, Jasper ? "

" You, Mr. Robin. To ax how long you are agoing to be your own ruination, sir ? "

" Until," answered Robin, clenching his fists, forgetting all save wounded pride, " yes, damme, until to all the smugly righteous, chastely virtuous, curst superior persons I make the name of Dale stink to highest heaven, Jasper ! "

" Sir, it does that already."

" Does it, b'gad ? Good ! Then until our primly austere and aristocratic Sir Oliver hears and duly appreciates it."

" Sir, he does that already ! "

" Aha ! Better and better ! But how d'ye know ? "

" By this here, Master Robin ! " and, doffing his hat, Mr. Shrig extracted therefrom a letter, which, having donned his hat, he unfolded, saying : " This is how he writes about——"

" You needn't bother to read it, Jasper. I can guess its contents and don't wish to hear."

" Then bung up your ear-holes, sir, ram your fumblers into your listeners, for to read letter aforementioned I now pro-ceed to do :

' MY DEAR JASPER SHRIG,

' Old friend, remembering your success in so very many difficult cases, I venture to ask your help on behalf of a misguided young man, once my loved Robin Goodfellow, who is pursuing such course as must in time lead to his misery, shame and probable destruction. You, having known him practically all his life—even longer than I have done—may thus have more influence with him than myself. Therefore do whatever you can and in your own way to check his present wilfully reckless behaviour. Tell him the love I thought dead was only shocked to insensibility ; whether or no it lives or dies depends on his future conduct. If you think proper to read this letter to him, pray do so, and know me your sincerely grateful friend

' OLIVER DALE.'

And how says you to this, sir ? "

" That I want nothing of him or from him. And you can tell him so ! "

" Werry good, sir, if it ain't werry bad. Anything more ? "

" Yes, you may also tell him that if I don't succeed in gracing the gallows as he so kindly predicted I may turn professional bruiser, a true cock o' the fancy, unless I enlist

—a soldier—foreign service and soon—that might be
best."

"Ar, p'raps it might—unless you get shot or flogged
for insubordination ! Howsever, talking o' gammon
rashers and coffee, tomorrow morn or, better, tea 's
arternoon."

"Now what on earth——"

"Along of our Lady o' Thames."

"What, with this infernal eye ? Not likely ! Besides,
she has probably heard of—of me—lately."

"Sir, she has so."

"Well, what has she heard ? "

"About Robert the Devil and your desprit fighting,
heavy drinking and——"

"Plenty of fight, Jasper, I admit, but hardly any drinking."

"Yet, Master Robin, 'tis said all along Thames-side
as you can down the drink as easy and hearty as you can
down a man."

"Cursed lies, Jasper ! "

"Ar, but sech lies are easy believed."

"Well, you know I'm not a drunkard and never could be.
You've always known that ! "

"Ar, I do, but she don't. Therefore s'pose you go and
tell her——"

"Not with this confounded eye ! Besides, if she has
swallowed such damned lies she probably—despises me,
eh, Jasper ? "

"Sir, since you ax me so eager, all as I can respond is—
ar."

"And what the devil does that mean ? "

"It means as how ' despise ' is the vord she used—vun
on 'em."

"Ha ! So she—she dares to despise me, does she ? "

"Master Rob, she's that high and noble o' sperrit she'd

dare you—ar, or anything in this here uniwerse, if put to it."

"Did she tell you she—despised me ? Did she ? If so, tell me all she said ; her exact words, mind ! "

"Werry good, sir. ' Jasper,' says she, and, mind you, she calls me by my baptismal these days, ' Jasper,' she says in that sweet woice of hers, ' Jasper,' says she——"

"And that's three times you've told me so."

"And, sir, I can't tell you nor nobody else too often. ' Jasper,' says she, sitting opposite me at her tea-table——"

"Ah, so you take tea with her, do you ? "

"Frequent, sir."

"Where ? "

"In the cottage."

"What cottage, man, and whereabouts."

"Vich, Master Robin, I are not at liberty to disclose. ' Jasper,' she says, ' next time you see that wretched, mis-guided, miz-erable young man '—meaning you, sir——"

"That is sufficiently obvious, confound you ! But go on."

" ' That miz-erable young man,' says she, ' pray tell him that I pity him for his shameful weakness, diss-pize him for his foolishness, and s-s-scorn him for so debasing himself. Tell him that, Jasper,' says she, looking as fierce as you are at this here moment. ' And tell him also,' she says, ' not to annoy me by his o-dee-us presence,' says she, ' until he is less——' "

"Eh—less ? Less what, Jasper ? "

"Master Robin, I don't hardly like to repeat all——"

"No matter ! Go on, man, let's have it ! Less—what ? "

"Less a object, sir."

"Ha, so now I'm an object, am I ? Well, go on, tell me all—every word she uttered."

"Less a object, Master Robin, of con-tempt, sir."

"And, by jingo, a pretty good effort, Jasper ! She can

lash with her tongue as hard, yes—harder than I can with
my fists."

"Ar!" sighed Mr. Shrig. "Vich took into con-
sideration, p'raps tea at four o'clock 's arternoon couldn't
hardly be recommended."

"And yet," said Robin, squaring his shoulders, "at
four o'clock this very afternoon she should see and hear me,
if only I knew where to find her."

"Sir, it so happens as I could tell you. But how about
your eye? Black John might doctor it for you."

"He can't. He's gone—left me in the lurch like all the
rest of 'em! I'm pretty lonely nowadays, Jasper!"

"But you've still got Sergeant Bob and all these here
black sheep o' yours and——"

"They don't count. And as for my eye—so much the
better! Yes, damme, I'll flaunt it at her. At four o'clock
she shall see it, and me behind it! Only tell me where to
find her, old fellow, like the good old Jasper you
are."

"Then, Master Rob, I happen to know as she'll be rowing
upstream to Brent's Farm at about about ha'-past three——"

"Good enough! Thanks, old friend; I'll be there to
exhibit this eye in all its mourning glory! Rather a pity I
haven't a cauliflower ear to go with it. The question is,
shall I trouble to shave or remain bristly—unshorn, un-
kempt and in my oldest togs—to show like the brutal
ruffian she deems me, an object of loathing and contempt—
eh, Jasper?"

"Her i-dentical vords, sir!"

"No hat, Jasper, and my shabbiest neckcloth instead of
cravat. Yes, b'gad, I'd better get used to shabbiness, for, if
you don't know already, Sir Oliver has positively disowned me, cast me off! If he stops my allowance, well and
good; if he doesn't, I shall return it. I can't and won't
touch a penny of his under the circumstances, not I!"

" Then, Master Robin, how shall you live ? "

" That's the confoundingly confounded question, Jasper ! I might sell this place. It's a valuable site, and yet—no, I can't do even that—his money bought it ! So the question becomes even more confoundedly unanswerable."

" Have you thought o' vork, Mr. Robin ? "

" Of course ! But the question still remains : what the devil can I work at ? I've neither trade nor profession, and I'm a perfect fool with a pen. The only thing I really know is just how and where to hit a man, so, if needs must, I'll turn professional bruiser and make myself champion of England—ay, of the world."

" D'ye think as you can ? "

" I'm sure of it ; aren't you ? "

" Yes, and so's Jessamy Todd."

" Aha, Jessamy ! By heavens, that's a grand idea, Jasper ! To help Jessamy hammer the Devil out of the ungodly, to fight beside him in his crusade against Old Nick ! "

" But what o' this here place and your black sheep ? "

" That's for old—for Sir Oliver to decide ; the place belongs to him. As for me—ah, for me—Jessamy, the open road with probably a good set-to at every town ! To fight beside a real, unbeaten champion like Jessamy would be a pure joy. Then, besides, there's good old Jerry Jarvis ; he might learn me to mend kettles and what not between whiles, and nowhere could I find two stauncher friends."

" Werry true, sir. And talking o' tea——"

" Eh ? Now what the deuce has tea to do with it ? "

" Everything, seeing as nothing's more companionable and soothing nor sociable than a cup o' tea, took leisurely by a fire, indoors or out. So, arter you've got rid o' they bristles and yourself into smarter at-tire, vith a cravat, don't forget kettle and teapot, Master Rob."

" Oh—ah, I see what you mean. But, Jasper, d'you suppose she'll—condescend to drink tea with a—dammit—an ' object of loathsome contempt ' ? "

" Not port nor yet sherry wine, nor yet ale nor beer, no ! The vord, sir, is tea ! No young fee-male, specially a lady tenderly nurtured, could find it easy to say ' no ' to a cup o' tea, properly brewed and offered vith doo humility and—at the proper time ! So, Master Rob, a shave, cravat and lump o' raw steak on your peeper should do you and it a power o' good ; sich is the adwice o' your oldest friend, same being J.S., take it or leave it, and good morning——"

" I'll take it, Jasper. And though I am outcast, deserted and pretty nearly destitute, the knowledge of you, old fellow, and your friendship is a mighty comfort and cheers me no end."

CHAPTER XXIII

Tells why Robin Threw His Tea-things into the River

AND SO, carefully shaven, combed, cravatted and dressed for the occasion, Robin, pulling upstream against the ebb, heard that same distant church clock strike four, glanced over his shoulder and beheld Her rowing slowly before him. Meeting his look, she frowned instantly, but did not alter her leisured stroke, therefore he had soon drawn level.

" Well," said she, frowning still, " drunkard ! "

" Wrong, madam ! " he retorted lightly. " Permit me to point out to your uninformed ladyship that hard drinking, like too much smoking, is extremely bad for the bellows. Hence I abhor drink and am never really drunk. All other sins and vices, mayhap, madam, but not the devastating foolery of drink. To thus inform your innocence or ignorance is one of the reasons for afflicting you with my detested presence ; another is to exhibit to your regard— my eye——"

" Oh, detested sir, it is mark of infamy only too shamefully manifest ! "

" Yes, it is pretty black, but I've seen worse. And my third reason is to invite your superbly immaculate and supremely dainty ladyship to sip tea with me in the nearest sylvan bower."

" But, Mr. Dale, my ladyship has no desire to sit and sip tea with brutal, fistic brawlers."

" Well then, madam, let us suppose you have enough imagination to deem my black eye a badge of honour and myself——"

" Quite impossible, sir ! Imagination totters at the mere suggestion ! "

" And that I myself, instead of brutal object for your ladyship's loathing, am neither better nor worse than— merely Robin ; would you then stoop to—to tea with poor Robin, not for your own pleasure, of course, but simply to comfort poor Robin ? Because, between you and me and Old Father Thames here, Robin was never so poor, never so woefully solitary as now. So—will you be so merciful, Bet ? "

" My gracious ! " she exclaimed, putting back the shadowy hood she wore. " Goodness me, what pitiful humility ! "

" I'm a truly piteous object, Bet. Oh yes ! For as a matter of fact I'm discredited, disinherited, disowned and deucedly dismally dejected—which, though alliterative, is too literally true ! "

" Indeed," she retorted, shaking her head disbelievingly, " you neither look nor sound in the least despondent."

" Because I'm looking at and listening to you ! " said he, urging his boat a little nearer. " For, somehow or other, I find you amazingly—stimulating. I suppose it's because you are so vital and—unexpected. Then—the way you move, your voice, your air——"

" You mean my hair, with an aitch, my so detested black hair."

" No, I can forget it when I look at the rest of you—in spite of that hood thing you have on today. Why do you wear it ? "

" Because I hate to be stared at—as you are doing now."

" Yes," he answered gravely, " I am and must, because the sight of you is doing me a power of good. You are becoming my necessity—almost."

" Almost—yes ! " she mocked. " For you have been well enough lately without your ' necessity '."

F

" No, I've done very badly."

" Meaning you were beaten in your horrible fighting. That black eye ! "

" Beaten ? " he repeated, with look of indignant amazement. " I—beaten ? No, most certainly not. I floored every man who dared me, so took them on two at a time. That was how I got this eye. But to win so constantly and with such ease loses its charm at last, and so——"

" ' Charm ' do you call it ? "

" Well then, ' attraction ', and so I have done with the whole business."

" Indeed ! Then because he is wearied with pummelling poor wretches into subjection for his brutal pleasure, I am now to be favoured with the presence of—Robert the Devil ! "

" Now what the—who——? Ah ! " exclaimed Robin, frowning. " I suppose Jasper Shrig peached. You have seen him often lately, I understand. What more did he tell you of my doings, pray ? "

" He explained why you were not compelled to take that long journey. Mr. Jasper is a most interesting and well-informed person."

" Yes, Jasper seems to know something about everything and everybody ; he always has. I suppose he told you what a most complete fool I was made to appear ? "

" No, not a word."

" Then I will—if you care to hear ? "

" Of course."

" First, how much do you know of the confounded business ? "

" Simply that you quarrelled with your best friend and challenged him to fight a duel—so wicked of you ! "

" That's as may be."

" Oh no, that was most certainly wicked ! But let me hear your side of the story."

" You shall—over yonder ! " said he, gesturing towards the tree-shaded bank nearby. " I've been wishing to tell you and ask your advice. I'll tell you all about it—over a cup of tea. So, Bet, will you—please ? "

She hesitated, eyeing him keenly, then turned her boat shoreward.

Thus presently they landed ; then while she set out the tea-things Robin, building the fire, enquired :

" Now that you know Jasper Shrig better, what do you think of him ? "

" That he's a perfect dear ! Yes, and most truly your friend, especially this afternoon ! "

" Ah, you saw him so recently ? "

" Yes, that is why I am here."

" Is it, by jingo ! Meaning he told you I should come hoping to see you ? "

" Of course ! How else should I be here ? "

" So, that was it ! Then blessings on his round old nob ! I'd hang a halo on that bullet head of his, if I could. Please, your ladyship, may I know what he said of me ? "

Here, sitting back on her heels, she mimicked Mr. Shrig thus :

" ' My Lady Bright, my young friend Master Robin, being so werry young for his age, is now his own fool, sorrer, regret and con-flummeration ; if he happened to be o' the fee-male sect he'd be veeping bitter tears for his own sorry self and them as he brought sorrer and woe upon, namely Sir Oliver Dale and the young Wi-count. At about four o'clock he'll come rowing upstream werry hard for sight o' you, my Lady o' Sunshine, so then p'raps you'll blame him as gentle as you think fit, because he ain't truly wicious, he's only a random fool, and—young ! ' And that," she ended, glancing at Robin's gloomy face, " so far as I remember, is exactly how and what he said. And now I suppose you are angry ? "

" Yes," answered Robin, scowling at the placid old river. " Yes, I'm furious with myself. Jasper is right. I was a fool, a most preposterous, superlative ass—because it all began with golden hair, Bet."

" Oh ? Whose ? "

" Surely I told you of her, the runaway lady named Phyllinda."

" Yes, I remember. You said her name was like a small, sweet song."

" Did I ? Oh well, I've told you I was an ass. However, for her sake I quarrelled with old Rags and Bones, my best friend."

" Because you were in love with her golden hair ! "

" Yes—she had the most glorious hair, Bet, very like—another's."

" And so—you love her."

" I did—at the time. But now——" Here Robin sighed and shook his head.

" Well, what now ? "

" I'm not so sure ; in fact I—don't believe I do."

" Yet you were going to fight your friend for her."

" At first yes, but afterwards when I'd had time to cool, not for her so much as because I—didn't want to fight." Here once again he tried to explain how a man who fears to risk his life is by fear compelled so to do or become his own shame.

" So you would have ventured your life and your friend's life merely to preserve your own self-respect ? "

" Yes, I suppose that was it."

" Then it was—abominable of you ! Yes, it——"

" But, Lord love me, Bet, what else could I do ? "

" Forgotten your egregious self just for once and begged your friend's pardon. I hope you did ? "

" No, I did not."

" So then you—fought ? "

" No again. Sir Oliver came and stopped it—tossed the swords into the river, and I standing there like the veriest fool. Ah, thank heaven our kettle's boiling at last; I'll brew the tea."

" No, I will, while you continue your tale. You were standing like—the veriest fool; go on from there." And so, unwillingly now, Robin told the story, ending with :

" Yes, I—even raised my hand against my governor, dear old Noll, one of the best, ah, one of the noblest men that ever lived. Oh, Bet, I—struck him, and with that blow killed all the regard he ever had for me—and no wonder ! So, there's the truth of it. Nothing can extenuate or ever excuse my damnable conduct. Whatever hardship is in store for me I richly deserve and am ready and willing to endure. But now the kettle's boiling, so let's——"

" And you refused to take the Viscount's proffered hand ? "

" Yes ! I wanted to, but—well, I didn't."

" That was worse than foolish ! It was as cruel and wicked as striking your benefactor."

" Oh well," he sighed, " it's over and done with ; so if you're going to brew the tea, pray do."

Instead, she rose, saying :

" I'm not inclined for tea—with you today."

" What ? " he exclaimed, starting up to his knees. " Are you leaving me, too ? Will you desert me, like all the rest ? "

" Not deserting you—yet," she replied gently. " But I am certainly going."

" Go then ! " he cried, and, snatching the purring kettle from the fire, he hurled it into the river, and after it the teapot, the plates and cups and saucers.

" How very silly of you ! " said she, stepping lightly into her boat and drawing on her hood.

" And here," quoth he, between shut teeth, " here ends our friendship ! "

"Does it ? " she enquired, taking up an oar. " I didn't say so."

" Well, I do ! If you can desert me now, like John and all the others, I've done with you and for ever ! "

" Have you, Robin ? " she enquired sweetly as she pushed out into deep water.

" Yes, damme, yes I have ! " he fumed.

" Gracious goodness ! " she exclaimed, pulling her hood closer. " What a wildly passionate young man you are ! Very young and dreadfully ungoverned——"

" Oh the devil ! " he cried, with hopeless gesture. " There's a curse on me ; I know now the curse of loneliness."

" No," she answered, shipping her oars. " You always have your good, wise friend Mr. Jasper ; go to him and ask his advice."

" Why his advice ? And what about ? "

Now as she rowed away, she answered and with sudden smiling glance :

" You and—me ! "

And so she left him to scowl down at the old river and up at cloudless sky and detest Robin Dale more than ever.

CHAPTER XXIV

How Mr. Shrig Banished Robin's Despondency

" SIR," said the sergeant, saluting smartly as usual, " beg to report as commissariat and general store is oncommon low."

" Sergeant," sighed Robin, shaking his head despondently, " I expect they'll be lower still, for, between you and me and this empty coffee-cup, our gamecocks will have to roost somewhere else, because we're closing, Bob."

" Closing ? Sir, d'ye mean—— ? "

" That we are shutting up—for lack of funds."

" I'm sorry for that, sir, very ! "

" So am I, Bob, bitterly."

" Things, sir, do seem to ha' gone wrong wi' us ever since Mr. John left us so sudden."

" Yes, Bob. Everything has gone devilish wrong. You'd better go and warn the men. How many have we this evening ? "

" Forty-one, sir."

" Then go and tell 'em to—to clear out. I can't—and won't. You must do this for me."

" Very good, sir ! "

And away stumped the old soldier, but presently came stumping back to salute again and say in voice somewhat harsher than usual :

" Sir, beg to report as men declare as they can raise four pound two shillings no pence and a farden, hoping as that may be o' service to you."

" Well now, Bob, hang me if that isn't downright handsome of them ! "

" Yessir. And beg to say as I can make it another twenty-three shillings and a groat, if so be you——"

" No no, Bob ! Thank you heartily, but no. Go back to the men and tell 'em I'm truly grateful to them one and all, but—it's no go ! Close today and this at once. Wish them all good luck, every man of them, Bob, and—goodbye ! " Uttering the word, up leapt Robin and, striding out into the courtyard, crossed to the old water-stairs and, here seated, bowed in the utmost dejection, gazed down at the ebbing tide with mournful, lacklustre eyes.

Now as he gazed down and listened to the rippling gurgle, this so familiar voice of his beloved river, he and old Thames, just now aglow with sunset, held communion, thus:

ROBIN (*enviously*) :   You look and sound uncommonly merry while here sit I beside you, old Father o' mine, as I always have done when anyways distressed.

THAMES :   What, boy, because she refused to drink tea along o' you, eh, eh ? And you pelting me wi' kettle and teapot, and cups, like petulant oaf ? Is she your—grief ?

ROBIN :   No—my own most detested self. For you were quite right. I am indeed my own trouble and curse—so much so that I'm sick of living and greatly minded to let you take me—out and away to the ocean and my final end.

THAMES :   That would not end you, Robin. Oh no ! In all God's creation there is no end, only change, for better or worse. Besides, I should refuse to drown you, because already you are changed and changing.

ROBIN :   I am ? In heaven's name, how ?

THAMES :   By scorning your baser self and wishing to amend it. So am I the more hopeful for the future of you.

ROBIN :   What future can there be for me ?

THAMES :   So great as your mind has power to imagine
   if backed by a will strong enough to make thought a
   reality. Whoso can greatly think and as greatly do
   must in the end greatly achieve.

ROBIN :   Suppose I don't wish to achieve ?

THAMES :   Then, of course, you were better dead than
   a do-nothing cumberer of the earth. But don't expect
   me to drown you, for I won't ! Try some pool or a
   pistol or a rope. Yes, better be dead and buried than a
   mere shadow in the sun ; far better change that
   powerful body o' yours into grass for cattle to fatten
   on and flowers o' the field for children to pluck, than
   rot in life to no purpose. Have you no ambitions, my
   poor youthful wretch ?

ROBIN :   No. I'm too low-spirited at present, anyhow.
   Have you any suggestions ?

THAMES :   Yes ! A letter to our good Sir Oliver craving
   pardon for that wicked blow.

ROBIN :   I'm such cursed dunce with a pen.

THAMES :   You are ! But no excuses ; do your best.

ROBIN (*unhappily*) :   I—I'll think about it.

THAMES :   You shall do more ; you must humble your
   arrogant pride—or I will.

ROBIN :   What will you do, Old Thing ?

THAMES :   Humble you, my cocksure lad, in spite of
   your strength and fistic might ! Yes, because you are
   my Robin I'll flatten you and your swaggering pride—
   flat as any pancake !

ROBIN :   Oh ? Indeed ! How and when, pray ?

The reply was a gurgle, a throaty chuckle ; and then into
Robin's range of vision stole the sharp prow of a speedy-
looking though weather-beaten boat, then his unwilling
eyes beheld the wide back of the man Bartrum and beyond
him a face neither round nor square, being that of Mr.
Shrig.

"Easy now, Bill!"

"Easy it is, Jarsper."

Very cautiously Mr. Shrig stepped out upon these ancient stairs green and slippery with age-old slime, nodded to Bartrum, who, nodding in reply, pushed off and rowed away.

"Well," demanded Robin, with sigh like a groan, "what d'ye want today?"

And mounting the stairs with very careful deliberation, Mr. Shrig replied, as once before:

"Robert the Devil!"

"Ha!" exclaimed Robin, scowling. "Now hearkee, Jasper. If you've come to lecture me again I'm in no mood to listen, so keep your confounded trap shut, or, better still—go!"

"Werry good, sir! But first am I free to utter—a—single vord?"

"Oh, if you must," sighed Robin wearily. "Say it and go." And the word Mr. Shrig uttered was:

"Fight."

"Eh?" enquired Robin, sitting up. "Where? When? And you'd better explain 'who' and 'why'!"

"Battle, sir. Murder, p'raps, and sudden death!" quoth Mr. Shrig sonorously.

"Well now," said Robin, his eyes brightening, "that sounds fairly promising. But how am I concerned?"

"As a public-sperrited citizen, Mr. Robin, for the law demands your ass-istance, the use o' they fists o' yourn in a matter o' life and death."

"No, Jasper; I've done with fighting."

"For the be-hoof of your enemy, Mr. Rob."

"Who? What enemy?"

"Your old friend Wiscount Ragvorth and——"

"So," cried Robin angrily. "You want me to fight Ragworth, do you? Well now, let me tell you——"

"No, Master Robin, I'm atelling you, therefore stow your whids, stint your gab and listen! I'm axing you to peril your precious blood and risk your dewoted life for your enemy Wiscount Rag——"

"He is not my enemy, Jasper; he never was—nor I his! But go on; what's this talk of peril and what not?"

"Werry good again, sir. Now—are you listening?"

"Yes, yes, of course I am! Go on."

"Then, Master Rob, this same friend as you meant to fight vith swords because he vasn't your enemy has—wanished."

"Good God! How, Jasper, when and——"

"This here arternoon about four o'clock the Wiscount sets out from Storringdean in his noo curricle along of the Lady Phillindy Mered——"

"Good great heavens! Has she vanished, too, Jasper?"

"Ar, hide and hair, Mr. Robin! At about five o'clock, not an hour ago; curricle aforesaid is found in the ditch, but—no horses, no Wiscount and no lady. But on the dashboard is a spot or so o' blood."

"Jasper, this is frightful! Was it an accident?"

"P'raps, and yet again—p'raps not."

"You mean they were stopped, attacked and robbed—footpads, highwaymen?"

"Stopped—ar! Attacked—ar again. But as for high tobymen——" Mr. Shrig pursed his lips in their soundless whistle and shook his head very solemnly.

"But who else would commit such an outrage—and in broad daylight? Ha—the Despards, dammem! Is this what you suspect, Jasper?"

Once again Mr. Shrig said "Ar", but this time with a gusty sigh.

"So?" cried Robin, leaping afoot. "You think, you suspect these cursed Despards have got—her—and poor old Rags! Well, let's get after them; you know where to

find 'em. Let's start now, this instant. Hurry, man, hurry !
Why stand here wasting precious time ? Come on, what are
we waiting for ? "

" My gig and Dan'l, sir ! Ah, but suspicion ain't fact !
Belief in guilt don't and can't prove same."

" Then what are you going to do about it ? "

" First of all, borrow they fists o' yours."

" And they're heartily at your service, Jasper."

" Not mine, sir ! If used, 'twill be to serve the law !
Vich I therefore must give you doo notice as 'twill be a
ticklish business, for, as aforesaid, you go to risk your
blood and precious life—if so minded. Are you ? "

" Well, of course, Jasper, and the sooner the better, for
the sake of old Rags and Bones and the Lady Phyllinda.
Besides, I'm hoping for a go at that great, powerful brute
the Count."

" Ar—but," quoth Mr. Shrig, beaming, " 'tis brother
Claude best pleases me, that smallish, soft-spoke, smiling,
ladylike gen'leman——"

" A contemptible fellow, Jasper ; a foul, crawling,
snake-like creature ! "

" Werry true, sir ; I took to same on sight most
asstonishing ! Snake's the vord, and snakes sting
occasional, or some do. Mr. Claude is a tip-top, reg'lar
out and outer—a capital capital cove is Mr. Claude,
therefore I have kept a ogle, or, as you might say, ' peeper ',
on him, constant, for 'tis him as is my vorry at this here
moment con-sidering that too-timid and tender young fee-
male and gentle lady——"

" Phyllinda ! " exclaimed Robin, clenching passionate
fists. " Yes, by heavens, Jasper, I—God keep her till we
can reach—her."

" Amen, Master Robin ! Vich I says werry solemn
indeed, her being a lamb so defenceless and him such a
creeping wolf all teeth and claws ! Now if she only had the

sperrit to strike in her own defence same like her sister, as you'll mind ? "

" Yes, Jasper, that poor unfortunate Lady Aramanthea who was drowned——"

" And—buried ! " nodded Mr. Shrig with emphasis. " I saw 'em bury her, and Mr. Claude so moist wi' grief ; ar, he shed tears so werry copious and con-wincing that I felt my innards yearn towards him—most sympathetic."

" You surprise me, Jasper ; mine would have heaved ! "

" Sir, I sap-rise myself, frequent."

" But, Jasper, what the devil ! Why waste time here, when are we going to do something ? If the Lady Phyllinda and old Rags are in such danger, when, man, when ? "

" Master Robin, it all depends."

" On what ? "

" My b'y Midge."

" Never heard of him. Your boy ? Good lord, is he your son, Jasper ? "

" Not hardly, sir, no ! Same being a werry small vaif as I've took under my ving same as I took Gimblet years ago, but he's even smaller than Gimblet—ar, so werry small I've named him ' Midge ', short for midget. He used to be the ill-used little slave of a chimbly sveep, therefore climbed chimbleys and consequent can climb anything else, pretty nigh ! And talking o' the Lady Arrymanthy, you didn't see much of her, did you ? "

" Eh, Lady Aramanthea ? Why no. My aunt showed her to me in bed, covered up to the chin, so all I saw was a face, Jasper, and, b'gad, a face that glared up at me most balefully—like a she-devil, and for no earthly reason ! Shocked me no end ! "

" P'raps she heard you call her ' a armful o' filth ', sir."

" Oh no, impossible ! And yet, come to think of it, the door was ajar. If she did hear me, no wonder she glared !

A pity, and I'm sorry, more especially as the poor young creature is dead——"

" And buried ! " quoth Mr. Shrig again.

" She was too young to die, Jasper—and such death ! I wonder how it happened."

" And here's my Midge ! "

" Eh ? The boy ? Where ? "

" Behind you, sir."

Turning hastily, Robin beheld a small urchin in his immediate rear, so very diminutive he might have been a child but for his eyes, large, wistful and aged by more than years, a boy this made wiser than his age by past suffering and remembered evils. And now, looking up at tall Robin with the keen gaze of one much too wise in experience of life, the boy took off his neat cap, bobbed his small, dark head, saying in voice unexpectedly sweet :

" Mornen, sir ; servink, sir ! Dan'l's 'ere, Guvnor."

" Werry good, m' lad, though you dropped your aitch ! "

" Haccidental ! Sorry, Guv."

" Anything to report ? "

" No, Guv, only me and gig's awaitin' along of Dan'l ! "

" Werry good again ! Now cut back to Dan'l and say as I'm coming along o' Mr. Robin—this gen'leman being same."

" I guessed as much," said the boy, surveying Robin from head to foot with his quick, bright glance. " I'm a off 'un ! " And off he sped.

" Now," said Mr. Shrig portentously, " seeing as we're setting out to do summat a bit different to picking nosegays in a flowery garden, the question is, are you armed ? "

" Yes, old fellow, with my fists."

" And, Master Rob, the best in all England—agin other fists, but not so apt agin steel or bullet ! So I'll ax you to favour me by taking this here." And from somewhere about his person Mr. Shrig produced, and with amazing speed, a small though very business-like pistol.

Whereat Robin laughed, and more joyously than he had done lately, and waved it aside, saying :

" No thanks, Jasper. I prefer nature's weapons. But if I must go armed, I'll take a good stout bludgeon."

" Vich same article you shall find in my gig, Master Robin ; and since you are game, as expected, to risk yourself on this here adwenture serving the law, toddle along o' Jarsper."

CHAPTER XXV

How They Set Out to Commit a Felony

" THIS HERE case," said Mr. Shrig, touching his horse to faster gait, " being no more than suspicion, ain't a case— eh, Dan'l ? " And from his perch beside the boy Midge in the rumble behind Dan'l replied and in tone mournful as his drooping " weepers " :

" Too true, Jarsper ; no case and no search warrant ! "

" Because no time for same ! " sighed Mr. Shrig.

" No matter," said Robin grimly ; " since we mean to rescue old Rags and the Lady Phyllinda, we'll act without any confounded warrant."

" Vich means committing a felony, Mr. Rob ! "

" ' Breaking and entering ' ! " sighed Dan'l.

" A werry hee-nious offence, sir ! "

" Means the noose or Botany Bay, sir ! " groaned Dan'l.

" Ar ! " quoth Mr. Shrig. " Transportation certainly ! "

" However," said Robin, squaring his shoulders, " if they have old Rags and Bones, I'll do all the ' breaking and entering ' necessary to get him out."

" You hear that, Dan'l ? "

" True blue as expected, Jarsper ! And, Mr. Dale sir, in your breaking the law and committing this here felony, the law, in the shape o' Jarsper and me, 'll stand by to back you up, sir."

" And me, too ! " piped Midge.

" Ay, all three on us, Mr. Dale."

" From a distance ! " added Mr. Shrig.

" Though not a very distant distance ! " said Dan'l, left eyelid flickering.

" Now if," quoth Mr. Shrig portentously, " as I guess
and hope, the Wiscount is there for you to rescue, Master
Rob, werry good indeed ! Ah, but to remove the lady from
the house and care of her lawful app'inted guardian is
another felony—the serious crime of ab-duction vich the
law comes down on werry heavy."

" No matter ! " said Robin cheerily. " A double-dyed
felon I'll be, Jasper, yes, by jingo, and all by reason of
associating with you and Dan'l."

" An' me, too, sir ! " piped Midge again.

" Yes, b'gad, and you also ! " chuckled Robin, turning to
nod at the eager boy. " And now, Jasper old friend, tell me
precisely what I am to do."

" Master Robin, I'm acting on suspicion only, vich
means p'raps as I'm acting like a nass—but said animal is a
stubborn beast and so am I ! At best, I'm only guessing, and
as a ordinary man I'd take a chance, but as a nofficer o' the
law I musn't and can't. For the law demands proof, and
proof ain't—no, never a tittle or jot, except for summat as
may be nothing, eh, Dan'l ? "

" Meaning the ship, Jarsper ? "

" Ar, the Lady Phyllindy's big yacht as is laying below
bridge ready to slip moorings at any moment ! From vich
fact I de-dooce as the lady owner and friends is going to take
a trip abroad. ' And werry nice, too,' says the law, ' and
werry nat'ral, the veather being so calm and sunny.' ' But,'
says I, ' suppose said lady, being so terrimendious rich, is
being took and compelled to sea and matrimony both agin
her desire ? ' ' Prove it ! ' cries the law, werry fierce. ' I
can't,' says I, werry meek. ' Then you have no case ! '
cries the law. " No more I ain't," says I, ' but——'
' Enough ! ' thunders the law. ' I admit no " buts " or
" ifs ", neither possibles nor probables ; facts and proof,
give me these or be off ! And remember " the liberty o' the
subject "—interfere at your own peril ! ' shouts the law,

fiercer than ever. And—there y'are, Master Rob; there's this case as ain't a case."

"Then, by heavens, Jasper old boy, tell me how and I'll make it one! Only tell me what I must do."

"Werry good, Master Rob. You'll enter Framling Manor by the old haunted tower so soon as 'tis dark enough for the flames to show nice and bright."

"Eh? Flames, d'you say?"

"Ar! There's a ancient barn as is going to ketch fire."

"Is there, b'gad!"

"Dry as tinder, Master Rob, and 'll blaze werry bee-ootiful indeed. And there's nothing like a good big blaze to draw folks!"

"Aha, Jasper, you mean——"

"That all folks being dooly drawed out thereby, you'll go in, free the Wiscount, if he's there, and ab-duct lady, if she ain't been took already, then out you'll come and find us standing by to aid, comfort, abet and ab-scond along o' you immediate."

"Good!" exclaimed Robin, eyes asparkle and fists clenched instinctively. "Aha, my old Jasper, most excellent tactician. I only hope you haven't made it all too easy for me."

"Easy?" repeated Mr. Shrig in shocked accents. "D'ye hear that, Dan'l?"

"Ay, I did so!" replied Dan'l with laugh like a moan. "Lord, Mr. Robin sir, and you alone agin all them murder-ous Eye-talians wi' their daggers——"

"Stilettas," sighed Mr. Shrig; "sharp as needles! No, you ain't agoing to find it too easy—werry much the rewerse."

"Good again, Jasper, for I want action, and if I'm to receive my—hum—quietus, as well or better this way than any other."

" No more cups o' tea, then, along of—Old Feyther Thames ? "

" Of course not," answered Robin, " never again ! " Here he sighed profoundly, at the which most unwonted sound Mr. Shrig shot a keen side-glance at him, saying :

" No more you could, being a stiff un, seeing as how cups o' tea and corpses don't hardly go together, leastvays not werry often."

" But," said Robin, and very wistfully, after they had travelled some little distance in a thoughtful silence, " you might tell—anyone who cares to listen that one of the last things I said was—that I could have grown quite—used to—black hair—in time. Will you remember this, in case, Jasper ? "

" Ar ! " replied Mr. Shrig, then turned away to wink very knowingly at nothing in particular.

CHAPTER XXVI

Tells What Befell Our Conquering Hero at Framling Manor

THE SUN was setting as Mr. Shrig checked his speedy animal to a walk and turned down a shady lane that presently narrowed to a grassy track shut in by dense leafage, beyond which gleamed the river.

"And now," quoth Mr. Shrig, reining to a stop, "the vord is caution!" So saying, he alighted, beckoning Robin and his boy Midge to follow, whereupon Dan'l, climbing into the driving-seat, took the reins and enquired :

"In the spinney, Jarsper ? "

"Ar!" replied Mr. Shrig, reaching for his knobbly stick. "Lay low till I j'ine ye. Now the dark lantern and Mr. Rob's bat." This proved to be a short, heavy bludgeon, which Robin twirled lightly, exclaiming :

"Aha, here are headaches for some o' these ruffians ! Lead on, old fellow ; I yearn to be at them."

"Plenty o' time, Master Rob ; there's a goodish half-hour afore the sun goes down."

"But why the deuce wait till then ? "

"Shadders, sir ; must have shadders to do justice to my bonfire. However, foller me close and use your eyes and ears—constant. If you see or hear anything, stop and don't move till I do and—norra vord ! Easy now ! "

He led them down to the river and along the bank, which hereabout was shaded by trees and thickets ; but on he went as though familiar with the place, following a path unseen amid this dense undergrowth, until, reaching the edge of this little wood, he halted to point with his stick and say, almost whispering :

" The boathouse ! "

" Lord ! " exclaimed Robin, also in hushed tone. " It looks more like an old Roman temple with that portico and those columns."

" Ar, mebbe it was, years ago, being so werry ancient ; old as the tower, I reckon. And it had a underground passage to same, vich has fell in and got itself choked, more's the pity. So your only entrance must be by the door vich is kept locked, bolted and barred night and day."

" Then how d'you expect me to get in ? "

" B' means o' my Midget here, oo so soon as 'tis dark enough is agoing to do a bit o' climbing ; eh, my b'y ? "

" Ar, Gov ; up the ivy like as you showed me las' night."

" Sounds pretty dangerous, Jasper ! "

" Cor luv a duck no, sir ! " piped Midge. " Not for me it h-aint ; it'll be h-easy as kiss me 'and. Mister Robin, I can climb h-anythink, I can."

" And you've got they aitches all mixed up again, Midge," sighed Mr. Shrig.

" Very sorry, Gov ! I tries 'eavens-'ard h-I do, but them h-aitches is allus adodgin' of me."

" Werry true, m' lad ; aitch is a oncommon slippery customer to tackle unless collared prompt ! And, Mr. Robin, 'twas hereabouts as Lady Arrymanthy flattened Mr. Claude vith her oar, like a reg'lar ama-zeen ! "

" Yes," said Robin musingly. " The more I hear of her the better I like her."

" Though a bit late, sir, seeing as how they've buried her—a slap-up coffin vith silver handles and a large silver plate on the lid vith her name and age in capital letters, and all covered wi' flowers and wreaths wi' cards tied onto 'em. ' From her heart-broke Claude ' says vun ; ' From her adoring Hugo ' says another, and all wrote so pretty, too ! "

" You seem to have taken mighty interest in her funeral, Jasper."

" Ar, I did—and—I do ! "

" But why, seeing the unfortunate young lady is—gone ?"

" Ay, ashes to ashes, Master Rob ; dust to dust, sir."

" Jasper, why so infernally dismal ? "

" Vich, sir, ' in the midst o' life us may be in death ', b' reason o' man-traps, spring-guns and trip-vires—so tread careful as I do, foller me close, and the vord now is ' mum ' ! "

More cautiously than ever he led them on again where leafage was thickest and shadow densest, until Robin espied a house that seemed all steep gables and twisted chimneys, a spacious dwelling flanked by the great, square tower hoary with years and clothed, more or less, with age-old ivy to its weather-worn battlements ; and, gazing up at this grim relic, Robin noticed that the loop-holes of its topmost story had been widened to latticed windows.

" Oh, Gov," whispered the eager boy, " shall I go now ? " Mr. Shrig glanced up at the sky, where a ruddy sunset was fading, then round about where shadows were deepening, and replied :

" Another ten minutes, my midget. So let's hear you repeat all as I've told you to do, and in a visper."

" Righto, Gov. I'm t' go up the ivy very quiet, get me onto the roof, creep me down the stairs, listen at every door, then creep me on down to the tower door, open it wivout a sound and cut back here t' you and Mist' Robin. And the sun's down at last, so shall I go ? "

" Another ten minutes, m' b'y."

" You says that afore."

" And I says it again. Ha' patience and heark to all as I now tell Mr. Robin. Sir, having got into the tower, you'll ob-serve a smallish door on your left as leads into the house, so pass it, then afore you in the right-hand corner you'll espy a spi-reel stair as 'll twist you down through the floor into the dungeons and up through the ceiling to three rooms above, each atop o' t'other, and so up to the battle-ments. And 'tis below in said dungeons as you'll find the Wiscount alive and kicking—I hope. Now, Midge, take precious good care not to be heered or seen. Off ye go ! "

" Righto, Gov ! " he whispered and sped away on sound-less feet to vanish in the ever-deepening shadows.

" D'you think he'll do it ? " enquired Robin anxiously.

" Lord love you, yes, he'll be up that old tower, sir, in a pig's-visper, Master Rob ! Keep your ogles on that theer ivy, though the shadders are nice and dense ! "

So Robin watched that grim old tower looming even grimmer in the gathering darkness ; and presently, half-hidden in that dense ivy, a shadow darker than the dark began to mount—up and up with surprising speed and with never a pause until that small nimble shape, outlined for a moment against the sky, vanished behind the battlements.

" Ah, bravo ! " exclaimed Robin under his breath. " B'gad, he's done it ! A smart, plucky little fellow, Jasper ! "

" Ar ! " quoth Mr. Shrig, busying himself to light the lantern.

" He's certainly surprisingly sharp, too, and mighty knowing for his age. How old is he ? "

" Master Rob, ekker alone responds ! Howsever, he took to the law same as he took to me—immediate ! "

" How did you come by him, Jasper ? "

" In a back alley, a little half-starved creeter being trounced by a chimbley sweep. So, arter I'd dooly trounced said sweep, ' Boy,' I says, ' could you eat a plate o' roast beef ? ' ' Oh, Governor,' he says, ' could I eat forty plates o' beef ? ' So I took him home along o' me to The Gun and Corporal Dick, and vith us he's been ever since."

"And, old fellow, I'm beginning to think he ought to be back with us now."

"Not hardly, Mr. Robin. That tower's a pretty big place for a small b'y to seek over and search."

"Yes, I suppose so. But damme if I like this inaction, this—this waiting. Suppose some of those Italian brutes catch him, how then?"

"He'll vistle!"

"Eh? What? How d'you mean—whistle?"

"Sir, he's got a silver vistle slung about his neck, and if in any trouble he blows it and I act—prompt."

"But if he whistled now, how on earth could you get in to help the little fellow?"

"Knock at the front door and demand to see Mr. Claude Despard."

"And suppose he has no chance to blow his confounded whistle?"

"Master Rob, I can't and don't never suppose no sich impossibility. So now let's hush and hark." Thus for some while they were mute, the dark lantern fuming between them on the grass. But, as the slow minutes dragged, and evening deepened to night, Robin grew ever the more restless, until, at last:

"Jasper," he whispered tensely, "if he doesn't return soon I shall go in after him."

"But how can you, sir, till he opens that theer door?"

"By the ivy-stems, of course."

"No, Master Rob; they'd never bear your weight!"

"I'll have a dev'lish good try, Jasper."

"At your peril, sir!"

"To peril life, old fellow, makes existence more interesting, at least for me. So I shall go after your midget boy unless he turns up before I count a hundred. One——"

"Thankee, sir, but you don't have to, Mr. Robin, 'cause

h-ere I h-am, sir," whispered a voice surprisingly near in the now enveloping darkness.

" Oho, good boy ! " exclaimed Robin. " What kept you so long, my hearty ? "

" She did, sir."

" She ? D'you mean—a beautiful lady with golden hair, boy ? "

" Yessir ! "

" Aha, so you found her in the tower ? "

" Yessir ; I seen and spoke with her, too, I did."

" Splendid fellow ! "

" Caution, sir ! " Mr. Shrig warned. " Now, Midge, make your report and speak soft ! "

" Very good, Gov. H-aving got me into the tower h-I creeps down some narrer stairs an' hears somebody sobbin' and moanin' behind a door as is locked. So I thinks she must be the lady, so I taps very gentle and hails her froo the key'ole very soft, and ' O oos there ? ' she says. ' 'Sme, lady,' says I, ' Mr. Jarsper Shrig's Midge,' I says, ' and I've come along of him and Mister Robin Dale to set ye free,' says I. So then she unlocks the door an' there she is—all tears and golden 'air ; and ' Oh, where are they ? ' says she, and ' 'Ave they got him, the Viscount Ragworth, safe ? ' ' Yes, lady,' says I, ' Mister Dale 'll 'ave him h-out, safe an' sound, so soon as I let 'im in,' I says. ' So now you come 'long o' me and run to Jarsper while me and Mister Dale lets out the Viscount,' I says ; and ' Oh, thank God,' says she and calls me a little h-angel, ' Which I ain't, ma'm,' I says. So then she tries to kiss me, but I ducks it. Then we 'ears futsteps and a voice callin' out ' Briggs, tell me the moment as Count Hugo returns ' ; and she sobs, ' Oh, it's Claude,' and pulls me in an' locks the door very quick. So then we h-ears h'm outside and 'e bangs the door an' kicks it an' shouts to 'er to come out or it'll be worse for 'er Viscount. But all she does is fall on 'er knees and cry tears all over herself. So I w'ispers in 'er ear'ole, ' Don't take on, lady ; Jarsper's awaitin' and Mister Robin's acomin',' I says. But ' Oh,' says she, ' listen to Claude ' ; and there 'e is, shoutin' again, sayin' as 'e'll fetch his men to chop down the door, and off 'e goes. So then ' Lady,' I says, ' now's y'r time to cut off along o' me to Jarsper.' ' Oh, I dassent,' she says. ' Very good,' says I ; ' keep the door locked and wait till me and Mister Robin comes for ye.' So then I skips down all them steps, unlocks the big old door, and h-ere I h-am ! "

" And, by jingo," exclaimed Robin, clasping his arm about this small, dim-seen speaker, " a regular little Trojan you are, a positive trump ; eh, Jasper ? "

" A sprig o' the law, Master Rob ; a shoot as promises."

" And the door's open, Mist' Robin, so shall us go, sir ? "

" ' Us ' ? " Robin repeated. " D'you mean you want to go with me, boy ? "

" Yes please, sir ! "

" But I'm hoping there may be a bit of a scrimmage, and if you got hurt——"

" I wouldn't, sir ; ho no, not me ! 'Sides, you'll need me to show the way, and, seein' as how I promised the lady, you should ought to lemme go with ye, sir."

" How say you, Jasper ? Suppose I run into these ruffians, as probably I may, and they show fight, as they certainly will—how then ? "

" Midge'll cut back and report same to me immediate. You hear m', b'y ? If Mr. Robin is set on, you'll run back here to me, fast as you can."

" Yus, Gov, like a arrer ! "

" Very well," said Robin, stifling a chuckle ; " come on, Midge, my small heart of oak."

" You're forgetting your bat, sir ! " said Mr. Shrig reproachfully.

" So I was ! " said Robin, taking the weapon and giving

it a preliminary flourish. "But I have the dark lantern. And what of you, Jasper ? "

"I'm agoing to fetch Dan'l, and then bide here for ye. And no bloodshed, if you please, Master Rob ; don't go looking for a fight. Go cautious, bring out the prisoners and —norra sound, if possible."

"Right you are, Jasper. And I'll take care of your little valiant imp."

"Sir, I'm hoping and expecting as he'll take care o' you ; eh, Midge ? "

"Yus, Gov, I'll keep my h-eye on 'im, I will."

"Come on, then," chuckled Robin happily ; "forward, Midge, my pocket Achilles, my budding Ajax, shoulder to knee." So forward they stole, close together in the darkness, until the grim old tower was looming before and above them, and here the boy drew closer to whisper :

"Is it ladies first, Mist' Robin ? "

"Usually, comrade. But tonight we'll have the gentleman first, because I know he'd like to help us rescue the lady."

"Well, 'ere we are, sir ; 'ere's the door."

"Yes, I feel it—banded with iron, b'gad, and studded with great nails."

"'Tis very 'eavy t' move, sir, and squeaks it do ! "

"Then gently does it. Here goes ! " But, despite his care, this ponderous door squeaked and groaned in loud complaint as he swung it gently open upon a darkness more profound than this moonless night. For a moment he stood hushed and still to listen, then, advancing a cautious pace, slid back the shutter of his lantern, whose beam showed a spacious stone-flagged chamber, its massive left wall pierced by a deep arch with a door that stood wide open. To the right in shadowy corner a narrow stair wound itself down through the pavement and up through the ceiling. Robin had taken a pace towards this stair, when he halted very suddenly, as from somewhere high overhead came a vague clamour of voices followed by thud of heavy blows, crash of splintering woodwork and a shrill scream.

" Ooh ! " gasped Midge. " That's the lady ! They're choppin' the door down, sir."

" Yes," said Robin, placing his lantern on the floor, " that will indeed be our Mr. Claude ! Go warn Jasper— run ! " Then with a leap Robin was on and speeding up that winding stair, for in his ears was a woman's voice upraised in supplication :

" No, Claude ! Oh no, for mercy's sake. Don't shame me ! Ah, for God's sake——"

Guided by these piteous outcries, on sped Robin, lusting for combat, on and up, until he beheld flickering lights that showed him a shattered door, and beyond this—Phyllinda struggling feebly in Claude Despard's merciless embrace and watched by men who laughed. . . .

" Ha—damned ruffians ! " cried Robin, and sprang at them to smite and conquer as usual—but was tripped by an out-thrust foot, staggered by an unseen, stunning blow, beaten to his knees ; then, lying sick, helpless and half aswoon, glimpsed the flash of steel. And thus, knowing at last all the shame and bitterness of defeat, he strove no more, but gasped :

" Stab me and—be damned ! Kill me and—make—an end."

" Oh no, no ! " cried a mocking voice, at sound of which the furious tumult around him was hushed. " Ah no, Master Robin Dale, I cannot allow you to be killed, at least not in the presence of my too-sensitive Linda. Were she absent and we in my beautiful Italy—ah, then, what exquisite joy to accord you the death you plead for so piteously. But alas, we are in your damnably dismal England and here it would be adjudged murder. Yet there are other methods whereby your plea may be granted ; an accidental fall properly contrived, for instance, or, better still, to lie dungeoned and forgotten in this aged tower—darkness, Mr. Dale, hunger and thirst, until—oh, admirable ! Thus shall we bestow the favour you desire ! "

Here Mr. Claude issued rapid orders in Italian and to such effect that Robin, bound and helpless, was dragged away and down those many stairs, to be tumbled at last into a place of utter and blinding darkness.

CHAPTER XXVII

Which is a Chapter of Counteraction

AFTER such complete disaster, the proudest Hero of Romance might have shed tears (manful and bitter, of course) for shame of his swift and most inglorious defeat, or raged (disdainfully) against his impotence and prisoning bonds ; but Robin, being merely himself, began to chuckle. Then he laughed, until from somewhere in the darkness nearby a woeful voice enquired :

" Who is the fool can laugh in such infernal place as this ? What idiot can think this accursed dungeon so funny ? "

And, laughing still, Robin contrived to answer :

" Not the dungeon, old boy ; I'm the fool I laugh at. Ah, but, Rags old fellow, dear old Rags and Bones, at least I've found you ! "

" Robin ! " cried the Viscount, in tone now anything but woeful. " Can this really be you ? "

" None other, old boy."

" But what brings you in this hellish place ? "

" You do, Rags, and this is what's so devilish funny. Here came I like a deuced conquering hero to your rescue, and now the joke of it is—here am I bruised, battered, helpless, trussed up like a confounded chicken, waiting for someone to rescue me ! Now laugh, Bones, laugh ! "

But instead the Viscount enquired and very seriously :

" So you came here for my sake, Robin ? "

" Of course, Rags, naturally, and for—your Phyllinda."

" Mine, Robin ? But didn't you—don't you——? "

" My dear old Bones, I've been no end and all sorts of a
fool ! She never loved me and never could ; it was and is—
you. She's yours, old boy—to have and to hold—in
marital bonds, and my blessings on you both ! Now I'll
roll over to you and we'll have a try at freeing each
other."

" But my hands are tied behind me, Robin, and feeling
pretty numb."

" So are mine, old boy ! However, we'll have a go at it.
Here I come ! "

Thus, in the darkness, unseen, they met, to twist and
writhe and fumble with the cords that bound them, until :

" It's no go ! " Robin growled at last.

" Not a bit ! " sighed the Viscount. " And, oh, Robin,
when I think of Phyllinda and that beast——"

" Yes, old boy, all delicately dainty beastliness is our
Claude."

" He—he needs—killing ! " panted the Viscount.

" No, whipping ! I agree he'd certainly be nicer dead.
But a good sound drubbing he'd feel more, and be able
to think upon, a fadeless, unforgettable soul-harrowing
memory, Rags."

" Yes, but when I think of him and Phyllin——"

" Then don't ! Tell me instead how it all happened.
They beset you on the road, I suppose ? "

" Yes, and we had only just left Storringdean—hardly out
of sight of the park gates when they were on us, six of them.
I did my best with the butt of my whip, yet I was soon down
and helpless. They drove off my horses and ran the curricle
into the hedge to make it seem an accident—and a fatal one
for me, because the egregious, too-dainty vileness——"

" Accursed Claude, yes ? "

" Would have had his fellows brain me but for the
Count. Yes, I should be extremely dead but for Count
Hugo."

" Then my blessings on the Count ! "

" So they brought me here and—ha, Robin, as I lay help-less, this dainty, smiling fiend stood over me and told me—how—he was going to—force her—— Ah, curse him, I cannot say it ! But boasted how she would beg him to marry her, yes—plead with him—on her knees—— Robin, I couldn't bear to listen. I shouted—screamed to drown his shameless words ! And now—God help me, here I lie helpless—in torment, knowing she is at his mercy. This evening he sails with her for Italy, and tonight——"

" Not so, Rags ; they'll do no sailing this night, because, though I've made such a completely damnable mess of things, Jasper Shrig won't——"

" Shrig ? " cried the Viscount in tone very like rapture. " Is he here, too ? "

" Old boy, he's standing by watching and waiting for the proper moment to act, and when he does—things will happen, as they always do when Jasper takes a hand. So, my dear old Rags and Bones, pluck up, because though I so miserably failed you, he will not ! So take comfort in our good old grimly cautious sure-as-death Jasper."

" I do and shall, old f'low, and be eternally grateful to you for venturing here on her behalf and mine. I cannot tell you—— God only knows what it means to me to have you again and here beside me in this hell."

" And yet," groaned Robin, " I failed you ! Yes, Rags, I'm a failure ! I that came here eager for battle—my only fear lest I should kill too many of them—am no better than a beaten hound ! Fighting is about the only thing I do well, and I fail even at that ! Ha, damme, I shan't be able to look myself in the face, because, at last, I am indeed my own shame."

" No no, Robin ; you were simply unlucky——"

" I'm a fool and a failure, I tell you ! "

" And I tell you," said the Viscount with vehemence,

" that as you lie here beside me, beaten and defeated, I never felt prouder of your friendship than now."

Thus they endeavoured to comfort one another, and the more easily and whole-heartedly because of the enveloping darkness.

" However," mourned Robin, " I'm no better than a confounded broken reed! The next time I shave, if I ever do, the sight of my phiz in the looking-glass will fairly turn my stom——"

Screech of key in lock, glare of sudden blinding light, a voice that whispered :

" 'Sme, Mist' Robin. I've come to git you out an' ris-cue bofe o' ye, 'cause Jarsper's bonfire's ablazin' so lovely it's drawed 'em all out and they're atryin' to put it out, so now's y'r time, sir, an' I got Jarsper's own knife t' cut them ropes, so if——"

" Oh, Midge, my blessed mighty atom ! " laughed Robin, though rather shakily. " Cut away, and the Viscount first."

The boy's small, eager hands wrought so deftly that very soon Robin was up and stretching his limps joyously, while the Viscount, struggling painfully to his knees, remained crouched thus and, stifling a groan, gasped instead :

" Oh, my boy, is the lady—safe ? "

" Jarsper says ' ar ', my lord, if you'll do as 'e says, and wot 'e says is for you bofe to cut away t' the spinney while the coast's clear becos o' the fire and wait for him there. So be quick, sirs, quick ! "

" Right, my amazing imp," said Robin, " we'll gallop forth forthwith ! So up with you, Rags, and come on."

" 'Fraid I can't, old fellow ; my legs feel as if they belonged to someone else. But off with you, Robin ; I'll follow—soon as possible. Oh, run, man, run ! "

" And leave you here ? Not likely, damme, no ! Let me lift you afoot. There now ! Try to walk. Ah, pretty painful,

G

eh, old boy ? And no wonder, considering how long you've been tied up."

" Ooh, sirs," whispered the boy, dancing with impatience, " Jarsper says as how you should be quick—afore they comes back from the bonfire."

" And here am I," groaned the Viscount, " tottering and feeble as an ancient greybeard."

" Poor old Bones ! Can you totter up that confounded stone corkscrew?"

" Not yet, Robin, though my pins begin to feel more like my own. I shall be all right soon now. So off with you, I shall manage better alone."

" I might carry you, Rags ; yes, b' jingo—pickaback, old man, so up you get and——"

" His-s-sh ! " whispered the boy in sudden alarm. " Somebody's acomin ' ! " Mute and motionless all three, they listened, until :

" What means that light down there ? Guiseppe, is it you ? " demanded a voice most hatefully familiar, at sound of which the Viscount gnashed his teeth and Robin clenched his fists. . . . The voice drew nearer, speaking now in Italian, feet tripped lightly down the stair, halted suddenly, and Mr. Claude Despard, uttering a gasp, turned to flee. But his slimly elegant leg was clutched by two small arms that, despite frantic kicks and buffets, clung fast—until Robin had seized him, saying happily :

" Welcome, Mr. Claude ! My lord Viscount and I greet you with joy ineffable ! For here are no trembling women for you to shame and terrify. Lately, sir, I heard a lady scream because of you. So now you shall howl because of us ! " Then, in spite of his most desperate though futile struggles, Mr. Claude was shaken and whirled face down across the knee of his merciless assailant, who cried, laughingly :

" Aha ! Poetic justice, Rags ! A dream come true, a

yearning satisfied—oh joy! Lay into him with the rope's-
end, old boy! Trounce him as he deserves, which is
impossible, of course, but do your best and hard, Rags,
hard!"

And forgetting his own aches and pains, the Viscount
did as suggested, until, after a season of violent effort, he
panted:

"Robin, old—f'low—that's done me—power o' good!
Arms and legs—my own again! I can walk now—even
run."

"Excellent!" laughed Robin and loosed his victim, who,
sliding from his knee, fell to the pavement and lay there
motionless and mute as he had been throughout this (for
him) most painful interlude; only he gazed up at Robin with
a quite dreadful intentness. And looking down on him,
Robin exclaimed in contemptuous disgust:

"Pah! You loathsome, venomous little pest, someone
who doesn't mind foul messes ought to tread on you, for,
b'gad, you'd be so much pleasanter as a corpse, so I'm
hoping someone will! Now, Rags, if you're ready, let's——
No, d'ye hear that shout? We're too late; they're coming
—and in force, too! Well, let 'em. It's do or die now, Rags,
so, shoulder to shoulder—— Midge, get you behind us and
lie low. Now for it!"

A vague hubbub growing rapidly louder, trample of
hurrying feet and down upon them, backed by his four
Italians, came Count Hugo, seeming more gigantic and
dominating than ever. And now at last Mr. Claude gave
tongue, for, lying pitifully outstretched upon the hard
pavement, he wailed in tones as piteous:

"Oh, Hugo, brother Hugo, strike them down! Oh,
Hugo, they have so brutalised me. Look at me. They have
nearly killed me between them. Slay them, Hugo, for the
murderous house-breakers they are and as the law allows
and expects in defence of hearth and home. You are armed,

so shoot them, or—better give me your pistols and I'll take joy to shoot."

"Werry wrong o' you, sir! Vich so being, the vord is 'No'! And 'tis the law as so commands!" Uttering these words, the law (deliberate as usual) in the form of Mr. Shrig descended upon them, saying as he did so :

"If there's to be any shooting, I'll do it!"

As he spoke, his right hand vanished, to reappear grasping a pistol, its muzzle seeming to threaten each and all while his bright, roving glance questioned every face. Thus ensued a hush wherein none moved or spoke until upon that winding, shadowy stair was shuffle of stealthy feet that crept—then a voice enquired, plaintively :

"Which on 'em do I shoot first, Jarsper?" Whereto Mr. Shrig responded :

"Dan'l, it all depends on this here Count Hugo. And, sir, in us you now behold the law as has got you each and every, sir, in a cross-fire, four barkers, Count, or, as you might say, 'pops', and vith fingers on triggers o' same. Therefore I adwise you to order your Eyetallyuns to drop their stilettas, also if you happen to have any veppings concealed about your person, obleege by handing 'em over."

"So ho!" exclaimed the Count, squaring his mighty shoulders defiantly ; then he laughed, saying : "Shrig, you are a ridiculously impertinent, most audacious and comical rascal."

"No, sir, I am a dootifully active limb o' the law, as aforesaid——"

"And pray, what are you doing here in the privacy of my house ?"

"I am here, sir, in Lady Meredith's mansion as in dooty bound——"

"Then I demand to see your search warrant. Come, show it." Here Dan'l, seated dejectedly on the lowest stair and with a pistol levelled above each knee, enquired :

" It'll be the two gentlemen as I pop at first, eh, Jarsper ? "

" Ar l " sighed Mr. Shrig. " But try not to kill 'em, to ving 'em, arm or leg 'll do l So, Mr. Hugo, Count and sir, I'll trouble you for——"

The Count laughed again, saying :

" Robbery with threatened violence, eh, Shrig ? My pistols or my life ? Well, take them, but you shall hear more of this."

" And, sir, you'll notice as my finger is on my trigger. Now your barkers, first right, then left, slow and easy."

And thus, perforce, from the deep side-pockets of his riding-coat, first one then the other, Count Hugo drew the weapons, and one after the other Mr. Shrig tossed to the Viscount and Robin, saying as he did so :

" Stilettas is now the vord, sir."

Count Hugo gave the word, in Italian, and the four stilettos tinkled upon the flagstones.

" Werry good l " quoth Mr. Shrig. " Sich things are better so, and, so being, I come now to the reason for my wisitation, vich is the late murderous assault and battery upon the person o' my lord Wiscount Ragvorth committed upon the King's highway about four o' the clock this here werry arternoon, my dooty being to examine and probably apprehend perpetrators o' said crime. Have you anything to say, sir ? "

" Not a word."

" But, sir, from information received, you, Sir Hugo, and brother Mr. Claude are chief parties con-carned in this werry heenious offence. And how says you to this, sir ? "

" That I was—and also, as in duty bound, Shrig, mark that, rescuing and protecting my ward from her abductor, who proved so extremely violent that I was compelled to restrain him and deemed it best to bring and detain him here until I had removed the lady safely beyond his reach, as any truly devoted and spirited guardian should ; and, Shrig, I am both ! "

"Howsever, sir, this brings me to this case of murderous assault, and I now proceed to——"

"Oh, enough—enough ! " exclaimed the Viscount wearily. "I have no wish to prosecute. On the contrary, the matter shall drop. All I desire is to be away and out of this infernal dog-hole and at once ! "

"Werry good, my lord, so be it ! Though your lordship is condoning a felony ! Vich shouldn't ought now nor never so to be, being by law to the law contrairy——"

"And here," boomed Count Hugo, in his deepest, most commanding voice, "I also cry ' enough ' ! Hold your foolish tongue, Shrig ; cease your futile babble and listen to me ! As a law officer I charge you with being inept, venal and corrupt, for it is you who are so shamelessly condoning, nay, indeed aiding and abetting, the abduction of my ward by these two young men—these paymasters of yours."

"Liar ! " exclaimed Robin. "Impudent liar ! Your unfortunate wards eloped alone and of their own accord ; fled the shame and terror of you. So, Count Despard, I charge you with being a scoundrel, a tyrant, a very probable embezzler and——"

Count Hugo leapt and struck so swiftly that although Robin expected and therefore eluded the blow he reeled backwards from the violent impact of that tremendous body, then he recovered, laughed joyously and in turn leapt to action.

So began this very terrible combat which was to be long remembered : Count Hugo's science, power and formidable size against Robin's speed of foot, strength of arm, natural skill and inborn love of fighting.

"Kill him, Hugo ! Oh, kill and don't spare him ! " wailed Mr. Claude. And such evidently was his gigantic brother's intention, for now, as they fronted each other, his wild fury was tempered to a cold and purposeful ferocity that made him the more deadly.

Of the titanic and desperate affray that now ensued, the Viscount (awed and anxious) and Mr. Shrig (serene and watchful as ever) could afterwards, and frequently did, recount every lightning shift of those splendid, agile bodies and every telling blow of those four mighty fists. It was as they broke away after some ugly in-fighting that Robin said mockingly :

" Sir, I would have you at your very best, and that long riding-coat is evidently hampering you. I'll allow you time to remove it."

Count Hugo smiled ; that is to say, he showed his teeth as he retorted :

" You desire a breathing space, Mr. Dale ? However, I may as well be rid of this encumbrance, and, doing so, I warn you that I shall——"

" Spare me your talk, sir, and save your breath that you may perform a little better, if possible, though I'm enjoying it pretty well, but—if you could put a little more devil into it——"

" Hell ! " cried the Count. " You shall have all hell ! " He wrenched off his coat, he flung it aside and with it all reasoned judgment and caution ; then, rushing in to smite the taunting smile from the mouth that dared so deride him, was met in full career by a left fist that stung and checked him, followed instantly by a jarring right that drove him reeling backwards to the wall ; and as he leaned there gasping, Robin taunted him again, saying :

" Pray take your time, sir, for I've no desire to end this pleasure too soon, and so venture to advise you to less passionate and more cautious play ! To lose your temper is to lose all ; remember this and you'll do better, I hope, and——"

Uttering a cry hoarse and inarticulate, Count Hugo

leapt at this smiling man who dared thus to jeer him, striving to close, intent now to crush and strangle him. Thus to fury brutality was added. So on and in he came— only to be lightly eluded or checked and driven back by fists that seemed never to strike amiss, yet confident in his might of body and scornful of hurts ; on and in he came. . . .

And now ensued such fighting as the onlookers (more especially two and a half) were never to forget, a duel without respite, a desperate life-and-death struggle becoming ever more viciously relentless. . . . Thus for a while it seemed that Robin's speed, skill and powerful fists availed not against his gigantic adversary, for even he breathed hard now, and both of them were bloody. . . . Yet they fought on fiercely as ever, but with this difference : the Count gasped and scowled, whereas Robin, though somewhat battered and short of breath, smiled so happily that the Viscount, clutching at Mr. Shrig's arm, exclaimed :

" Shrig ! Oh, Jasper, I believe he really is enjoying it ! "

And Mr. Shrig replied :

" Ar ! That, m'lud, is the reason as he's let it go so long ! He ain't used that right of his yet—not properly ; and when he does, all as I hope is as he don't hit too hard."

" But he must, Shrig, he must ! The Count is so devilish good. Look at that frightful blow—and that—and he looks like murder ! "

" Werry true, m' lud ! "

" Ha, look, Jasper—look ! Robin's tiring ! Good God —he's done ! "

" Not him, m'lud ! Keep your ogles on his right ! " But, as they watched, this right fist seemed to waver, to drop feebly. . . .

" Now ! " quoth Mr. Shrig.

And now indeed it was ! For, deceived and lured by this feint, Count Hugo gave the expected opening—and up flashed that same right fist with all Robin's strength and weight behind it, such blow as nothing human could with-stand, for over and down went Count Hugo Despard, to lie speechless and inert as if poleaxed. And now was a mo-mentary hush, a quite dreadful stillness. . . .

Then Viscount Ragworth was kneeling beside the fallen giant and from his bloody face glanced up fearfully at panting Robin, who stood flexing his bruised hands.

" What—what is it—Rags ? " he enquired breathlessly. " Why d'you—look at me—so ? "

" Robin, you hit him—with all your strength ! "

" Yes—yes, I did, and—in the right place ! "

" Come and look at him ! "

" Eh ? Oh, good God ! " exclaimed Robin, in sudden dismay. " You don't mean—— Oh, Rags, you can't mean—— "

" Murderer ! " wailed Mr. Claude. " You've killed him."

" If," sighed Mr. Shrig, standing to gaze down at this great motionless form, " sich be so, Master Rob, I must here and now arrest you for manslaughter, sir, as in dooty bound. Though first I suggest vater—in a bucket, poured over your wictim nice and slow ! "

" Yes," cried Robin anxiously, " let's try dowsing the poor fellow. Water in a bucket, somebody, and hurry, hurry ! "

" No need," quoth Mr. Shrig ; " gen'leman's stirring and werry much alive ! " In proof of which, Count Hugo sighed deeply, opened swimming eyes, and with the Viscount's ready aid contrived to sit up and, blinking at Robin's anxious, down-bent face, said very feebly :

" Sir—must congratulate you ! No man—ever downed me till now ! "

" Oh, Count," exclaimed Robin, sighing his deep relief, " you speak as only a true sportsman could, and as such I hon—— " He recoiled, dumbstruck, as with motion incredibly quick the Count's hand darted towards one of the stilettos that chanced within reach, a hand snatched back only just in time to escape Mr. Shrig's heavy boot.

" Fool ! " cried the Count, glaring up at him. " I meant it for myself. I am unused to being worsted in anything, and abominate failure even in myself."

" Howsever, sir and Count," sighed Mr. Shrig, kicking the weapon further away, " seeing as how—the law shall impound these here stilettas. Pick 'em up, Midge. So, gen'lemen, afore bidding ye good night, I am to inform you that unless you return to Italy and there abide you are to be pros-ecuted for embezzlement and cited therefore by the Lady Arrymanthy Meredith."

" If you mean—my beloved Aramanthea, she, alas, is dead."

" Ar, and buried ! "

" Very well then, you chattering fool, what the devil do you mean ? "

" Sir, since you ax me so p'inted and polite, I answers you full and free—as how for the present ekker alone responds." Then with a farewell flourish of his pistols, he led the way up that winding stair and out into a fragrant night, where a great moon was rising.

" And now," said he, glancing at this ever-brightening glory apprehensively, " the vord for all on us is speed, afore they begins shooting. My lord, you'll find your lady in my gig ; and, Master Rob, Bill Bartrum is standing by for you in his boat. And I says again, and werry fervent, speed ! "

CHAPTER XXVIII

Of Clia, Lady Dale and "Angel of Mercy"

IN THE Gamecock's Roost, this now dreary solitude where no birds, feathered or otherwise, were ever destined to roost, Robin sat hard at work with pen and ink, to him always a labour most detestable and more especially now, for he was writing to Sir Oliver Dale.

The tall old grandfather clock in the corner nearby, whose deliberate tick sounded so strangely loud in the pervading silence, informed him that more than an hour of life had elapsed since he had set pen to paper. The floor around him was littered by past efforts, and still this letter was unfinished. So Robin scowled, sighed plaintive curses, ruffled his hair, bit savagely at the feather of his pen, glowered at his stained right hand, but, noting the bruised knuckles of this same hand, was reminded how well it had served him four days ago, and smiled grimly. Cheered and heartened by this memory, he set his chin, squared his elbows and, using his pen with the utmost determination, finally produced such result as he deemed might fit the occasion, as thus :

" To Sir Oliver Dale, Bart.

" MOST DEAR SIR,

"I am riting to aknowledge reseat of quarterly alowance just to hand, but beg herewith to return it as under the present unhapy cerkomstanses I cannot akcept any more favers from you espeshally money.

"Hereafter I propose to exist by my own eggsertions and am, sir, your most humbelly graiteful and sincere well wisher, " R. D."

He was gazing very dubiously at the last lines of this screed, when suddenly he held his breath the better to listen as he had done so often of late, for once again he had an uneasy feeling that he was not alone—that in this great, rambling structure was a presence, a creeping, furtive menace, that eyes unseen were watching him, feet unheard would follow him. . . .

And now, sitting thus motionless, he became aware of many vague sounds above and all around him—faint creakings, stealthy rustlings ; the old place seemed talking to him with its every ancient timber and beam. Was it trying to warn him ? If so, of what ? From beyond these age-old walls that shut him in came the distant stir of life, the bustle of wharf and never-ending traffic of the river ; yet what he listened to was something nearer. And now there recurred to him the memory of Mr. Claude's upstaring hateful eyes. His own contemptuous laugh startled him so that he laughed again and, relaxing, leaned back in his chair ; and he was about to fold and wafer his letter when he was arrested by sounds there was no mistaking and of all others the most unexpected—light, quick footsteps, a rustle of silken petticoats—and there before him stood Clia, Lady Dale, adorable as ever, from plumed bonnet to slender sandalled foot, though beautified by the new dignity of wife and motherhood.

" Clee ! " he gasped, leaping up in rapturous surprise.

" Oh, Robin ! " said she, glancing from his now radiant face round about the untidy room. " What an unholy mess—like your life ! "

" My life ? " he repeated, bowing his head in sudden dejection. " Yes, unholy is right. I suppose old N—Sir Oliver told you—about me ? "

" Of course, that's why I am here, though he doesn't know. Yes, I made him tell me, because he was grieving so very bitterly ! "

" Well, so am I."

" And so you should ! He was so proud of you, Robin, and loved you so dearly——"

" And this is why I grieve now and always shall. Oh, Clee, sometimes at night I dream of it and, waking, curse myself for it."

" For what ? "

" That most damnable blow ! "

" Blow ? " she echoed, widening her lovely eyes on him.

" Didn't he tell you ? Did he spare me the shame of it ? "

" Ah ! " she gasped, recoiling instinctively. " What more of your wickedness is there to tell ? "

" That I—struck him, Clee ! Yes, I raised my cursed hand against this one man to whom I owe everything, the man I have always loved and honoured—as I do and always shall. I struck him ! Now say you hate me ! "

" No," she murmured, clasping her hands. " Now I say this makes me love him all the more, were it possible ! He would never have told me of this—your crowning shame."

" My—crowning—shame! " gasped Robin. " Yes, and it is a crown that scorches me ; it has done ever since—and will do always, always ! " So saying, he bowed head to hide his face in both hands.

" And, oh," she exclaimed tearfully, " to think we used to play together as children so happily, and all—all because of his goodness, his loving, gentle care.[1] You were quarrelsome even as a boy, though never with me. You were headstrong and wild as a youth, but always gentle with me. Ah, but now, now that you are a man, what are you, and what are you going to be ? "

And, with face still hidden, Robin answered miserably :

" My own despair, it seems ! "

[1] See *The Happy Harvest.*

" But why, Robin ? Oh, why have you let things go so—
so dreadfully wrong with you ? Why have you become so
brutally wicked ? Because you are, you know ! "

" Yes," he groaned, " I know it ! "

" Well, why ? Tell me and I'll try to help you ; so—
tell me."

" You ought to know ! " he muttered.

" Well, I don't ! So let me know."

" Very well ! " said he, raising his head to look at her.
" When you married Oliver, I was lost. I told you it
would be so, and it is ! "

" Oh, hateful !" she exclaimed in sudden anger. " For
this, instead of pity, I begin to despise you ! "

" No wonder," he sighed, " for I despise myself far
more than ever you can."

" Abominable ! " she continued. " To lay the blame of
your own wrongdoing on me is contemptible, disgraceful
and——"

" Well, I am disgraced."

" Oh," she cried furiously, " don't be so dis-gustingly
meek and humble ! "

" Then tell me how I should be."

" Regretful, remorseful and truly repentant."

" I'm all that and more. The memory of that accursed
blow has haunted me ever since. I haven't known a moment's
peace or respite, except now and then, otherwise I'm pretty
sure I should have gone mad ! "

" Tell me of those ' now and then ' moments of peace and
respite, Robin ; the ' how ' of them."

" Oh, no matter——"

" Oh, but it does matter, if I am to help you. So be
frank with me and explain."

" There's nothing to explain except that occasionally
I have been enabled to forget."

Here and instantly she demanded :

" When ? How ? And—who ? " And as instantly he replied :

" Tea. A friend. Conversation." Now at this my lady Dale sank gracefully into the nearest chair, adjusted her frills and furbelows, resettled her coquettish bonnet and enquired :

" Who is she, pray ? "

" Eh ? What she ? I didn't mention——"

" Tea, Robin, conversation and a friend ! So who is she ?"

" Oh well, her name's Bet."

" Then I hope she's better than she sounds."

" Her other name is Tracy, and she is a lady, as dainty, and so forth, as you are."

" Are you in love with her ? "

" No, of course not ; she has black hair ! "

" Does she live hereabouts ? "

" No, upstream in the country."

" What colour are her eyes ? "

" Blue."

" Light or dark ? "

" Light, though sometimes they alter and seem to darken."

" Is she beautiful ? "

" Yes, I—suppose so, in a dark sort of way."

" Well, Robin, I'm glad, very glad for your sake."

" My sake ? But why, what on earth——? "

" I'm happy to know you love her, because she may be your salvation."

" Oh indeed, how ? "

" As your wife. Because, you poor, dear great helpless baby, Robin, you need marrying."

" What an utterly preposterous idea ! " he exclaimed. " For don't I tell you——"

" Yes, Robin, yes, you do indeed ! You have always told me far more than you imagined or intended."

" Because, Clia, you have always understood me better than anyone else—yes, better even than myself ! You still seem able to read my mind as you could when we were children."

" Yes," she sighed, " that is why I am here—and—without my beloved Oliver knowing ! "

" But, Clia, why the secrecy ? "

" Because he must never have the faintest suspicion I had anything to do with what you are going to do. He must believe it entirely your own act."

" Oh ? Well ? What am I going to do ? "

" Write him a letter."

" I have ! " said Robin triumphantly. " And the deuce of a time I had with it ! "

" Evidently ! " she laughed, stirring the nearest " efforts " with daintily shod toe.

" So will you please look it over, Clee, and see if it will do ? "

So she read the letter and laughed, saying :

" Oh, it's quite as Robinish as usual ! "

" I suppose," said he, shaking head ruefully, " I'm the worst letter-writer who ever dropped a blot."

" No, the funniest ! From your schooldays your letters have been a joy to me. But though this one is so perfectly you-ish, it won't do."

" Why not, pray ? "

" Because it's so perfectly wrong."

" You mean the spelling ? Well, lend me a hand as you did so often years ago."

" No, most decidedly not, Robin ! This particular letter must seem all you at your Robinest, but I'll tell you what to write. So take another sheet of paper, child, trim your pen, try not to drop too many blots, merely one or two, and begin : ' Best and dearest of all Governors——' "

" No ! " sighed Robin. "That'll never do. After what happened it would be too familiar and fulsome, don't you think ? "

" No, I do—not."

" However, I think, if you don't mind, that we had best begin with a simple respectful ' Sir '. Do you agree ? "

" That depends. Because this letter must be either an impassioned plea for forgiveness or humbly suggestive of your remorse for the past and hope for the future."

" God knows I long to be forgiven, but what I don't know is how to beg and plead for it—at least not yet. So will you tell me how to express a remorse that I find quite beyond expressing. Will you show me how ? "

" Give me quill and paper and I'll try. Goodness me, what a frightful pen—no wonder your letter is so blotty ! "

Yet, despite this handicap, she contrived to scribble so rapidly that very soon she dictated these lines which Robin forthwith penned in his own original way thus :

" DEAREST OF SIRS,

" I am, as usual in reseat of your generous alowance which considdering what happened when last we met, I think is so truly magnannymus and so like only you that I feel the moor unworthy.

" Thus, under the present unhapy and most greevous cerkumstanses I cannot aksept it unless you permitt me to earn it by some or any laber the harder the better so long as it may bennyfit you.

" Should I suckseed in so doing, my fervent hope is that someday you will forgive a very contrite Robert and know and believe him to be again most sertinly your ever most truly devoted and dutiful

" ROBIN GOODFELLOW."

"Grand!" exclaimed Robin in awestruck tones as he laid down his pen. "Perfect! Oh, Clee, how wonderful you are! But then, of course, you always were!"

"I think it will do!" she murmured. "I'm sure it will touch the great tender heart of him, because it is written from both our hearts—and because again, knowing you as I do, Robin, I am so very sure that deep down in that odd nature of yours is a great, undying love for him which makes you, really and truly, his Robin Goodfellow."

"Oh, Clia," he muttered brokenly, "oh, Clee—you dear, lovely angel of mercy. I was lost in the dark and you have shown me a light and blessed me—with hope. And I can't find words to thank you—for how can anyone thank an angel?" At this moment the old grandfather clock, wheezing to sweet utterance, proclaimed the hour; whereat my lady, preparing for immediate departure, exclaimed:

"Goodness me! And my dear, patient Sophronia waiting for me in the carriage all this time! Will you come and greet her?"

"Not after being blessed by my good angel. So give her my love and say I hope to see her and dear old Inigo[1] pretty soon!"

"Well, goodbye," said Clia, giving him that small but extremely vital and very capable hand of hers. "Goodbye, Robin, but only for the present."

"Bless you again for the suggestion!" he replied. "I shall live in hope that someday you and Oliver may welcome me again at Abbeymead." And so bowing head reverently, he kissed this hand with fervour, then stood to watch her cross the courtyard and so—vanish.

Sighing, back went he to his loneliness; and, having nothing better to do, began to set the untidy room into some sort of order. He had scraped the "efforts" into a heap with his foot, when he was arrested by sound of hoofs,

[1] See *The Happy Harvest*.

wheels and a cheery "view-halloo", so out he went—to behold the Viscount in his curricle (this two-horsed, resplendent vehicle), who, tossing the "ribbons" to his smart groom, had leapt down and was shaking his hand, all in a moment. And the Viscount's eyes seemed brighter than usual, his step, like the angle of his modish hat, was jaunty, in his voice such ring of gladness that Robin, holding him at arm's length the better to look him over, demanded :

" Old boy, when is it to be ? "

" Eh ? " exclaimed the Viscount, actually flushing. " When is what ? Oh, I see—you mean——"

" Yes, of course ! When ? "

" In a month, Robin. She said six, my governor three, I a week, and the Duchess a month, so—a month it is."

" Grand ! " exclaimed Robin, linking arms and leading him indoors. "This demands a bottle, and I believe there are one or two somewhere about, if we can find 'em."

" Thanks, Robin, thanks ! " sighed the Viscount gratefully. " You make it very easy for me, because, all things considered, I was afraid my joy might be your pain, and, well, I mean to say——"

" Rags, your happiness is mine, in lesser degree, of course ! She'll make you a perfectly lovely viscountess ! The bottles should be in this cupboard, top shelf—no, here's where my confounded riding-boots have been hiding ! Have a look in that sideboard while I try under the kitchen sink."

The bottle (only one) having been discovered eventually in that dim niche where stood the clock, Robin extracted the cork (more or less) by means of penknife and bradawl, filled the glasses (one of them footless) and proposed :

" Phyllinda, future Viscountess Ragworth, long life, happiness and—God bless you both."

And when the Viscount had duly acknowledged this toast, he glanced up and around uneasily saying :

" This place seems uncannily silent, Robin."

"As death, Rags ! " sighed Robin, shaking his head. " For dead it is. Yes, the Gamecock's Roost has ceased to be. You behold me here all alone in my confounded glory ! "

" Alone ? But where's Black John ? "

" Gone, old boy ! We had words and I—oh, damme, I sent him away ! "

" You mean—you actually got rid of——"

" I did ! Hence the general untidiness, nothing where it should be, everything where it shouldn't ; the corkscrew, for instance——"

" Oh, but—my dear old fellah, I mean to say—Black John was such a——"

" Splendid fellow, yes ! That's precisely why I got rid of him, old boy, and have missed him so damnably ever since ! You see, Rags, he refused to second me in my affair with you because you were you and he is the grand cove he is and I the asinine fool I am ! "

" Do you think he may come back to you—in your loneliness ? "

" Not likely—I can only hope. Oh well, let's talk of something else, yourself preferably."

" Well, Robin, I have been blowing your horn to all and sundry, such a fanfare that my governor made me recount that fight twice over, once to himself and again to your Uncle Roland who happened to drop in on us. Now don't scowl at me, old fellah, because it may do you no end of good in other quarters. You know of old what a powerfully effective person my father is, more especially where his personal feelings are concerned, and he has always had the warmest regard for you. Which reminds me, I bear you a letter from him—no less ! Here it is. " So Robin took this letter and, breaking the seal, read :

" My dear Robin,

" Though Ragworth is no fool hero-worshipper, he tells such epic tale of your late exploits that I desire to grasp that fist of yours.

"Come with him to Storringdean and be welcomed again by your frequent host of earlier days,

" Storringdean.

" PS. I suppose you will play best man again, though in gentler sense, a month hence."

" It will be like old times ! " said the Viscount, as Robin refolded this letter. " Plenty to do at Storringdean, as you'll remember, and, besides, we can ride to town, clubs, theatres and so on, and visit Her Grace of Camberhurst—and Phyllinda, of course ! You are acquainted with the little Duchess, aren't you ? "

" No, I was always absent when she visited Abbeymead. I'm glad to know your Phyllinda is safe with such an extremely potent lady."

" Yes, thank God ! Well now, Robin, what I propose is a meal in town, an hour or so at my place and riding to Storringdean in the cool of the evening."

Robin's eyes gleamed. He rose lightly, frowned woefully and sat down again heavily, saying :

" Sorry, Rags, and thanks ; but it's no go, I can't."

" Can't what ? "

" Accept your and the Earl's kind hospitality."

" Why—on earth—not ? "

" Because such pleasures are not for me—at present."

" Old fellow," enquired the Viscount, glancing at his friend's downcast visage anxiously, " just what do you mean ? "

" That I'm neither fit nor worthy—if you get the idea."

" I'm afraid I don't, my dear fellah ; you must be more explicit."

" Very well," sighed Robin, folding his arms resignedly, " I'll do my best, though I'm no hand at explaining ; but— well . . . Rags, old boy, you saw me strike my—more than father, the grandest, noblest man of my life. I struck him, not with my fist, thank God I opened it, but—I struck him, and that blow has cursed me ever since. His look of grief. . . . Oh, my brutal ingratitude is a sin I must pay for—somehow a shame that can only be atoned for by my own physical suffering, a sort of penance. This is why I refuse the—the comfort of you, the solace of your companionship, the honour of your father's welcome. All such must be denied me until by chance or my own efforts I feel myself less of a graceless brute. Now d'you see what I'm driving at ? "

" My dear fellow, yes, though I think you are much too hard on yourself——"

" Not so, Rags ! Quite impossible if I am to work out my own salvation, redeem myself in my own eyes, save myself from my own damned self ! "

" But—how—and in this ghastly solitude ? "

" Part of my penance, old boy. And I can't remain here ; Sir Oliver's money bought it ! So I must find other quarters, any place I can call my own, for d'ye see, from now on I must work to live."

" Eh ? Work—you ? But how, what at ? "

" I shan't be over particular."

" Oh, but—great good heavens, this is simply frightful ! "

" I hope it will be, since this is all part of my penalty."

" My poor dear old fool, this is out of all reason ! You know I shall be only too proud and happy to lend——"

" I know, Rags, I know. But if I let you finance me it would make it all too damn easy. So, as Jasper Shrig would say, 'the vord is "no"' ! For there's a certain cove known to some few as ' Robin Goodfellow ' who means to make Robert the Devil wish he had never been created."

" Yes, but how, Robin, how ? "

" By the infliction of such pains and penalties as shall hurt him most. For instance, when Robert the Devil in some garret or cellar has to draw in his belt on an aching void, as he will, or labour until the sweat pours from him, as it shall, then Robin Goodfellow will be all the happier."

" Does this mean you intend to disappear ? "

" Yes, my old Rags and Bones, it does."

" For how long ? "

" Until Robin has driven the devil out of Robert."

" What an odd fellow you are, Robin."

" So odd that I'm my own curse, Rags."

" Have you any idea where you are going ? "

" Oh yes, certainly. Down, of course, and down—to the submerged tenth, the dregs, the wrecks and castaways ; rookeries, old boy, back courts and alleys."

" Then, Robin, promise that, however deeply you submerge, you will keep in touch with me. Give me your word."

" Yes, I can promise this."

" And I wish to God you were not going alone ! "

" Atonement, old boy, part of."

" Well, is there anything I can do for you now, anything in this world ? "

" Not a thing, Rags, no—that is—yes, b' jingo, you can look after Cannonball for me and such few other effects as I possess, clothes and what not, if you will."

" Well, of course ! Don't I tell you——"

" Thanks ! Then now, since our bottle's empty, if you'll bear a hand—one chest smallish, two portmanteaux and one horse. . . ."

Thus after some while, his smart groom having driven away with the baggage, the Viscount, astride Cannonball, checked this mettled creature's exuberance to say, and more anxiously than ever :

" Robin, I hate to leave you in this very damnable solitude. Can't I persuade you to come with me for tonight at least ? "

" My dear old Rags and Bones, there's nothing I should like more, and consequently there's nothing more impossible, the answer being therefore a gratefully regretful no ! "

" Have you any idea when you leave ? "

" Not precisely—a day or so hence."

" Then, for the present, goodbye, old fellow, but only for the present ! And remember your promise to keep in touch ! "

" I will," answered Robin, as they clasped hands.

And so Viscount Ragworth rode away, leaving Robin to endure such pains and penalties as were to bring him to the very threshold of Death.

CHAPTER XXIX

In Which Old Father Thames Gives Warning

NOW WHEN all sound of his friend's departure had died away, Robin crossed to the old waterstairs and, there seated, gazed down at the river and enquired wistfully :

" Well, Father of Wisdom, you heard what I told my old Rags—pains, penalties and what not, atonement and so forth. Am I on a right course at last, think you ? "

And from the lowest stair Old Thames gurgled and lisped :

" Po-sitively ye-s-s-s ! "

ROBIN : Well, that's some comfort !

THAMES (*chuckling*): Though you don't know what's in store for you, my Robin !

ROBIN : Nor do I want to know !

THAMES : I could tell you very briefly.

ROBIN : Then please don't.

THAMES : Would the knowledge frighten you ?

ROBIN : I don't think so. It might shock me, but then I'm prepared and expect to suffer.

THAMES (*hissing*) : Even death s-s-sudden and sh-sh-arp ?

ROBIN (*more positively*) : No ! No indeed ! That would be too much of a bad thing, too devilish unpleasant.

THAMES (*whispering*) : Then I had better warn you that Death, with a capital " D ", my boy, whose other name is " Murder ", crawls in your shadow, awaiting to strike.

ROBIN (*glancing instinctively over his shoulder*) : Is it, b'gad ! Oddly enough, Old Thing, I've felt something of the sort lately, a kind of premonition, but deemed it merely a ridiculous fa——

THAMES (*sternly*) : Don't say " fancy ", my poor blind one ; that warning was of and by—me, for it is very real—ar, a menace creeping all too near.

ROBIN (*glancing behind him again*) : A menace ? Well, that ghastly little Claude looked " murder " at me ! Is he my danger ?

THAMES : Only one of many.

ROBIN : Which sounds extremely dismal ! What am I to do about it ?

THAMES (*gurgling throatily*) : Hop the twig, fly the perch, take French leave, cut and run.

ROBIN (*grimly*) : Not I—no ! If by this I can atone——"

THAMES (*gaspingly*) : By a knife in the back, by unseen bullet, by flood, by fire, by poison, by——

ROBIN : Hold hard, old friend ! Don't chuckle and gloat. You're too used to death of all kinds, but I'm not.

THAMES : Are you afraid of such deaths ?

ROBIN : Yes ! Yes, b'gad I am !

THAMES (*soothingly*) : Very right and proper, my boy ; such fear being natural——

ROBIN (*mournfully*) : And yet, Old Thing, if this is the only way to be rid of this cursed feeling of unworthiness, the only method of redemption, I'll meet old man Death like a friend, or try to. And, by God, I mean this, Father Thames !

THAMES : And, by God, Robin, I know you do. And therefore I will utter this prophecy. By my help one shall lift you from clutching Death up to new life and awareness of Truth at last. Ask me " who " and I shall merely bubble.

ROBIN : Well, I'm not asking, though I should like to——

THAMES : Of course, naturally. So instead I'll speak you
three words of comfort.

ROBIN : No, don't. There must be none o' that for
me until I prove and know myself fit and worthy
of——

A voice, clear and sweetly familiar : " Aho ! " Smitten
thus to joyful silence, Robin glanced up—and there she
was, coming down on the ebb and looking up at him across
her shoulder. Robin was afoot and down the stairs in one
movement almost.

" Well, Jack, are you indeed well ? " she enquired.

" Thank you, yes. But why ' Jack ' ? "

" Because he also used to beat giants."

" You mean—but how on earth—ha, Jasper, of course,
he's been talking ! "

" He has indeed ! He also sent me to collect and row you
to him, if you will favour——" Even as she spoke, Robin
stepped lightly into this boat with its letters B. E. T. and
away they went.

She was clad as he had first seen her, also she wore a long
cloak back-thrown for rowing but with a hood so drawn
that each time she bent to the oars her face was hidden.
So Robin watched the lovely, gracious shape of her instead,
and with such perfervid gaze that at last she thus admonished
him :

" As a child I was taught it was extremely ill-mannered
to stare at anyone."

" Ah, but," he sighed, "you are no longer a child, thank
heaven ! "

" Of course not. But why the fervour of gratitude ? "

" Because you have grown into such a perfect Bet, that
to lounge here at my ease and watch you at work is a joy.
Though why do you wear that hood thing ? "

" To protect my modesty from eyes that stare too boldly !
Besides, it hides your detestation—my hair."

"But I do—not detest it; quite the reverse."

"Can this possibly mean you are beginning to—forgive me for having black hair?"

"I could forgive you anything nowadays—almost."

"What could you not forgive me, pray?"

"Rowing any other fellow on this good old river of ours, for we are his children, you and I. So now while his daughter rows his son, let your oars caress him tenderly as the oars of a truly dutiful daughter should—which means row as gently, slowly as possible."

"So I am, so slowly indeed that Jasper Shrig will be wondering——"

"Well, let him! By the way, where is he?"

"Waiting where we used to have tea—until you threw the cups and things into the river."

"Because you had disappointed me so very bitterly!"

"Because you had behaved so very shockingly to your poor friend the Viscount and——"

"Too true!" sighed Robin. "But that's past and done with, more or less, so let's talk of something more you and me-ish."

"Very well—your face!"

"As you will, my lady! It's not much as faces go, but it's my one and only, so pray what of it, madam?"

"It is—no, not marked so badly as I expected, considering that—terrible giant!"

"Because I managed to keep away. Ah, but he was a demon at close-quarters, in-fighting and what not. You should see my bare chest and——"

"Merciful heaven, what a suggestion!"

"All I mean is——"

"Bruises and what-nots, yes, sir! Yet Jasper Shrig says his only fear was lest you should kill this gigantic——"

"Oh well, enough of him. Tell me about yourself."

"You mean my horrid black——"

"I do—not! The more I see of it, the better it seems to suit you."

"Oh, Master Robin, sir! You cannot possibly admire a black mane, especially mine!"

"Well, it needed getting used to, of course."

"Naturally, sir, considering your passion for golden tresses—such as adorn the lady you rescued so gallantly."

"But I didn't, Bet. No, my pitiful effort ended in the most complete and abject failure! It was Jasper who was the absolute success, as usual. Which makes me wonder what the deuce he can want with me today. Not that it matters so long as you are there while I am here and both of us in the embrace of our Old Father Thames."

"And pray, Master Robin, what of your golden lady?"

"She will be—another's very soon. So you see, I was a failure there also. I'm poor little Cupid's despair; his arrows simply bounce off me—no, I suppose it's the other way about. Women like me enough not to love me! Yes, by George and his confounded dragon, I'm an utter failure in most things."

"Except, poor Robin, in smiting down giants and other brutish monsters."

"Which is about my only accomplishment."

"Poor Robin!" she repeated.

"Yes," he sighed, "poor indeed am I." By now they were beyond sight and sound of the Great City. Instead were shady trees and fair green meadows, with the ripple and splash of their progress as the boat glided smoothly along this now crystal highway; and as Robin looked mournfully down at these placid waters she gazed as earnestly at him until, lifting his head suddenly, their eyes met and he said in voice like a groan:

"Oh, Bet, it's pretty damnable—to be—a failure, such as I."

"Who says you are?" she demanded.

" I do ! " he sighed. " The conviction is forced upon me at last ; I say it because I know it."

" Yes, but," said she with a new and strange gentleness in look and tone, " it is only poor Robin who happens to think so just at present ; but there are others who know you are neither hopeless nor a failure—nor ever can be, with those eyes, that mouth and chin. I know of two people who so believe in you and neither of them is a fool, because Jasper Shrig is one and I am the other."

" You ? " exclaimed Robin, leaning towards her so eagerly that the light skiff rocked. " Oh, Bet, have you truly such faith in me ? "

" So has Jasper Shrig, as I tell you."

" Ah yes, but you, Bet, you——"

" And Jasper Shrig ! "

" Good old Jasper ! "

" He is indeed your friend, as I said before, Robin."

" And yours, too, it seems, or he would never have told you anything about the Framling Manor affair. I'm amazed that he did."

" Oh ? Why shouldn't he, pray ? "

" Because it was all pretty irregular on his part as a law officer, forcible entry and so on ; and then, besides, he is usually so confoundedly close-mouthed and mysterious, hates answering questions or giving information of his doings as a rule. Did he tell you of the frightful mess I made of my part—beaten, bound and pitched helpless into a dungeon ? "

" Yes, though quite differently. He talked mostly of you and the coun—giant, like this ! " Here she ceased rowing the better to mimic Jasper Shrig, thus :

" Ah, my Lady Bright, as a nofficer, I should ought to have stopped same, but, though a limb o' the law, I am also a mere huming being and—ah, 'twas a grand and glorious fight, ma'am ! "

"Well!" exclaimed Robin. "All I can say is that you must have bewitched him, Bet. And grim old Jasper of all people! Yet this doesn't surprise me; at least—not much."

"Why not?" she enquired, glancing up at him from shrouding hood as she swayed back with leisured stroke of oars.

"Because," he replied, "strange to say, even I sense an odd sort of—yes—bewitchment about you every now and then."

"Do you really, Mr. Dale?" she murmured, face hidden as she swayed forward.

"Yes, I do, and—Bet, are you laughing at me?"

"Oh, Mr. Dale—the idea!"

"Well, anyhow, I wish you'd put off that confounded hood."

"So I will, later on."

And now they progressed a while in silence, until Robin enquired suddenly:

"I'm wondering if Jasper told you anything of something that has been puzzling me no end—are you listening?"

"Yes, of course I am."

"Then stop rowing and look at me."

Mutely she obeyed and, leaning across the stilled oars, look at him she did—such look that Robin quite forgot to speak and almost to breathe; for as they gazed upon each other, eye to eye, realisation smote and shocked him—of her beauty and of something even more amazing—then he drew a deep breath, she closed her eyes and bowed her head, though not before he had seen the betraying flush that, like her shyly averted eyes, made her the more lovely. Then she went on rowing, rather unevenly at first, yet saying in quite casual tone:

"I'm still listening."

"Listening?" he repeated in tone anything but casual. "What for?"

" You were going to explain how Jasper Shrig puzzled you."

" Ah yes, so I was ! It happened that night just before we left Framling Manor that Jasper said a very strange thing, for he warned those precious brothers that unless they returned to Italy and remained there they would be indicted and prosecuted for embezzlement by—the Lady Aramanthea Meredith."

" But, Robin, this doesn't seem so wonderfully strange— to me."

" It will seem more than strange, Bet ; it will become quite ghoulish when I tell you this poor Lady Aramanthea is dead and buried, as Jasper knows ! So what on earth could he have meant ? Have you any idea ? "

" How could I have—unless—perhaps he believes she is—neither ? "

" Neither what ? "

" Dead nor buried."

" But I tell you he knows, and so do I, that this most unfortunate lady is both."

" How can you be so positive, Robin ? "

" Because—ah, Bet, I saw the poor creature when they brought her ashore—drowned ! "

" How—horrible ! "

" It was ! I—Jasper persuaded me to view the—the poor thing for purpose of indentification."

The oars faltered in their rhythmic rowing and now dripped motionless.

" And—did you—identify her ? "

" Yes and no—at the first glance yes, and then I wasn't quite sure."

" But how could you ? Did you know her so well—by sight—this lady ? Had you seen her often ? "

" No, only once properly—in bed, which sounds improper but isn't. No indeed ! I merely saw her face and then she, b'gad—she glared up at me like any feminine demon ; yes, a positive she-devil ! "

" Did she, Robin ? How dreadful ! "

" Yes, it gave me quite a shock. I took one look and bolted."

" Was she good-looking, Robin ? No, she couldn't have been, of course. But was she handsome ? "

" I hardly noticed, but Aunt Rosamond said she was ' dangerously beautiful '—perfection of form and so on."

" And you were unable to identify her positively ? "

" No. But the Despards were and did, both of them, instantly ! Yes, so surely that they claimed and buried her. Oh, but enough of this ! Let's talk of something sweeter, lovelier, of bewitching Bet, for instance." Here again the oars faltered, stopped as she looked up at him to say :

" My word, you are very suddenly most unexpectedly complimentary today ! "

" And you," he retorted, " are what they would describe as a very handsome young woman."

" Oh ? Would they ? "

" Undoubtedly ! "

" Then it's very flattering of them, whoever they are ! Do you agree with them ? "

" Certainly ! Though I am no flatterer, not I ! No, I say only what I mean, often too bluntly, I'm afraid. How-ever, I'm no ear-tickling flatterer."

" Then what more are you, please ? "

" A mere onlooker who can best enjoy all loveliness from a distance."

" Meaning, distance lends enchantment to——"

" No, Bet, I do not ! I mean that a too great near-ness and familiarity can upset cool and reasoned judgment ! "

Now at this, and for no reason that he could perceive, she laughed, and when he demanded why, she splashed him

H

with each oar and began to row quite speedily. When he enquired the wherefor of this sudden haste all she said was : " Tush ! " and made a face at him ; in which moment a hoarse voice hailed, and, glancing unwillingly thitherward, Robin opened his eyes wider than usual and for such reason as demands a new chapter.

CHAPTER XXX

In Which Mr. Shrig Advises

IN THIS leafy remoteness, this bower shut in by drooping willow and alder, perched at ease upon that same fallen tree that so frequently served Robin to the same purpose, Mr. Shrig of Bow Street was feeding a blazing fire with dry sticks which crackled cheerfully. As the boat turned shorewards, he rose with wide-armed flourish of the famous hat.

"Well!" exclaimed Robin, returning this salute. "All I can say, my grim old limb of the law, is, what next?"

Whereto Mr. Shrig replied:

"Tea, Master Rob, drank along of Beauty, Friendship and Old Feyther Thames."

"Which," said Robin, aiding Beauty ashore, "is a trinity nothing on earth can better."

And presently all being ready, they began to eat and drink in a speechless enjoyment until at last sighed Robin, cup at lip:

"This is a pleasure wholly unexpected and therefore the more delightful!"

"This here J.O.Y. j'y," quoth Mr. Shrig, beaming fondly on the dainty slice of thin bread and butter he was folding delicately, "is owing to our Lady o' the River."

"This meal," said she, glancing from one to other of her guests, "will be most interesting if, when you ask your question, Robin, something more human than 'echo alone' responds, Mr. Jasper." In the act of biting into his bread and butter, Mr. Shrig chuckled instead, while Robin, setting cup in saucer, instantly and briefly put his question, thus:

" Why threaten the Despards with a dead woman,
Jasper ? "

And as instantly Mr. Shrig replied :

" Master Rob, 'tis you have said it ! "

" Oh ? What did I say ? "

" ' Dead voman ', vich I did not ! "

" Eh ? What didn't you ? "

" Say ' dead voman '."

" Jasper, what the deuce are you driving at now ? "

" The truth, sir, fax now as ever."

" Well then, suppose you answer my question."

" Sir, I have so, having told you as how I never
did."

" Never did what ? "

" Say ' dead voman '—not me ! And so, may I ax you
for more tea, my Lady o' Sunshine ? "

And, taking his cup, she replied :

" Oh man, of comfort and hope, of course you may."

" Yes, but," said Robin, " instead of answering my
question, Jasper, you've twisted it out of all shape and
meaning. What I wish to know is why you told those
Despards they would be prosecuted by the Lady Aramanthea when you know she is dead ? "

" Sir, I so said for the sakes o' both."

" Both who ? "

" The dead, sir, and the living. So—there y'are ! "

" Which is no answer, Jasper."

" Howsever, 'tis the best as I can do, Master Rob ; so
now talking o' boots, don't——"

" Great heavens, man ! What boots ? Whose boots ? "

" Your boots, sir. Don't go to bed in 'em—no. Sleep
in everything else, but take off your boots though keeping
'em handy."

Robin laughed, then frowned, saying indignantly :

" I'm not in the habit of sleeping in my boots like some

drunken sot—ha, now confound you, Jasper, what are you suggesting ? "

" Windictiveness, Master Robin."

" And what the deuce has that to do with my boots ? Well, suppose you trouble to explain."

But instead of so doing, Mr. Shrig sat gazing pensively into his recharged cup, head bowed and aslant as if listening intently for some expected sound.

" Boots indeed ! " exclaimed Robin. " Such ridiculous nonsense ! How say you, Bet ? "

And with her gaze upon Mr. Shrig's intent face, she answered :

" I'm—afraid he is—warning you, Robin. Tell me, please, dear Mr. Jasper, is there any cause for anxiety or alarm ? "

Mr. Shrig beamed on her, took off his hat to her, waved it once, put it on again and said :

" The lightning-flash ain't brighter nor yet speedier than the int-lex as fills your bee-u-tiful tibby, ma'am, nor the sperrit as anny-mates your werry lovesome, ladylike form."

" Oh," said she, with quick-drawn breath, " then I'm right—you do sense danger ! "

Mr. Shrig nodded, saying :

" Lady o' Sense and Beauty, ar ! Danger's the vord, spelt vith a werry big D ! Hence this here tea-party."

" Does this danger menace Robin ? "

" All on us, my Lady Bright, even to my b'y Midget ! "

" Well now," said Robin, squaring his shoulders instinctively, " this promises action, something in my line, eh, old fellow ? "

Mr. Shrig took a leisurely sip of tea, sighed, nodded and answered :

" Master Rob, Willainy is afoot ! Wiciousness is up and eager to be ' at it ' ! Windictiveness lurks for chance to strike. Therefore all sich chances must be denied and awoided till the law, armed by proof positive, claps its daddles on Willainy, lays Windictiveness by the heels and sets vould-be Murder a-dancing on air, the Tyburn jig, sir."

" Well and good, Jasper, but how and when ? I don't ask who, but how shall you procure the so-needed proof ?

" I shan't ! Willainy shall down Roguery, and Murder shall polish off Windictiveness, neat as ninepence—I hope ! "

" Same here, Jasper ! Ah, but how shall you contrive such a——"

" Traps, Master Rob ; I have dooly set and am setting same."

" Yes, but——"

" Sir, I have answered you full and free, so if you should——" He checked suddenly to sit listening again, until out from the dense leafage stepped the man Dan'l as mild and meek-seeming as usual. He bowed gallantly to Beauty, touched his hat to Robin, shook his whiskers at Mr. Shrig, and said mournfully :

" Jarsper, our birds has flew ! "

" As expected, Dan'l."

" Ah, but, Governor, from information received they've quit for good. All the servants, nine and a half of 'em, counting the boot-boy, has been paid off and the house is to be shut up."

" Anything more, Dan'l ? "

" Ay, from report just received, they are now aboard ship."

" Vich is rayther sudden, and sooner than expected. And said ship is ready for sea?"

" Sails on the flood, Jarsper."

" And that," quoth Mr. Shrig, consulting a ponderous silver watch, " that'll be in an hour and say fifteen minutes, giving me oceans o' time to wisit same and bid a-doo."

" And," said Robin " a very good riddance, if you and Dan'l mean——"

" Naming no names, Master Rob, I say ar ! But in this

here wale o' trouble and grief there's always a 'but' and generally a brace of 'ifs', and, if so, then that as should ought to be, ain't, vich, so being, ends in general conflummeration and there y' are! So, remembering as how chickens ain't till they're hatched and cups can't always be expected to reach lips, the vord I still give you is—Caution vith a wery large capital C. And now, my Lady o' Thames, thanking you for this blessed hour of peace and kindly fellowship, not to mention tea and bread and butter, I'll follow the call o' dooty, hoping for another sich-like hour pretty soon. But, Master Rob, talking of they 'ifs' and 'buts' aforesaid, there's always a bed for you at The Gun along o' me and Corporal Dick, as you know."

"I do indeed, Jasper, and a right hearty welcome. How is Dick?"

"Prime, sir, and so's the bed, feathers as you'll remember, and I should adwise you to occipy same for the next night or so; cosy quarters and good fellowship, eh?"

"Thanks, Jasper old fellow, I should like to, yes, I should like to so very much that precisely for this reason I must refuse and—return to my damn solitude; and if you ask me why—only your confounded echo will reply." Mr. Shrig seemed about to argue the matter, but, nodding instead, whistling the opening bars of the old song, "Barbara Allen", this answered almost immediately by sound of oars; then through the drooping alder screen stole the prow of a weatherbeaten boat urged by Bartrum, that much-bewhiskered man of whom Mr. Shrig enquired:

"You brought it along, Bill?"

"Ay, 'tis a-starn o' me now, Jarsper."

"Your boat, Master Robin," he explained. "I took the liberty of having it towed up here-along for you, seeing as how."

"Very thoughtful of you. Thanks, Jasper! And I'm still wondering why you sent for me so urgently."

"Vich, sir, circumstances at present forbidding, 'tis a story yet to unfold."

"More mysteries, eh, Jasper? Well, for the present goodbye and good luck, old fellow."

"And how says you, my Lady Bright?"

"Dear Mr. Jasper, I say God protect you always but especially—these days!" Mr. Shrig took off his hat, stared at it, put it on again, and said:

"Lady, for sich kind thought, I—no, there ain't no vord for it! Ha, Dan'l, get aboard and take the spare oars. I'll need as much time as possible for my wisit." Thus presently Mr. Shrig took his place aft and, there seated, nodded again, saying:

"Now give way, my lads, and put your backs into it."

So together the four oars dipped, leafage rustled, and the boat with its occupants vanished.

CHAPTER XXXI

Chiefly Concerning the Powers of Darkness

" AH ! " sighed Robin when the rhythmic beat of oars had died away. " Now, if there is any more tea, fill and let all be revelry and joy. But why so sombre, thou dark-browed goddess of this sylvan grove ? Why so thoughtful, Bet ?"

And, reaching for his empty cup, she answered :

" He—Mr. Jasper—evidently suspects some danger . . . something evil . . . still threatens you, Robin."

" Because Jasper is the most suspicious fellow alive."

" Yet, never without cause, I'm sure."

" You like old Jasper, don't you, Bet ? "

" Yes, yes, I do, very much."

" And he, b'gad, has taken greatly to you."

" Does this astonish you ? Is it so marvellous ? "

" Well, grim old Jasper is scarcely a lady's man—but you are so wonderfully changed."

" Because I speak King's English ? "

" No, because you are so much gentler, sweeter, kinder, and——"

" And what, pray ? "

" More lovable ! "

" Oh indeed ! Well, I think—no, I'm sure this change is in you."

" True enough, Bet ! Changed I am ; yes and changing, and for the better—I hope ! What do you think ? "

" Just at present I'm thinking of Jasper Shrig."

" Well, don't ! Think of me instead."

" Very well. Answer me this. What is the evil that I am perfectly sure you know is threatening you ? "

" Myself, Bet, my brutally unworthy self."

" Very well again ! But what is the danger Jasper Shrig warned you against and which I am perfectly sure you know exists ? "

" Well, most perspicacious astute and inquisitive Bet, I hardly know, but between you and me and the tea-pot I must confess that just lately I've been haunted by a feeling, an odd sense that I am sometimes very truly haunted, that in my solitude is a kind of watchful presence, that in my loneliness I am not alone, that eyes unseen are watching me, feet waiting to creep after——"

" Don't ! " she gasped. " It is too ghastly—too horrible —too dreadful."

" Yes," sighed Robin, turning to scowl at the river, " it might be and would be, perhaps, if I didn't welcome it."

" Welcome it ? " she repeated with look of horror. " How can you—why should you——? "

" As a penance, Bet. This is why I refused Jasper's hospitality and, instead of comfort and joviality, shall go back to my haunted solitude."

" But why, Robin ? Oh gracious goodness, why so cruelly afflict yourself ? "

" Because," he replied in voice like a groan, " of this hand, this damned hand of mine ! I raised it against my— more than Father. I—struck him ! And for that I must pay. You said I was a brute, and so I am—so I'll tame this brute by hardship and suffering. This is why I must dare anything, endure everything to work out my own redemption."

And now she also turned to gaze down at the river, where the first shadows of evening had begun to creep ; and so for a while they remained mute and very still. When at last she spoke it was in an awed whisper :

" To—dare anything ? To endure everything—even death, Robin ? "

" Yes," he answered grimly, " even that if I needs must —anything to be rid of this feeling of unworthiness." Here he paused, but, finding her silent, continued : " The idea being to make amends, to atone by something more than mere words, because, d'you see, Bet, I am so bitterly remorseful that I hate and despise myself and consequently mean to deny myself such comfort or happiness as may offer." Here ensued another silence which he broke at last to enquire and very diffidently : " I hope you don't think me a fool."

Instead of replying, she began to collect the tea-things, but in such odd clumsy manner that he knelt to help, and thus saw her eyes abrim with blinding tears. So, very naturally, he took her to the comfort of his arms and, her face being hidden, quite instinctively began to kiss the braids of silky hair that crowned her. But :

" Ah no—don't ! " she murmured, yet with such evident repugnance that he released her instantly, saying :

" No no, of course not ! Pray forgive me, though I was merely trying to comfort you."

Here, to his profound surprise, she laughed, though her lashes were still heavy with tears :

" Oh ! " she exclaimed. " How brave, how nobly unselfish of you—considering my detested black mane ! Now please lift the hamper into my boat for me. I must go."

" So soon, Bet ? "

" So late, Robin ! See how the shadows deepen about us."

" But there will be the moon later on. I suppose you— have never tried rowing by moonlight ? "

" Yes—once, and I hated it."

Now when she had stepped lightly into her boat and was seated at the oars, he propounded that same question rather differently, thus :

" Bet, please tell me, do you consider I am all kinds of a fool ? "

Now looking up into his solemn face, she answered gently :

" No, Robin, you are only—one kind ! And if you ask what kind, ' echo alone will respond '. And this reminds me. I wish, yes, with all my heart, you had accepted Jasper Shrig's hospitality, his invitation to——"

" With all your heart ? Oh, Bet, does this mean——? "

" That I hate to think of you alone in that great empty place."

" Is this why you deem me one kind of fool ? "

" Oh no ! " she replied, ruddy lips upcurving to the smile he though all too rare. But even as he watched, this smile vanished as she enquired, and with look suddenly troubled : " Are you quite determined to—make dreadful solitude and darkness your penance tonight ? "

" Yes," he answered grimly, " yes I am, I must and shall, because—I hate the very idea ! And so tonight, Bet, will you please—think of me, and as kindly as you can ? Will you ? "

" Yes," she sighed, drawing the hood of her cloak so that her face was in shadow, " you poor, harassed Robin, I shall pray for you."

" Oh, my dear," said he very reverently, " then no Powers of Darkness can prevail and I—well—my gratitude is beyond words, and," he continued haltingly, " you are—becoming very—precious to me, Bet ! "

Her oars dipped gently, yet she remained very still and with head bowed.

" ' Powers of Darkness ' ! " she repeated. " Oh, Robin, God bless and keep you this night and—every night ! Goodbye ! "

Then beginning to row, she smiled up at him, but, even so, once again he saw the glitter of those most precious tears ere she vanished beyond that dawn-drooping, leafy screen.

And so while evening deepened to night, Robin stood very still listening to the rhythmic stroke of her oars growing ever fainter until at last they had died away. With the ensuing silence came a loneliness such as he had never felt until now. Thus, gloomy as the shadows thickening about him, he got into his boat, shipped oars and began to row towards that desolation of roof and walls which was the only place he could call " home ".

Now as he plied leisurely oars, night fell—a spacious darkness wherein a small, chill wind stirred ever and anon, waking stealthy rustlings where trees and hedges loomed blacker than the all-pervading dark, dread shapes that seemed to menace with arms upraised to smite, bony hands down-reaching to clutch and rend—monstrous things that crouched, to leap and destroy.

Thus as he rowed, heedful of these now fantastically unfamiliar things, Robin began to recall such tales as he had heard and read concerning " The Awfulness of Night ", this dread season when spirits steal abroad to fell and direful purpose. . . . The Powers of Evil grim and ghastly, intent on foul and frightful . . .

From the darkness above something clutched and tumbled his hat off, startling him so greatly that he gasped and cowered, then swore in a fury, then laughed and pulled away from the river bank to avoid other such twiggy obstacles. And now, going downstream on the ebb with hardly an effort, he began to converse with the old river (and himself) thus :

" Father Thames, of your vast wisdom, tell me—what are the Powers of Darkness ? "

THAMES (*bubbling at oar-blades*) : Bub-boy, don't you ever read your Bub-bible ?

ROBIN : Not very often lately, I'm afraid.

THAMES : Shocking! Howsever, Matthew, twelve and forty-three, writes of them as unclean spirits who wander through dry places seeking rest and finding none. Then poor old Job, four and thirteen, tells how he was " terrified by visions of the night when deep sleep falleth upon men, fear came upon him and trembling which made all his bones to shake—then a spirit passed before his face and the hair of his flesh stood up ".

ROBIN : A nightmare, of course. The old boy had eaten too much supper.

THAMES : Don't be too cocksure, young un! Read in Genesis thirty-two, how Jacob wrestled all night with an angel.

ROBIN : I humbly suggest if he wrestled in a night as black dark as this he probably mistook some ordinary shepherd cove for an ang——

THAMES : Read Acts twelve, how an angel delivered Peter the Apostle out of prison.

ROBIN : Again and as humbly, my aged one, I suggest brave old Peter would have deemed anyone an angel who so freed him. But if these were spirits they were pretty good ones. I want you to tell me about the bad, these Powers of Darkness ; and first, do you believe in such ?

THAMES : Naturally, certainly and of course I do.

ROBIN : Then, my dear Old Thing, you surprise and disappoint me no end.

THAMES : Then listen, my cocky young cock! Spirits of Evil and Powers of Darkness are truly the evil engendered of our baser selves which, waking, we heed not ; ah, but when Sleep, that kindly brother of Death, enfolds and cradles us, then these latent evils are made real in dreams and so become Powers of Darkness to agonise us and terrify.

ROBIN : Now that sounds more common sense and therefore believeable. But no " terror that walketh in darkness " can trouble me, because, O Father Thames, She is going to—pray for me.

THAMES : I know ! I heard !

ROBIN : Well ?

THAMES : Ar ! Well it is, and exceeding well ! For otherwise it would be otherwise indeed with you, seeing you are not overwise——

ROBIN : You needn't labour the fact.

THAMES : Have you faith in her prayers and——

ROBIN (*fervently*) : Of course.

THAMES : Then, O Robin, cling fast to that belief, and when the horror of death comes at you, as it will, remember then and shield you behind her prayers—if you can ! Ho, Robin, I warn you !

ROBIN : Of what now ?

THAMES : How the Ancient Evil can and will make the Powers of Darkness very real and deadly.

ROBIN : But what is the Ancient Evil ?

THAMES : One of its names is " Hate ".

ROBIN : Which is a dev'lish arresting thought.

Having pondered this a while in some disquiet and to no purpose, Robin banished the worry of it to ask :

ROBIN : One other question you can answer for me if you will, being so all-wise.

THAMES : After all these ages and aeons of time I should be very fool of a river were I not brimful of wisdom. So ask your question. I know it, of course, but ask it ; 'twill pleasure me to respond.

ROBIN : Thanks, old companion ! Now I beg you'll tell me precisely what kind of fool she thinks me and why ?

THAMES : Fie and fiddlededee, young Rob ! Thinkest thou I would betray a woman's confidence, especially this adorable creature who hath more wit in her little finger than thou in all thy big carcase? Tush, boy, pish and bah! However, good night to thee, and sleep not in thy boots.

ROBIN: Well now, why—why on earth should you, a great and most famous river, echo the words of Jasper Shrig, why?

But now the only sound that broke the night silence was the plash and ripple of his leisured progress. Thus it was in pitch darkness that he secured his boat, felt his way up the waterstairs, crossed the courtyard and entered his Gamecock's Roost, this echoing desolation, to stand a moment listening, then, acting on sudden impulse, not only locked but bolted the stout old door against—what?

Stumbling in the dark, he groped for, found and presently lighted a candle.

In this dreary solitude he sat down to an unappetising supper of stale bread and cheese, of which, being hungry, he ate heartily and thereafter climbed the narrow stair to his small lofty bedroom (once indeed a hay-loft) high in the gable.

Beyond the little window, wide open as usual, a fitful wind was abroad, filling the night with stir and tumult, as suddenly hushed; a fretful, blusterous wind that shook and rattled crazy casements with vicious gusts, that whispered, sighed, rose to a wail and was gone, leaving a silence the more profound.

It was during one of these momentary lulls that Robin, in the act of removing his boots, checked, suddenly conscious of vague, inexplicable sounds from the courtyard immediately below—a fumbling rustle of stealthy movement . . . creeping footsteps. . . . Were the Powers of Darkness about him at last? Could such things truly be? To be sure, the wind was rising; that chill breath which had met him on the river had gathered strength and was making strange clamour out there in the dark. Ha, but was that merely a wind gust or—stealthy hands groping and fumbling at the door below ? And there again—was that the sibilant rush of wind in the thatch or—voices that whispered ?

Up leapt Robin and, coming to the little window, thrust as much of himself as possible out through the narrow casement to peer down into a vague glimmer that was the courtyard, and beyond this a murmurous blackness that was the river. And now though he could neither hear nor see, he knew that someone or something moved in the blinding darkness below. So sure was he of this that he cried sharply :

" Who's down there ? Who is it and what d'you want ? "

He was answered only by the bellowing clamour of the wind ; but still Robin leaned there, his every sense strung now to an almost painful alertness, watching and waiting impatiently for the moon to banish this very ominous darkness. And at last up she came in an ever-brightening glory to show him merely the empty courtyard and the ever-flowing river, his dark tide lit here and there by a myriad sparkling gems.

For some while Robin leaned thus to gaze upon this peaceful splendour and hearken to the buffeting wind, but when at last he went to bed it was in his boots, and thus, expecting wakefulness, fell asleep with this comforting thought : " She will pray for me."

CHAPTER XXXII

How Robin Came Out of Hell

" WAKE, Robin, wake ! "

Surely that was Her voice ! The vague creature of his dreams, now the very woman of his life and love, was calling to him out of the half-forgotten past, across vast distances, crying to him in voice very faint yet clearly sweet and with an urgency that troubled him greatly.

" Wake ! Oh, Robin—wake ! "

The beloved voice was nearer now and in it a note of terror. Why then, of course he must go to her ; he must hasten, now, this moment. Ah, but what was this that forbade ? What was this frightful, unseen presence that was clutching, holding him inert, stealing away his strength, stifling his will to move ? What was it ?

" Oh, Robin, if you love me—wake ! Oh, my dearest, in God's name—wake ! "

Yes, indeed, he was being stifled ; the dread Powers of Darkness were upon and all about him very really at last, crushing and choking him to terrified helplessness.

" Robin—Robin, fight now—for your life and mine ! Wake—oh, wake before it is too late ! Wake—wake and fight for your life and our future ! Up, Robin—and fight ! "

Her voice now was very near and shrill with such agonised appeal that fight he did and with very fury of desperation, since it seemed he battled for more than mere life. . . .

So thus, breaking at last from the deathly clutch of this most dreadful nightmare, Robin opened smarting eyes upon a swirling dimness lit by the pallid moonlight inflooding through the open lattice and, rising from his tumbled bed, staggered thither, coughing and choking.

Now leaning from this all too narrow casement, he beheld the empty courtyard lit by a red, palpitant glow and the river veiled in billowing, wind-driven smoke. Recoiling from this dreadful sight, he leapt to the door, to be met there by denser smoke uprising from the narrow stairway.

Checked thus, he stood appalled, for down there amid this thickening smoke was that same terrifying glow. Death was there and all around him . . . somewhere beyond, flames crackled to a deepening roar.

Catching up the bed-quilt, he swathed it about his head and shoulders and, holding his breath, plunged down this narrow stairway that would soon be a raging furnace. Down he sped, despite scorching heat and bite of flame, leaping, stumbling, until for the moment he was through the worst of it and able to breathe—only to find his one hope of escape from this merciless destroyer was and must be the small side door opening upon the courtyard. So thitherwards he fled, pursued by this same remorseless foe through a dreadful, red-shot dimness. Driven thus, onward he went, blundering into furniture, stumbling over unseen obstacles, while behind him this red death roared nearer and louder.

Coughing, choking, his smarting eyes half blinded by painful tears, he reached at last the passage leading to the door that was his only hope. Towards this he struggled through smoke that was strangling him, killing him now with his every failing step. But, dying, he reached this door of life at last. With weakly fumbling hands he turned the key . . . drew the bolts . . . raised the latch, and all to none avail. The door refused to open. Despite the wild fury of his efforts it stood fast—shutting him in with death.

And now because he must die so frightfully, despair seized him and panic.

With his last strength he beat upon this door, he kicked, shouted, screamed, and, knowing this all quite vain, sank to his knees, to his face, and, lying thus prone, found he could breathe again, for between smoke-cloud and floor was a gush of pure air. So, thus lying, he shouted once more—high above the hoarse roar of the cruel death that was creeping ever nearer. And in this moment of horror and despair, it seemed to him that even Her prayers were unavailing, and so died Hope. . . . But . . . suddenly upon this forbidding door came the thundering shock of a tremendous blow . . . another . . . and another. The stout oak splintered, was riven asunder at last. . . . Through the wreckage mighty hands reached and seized the dying man, lifted, dragged and bore him up and out from that fiery hell, out to the sweet, cool night, up and away from ghastly death to a new life.

Now presently, as speech and sight returned, Robin looked up at the down-bent anxious face of his deliverer and contrived to gasp :

" John. . . . Oh, Black John, my faithful . . ."

CHAPTER XXXIII

In Which Black John Makes a Promise

CHEEK by jowl, they were seated on the waterstairs close above the tide, yet sheltered from heat and glare by the graceful arch above them. And thus gazing at the river all aglow with the fire that, now fanned by the wind, roared in one huge, seething flame, Robin said :

" Well, old fellow, someone or other has contrived to set the Thames afire at last."

" And, sir," quoth John, shaking his black head mournfully, " I'm awondering how it happened."

" And I," said Robin, knitting his singed eyebrows, " I—am wondering—who ! "

" Who ? " repeated John, turning to stare in amazement. " Master Robin, d'ye mean as you think somebody set yon fire agoing ? "

" Yes, John, I do. Why wouldn't that cursed door open? That fire was meant to be my death, and would have been but for you, which makes me wonder how you came—and in the very nick of time, John ? "

" Chance, sir ! Tonight I happened to work uncommon late—I've a riverside job—and, being done, I chanced to look this way, as I often do for old time's sake. Ah, but in that very moment I spied smoke and a tongue o' flame ! So I came arunning, for, thinks I, Master Robin's been and done it at last ! "

" Done what, old horse ? "

" Set the place afire ! For, sir, you was ever a bit careless like wi' lamps and candles and sich."

" However, this was none of my doing, John, for why was the door made fast against me ? Why wouldn't it open ? "

" Ay, to be sure, sir, this looks very ugly ! "

" Besides, I—heard them at it ! Just before I went to bed I fancied I heard someone down here—soft footsteps, John, then—a fumbling at the door. I wasn't quite sure then, but I am now ! Did you see anyone hereabout as you came ? "

" No, sir. And the fire gave light enough to see if there had been."

" Ha, John man, just look at it now—one all-devouring flame ! Had you not come, I should be in that fiery hell—a few charred fragments. Not a pleasing thought."

" And, sir, I come only by chance."

" So by chance I am alive—yet no ! Oh no ; here was far more than mere chance—yes, by God and all that's holy ! John, do you believe in the efficacy of prayer ? Do you ? "

" Master Robin, I dunno as I've ever thought about it. My blessed mother used to pray and learned me how, but she died years ago and since then I haven't give it a thought."

" Well," said Robin very gravely, " I do believe, I shall and must, for sure am I 'twas only so that I escaped that flaming death this night. Look at it—listen to it ! And, by jingo, the whole neighbourhood is astir ! "

And now indeed as the flames soared amid billowing smoke and sparks plain to hear above rush of wind and the fire's dreadful roar was a growing tumult near and far, ashore and afloat, the hoarse clamour of many voices, shouts and cries from the river, where boats and barges were being urged and towed to more distant and safer berths, while wharfs and foreshore, streets and alleys were athrong with jostling crowds.

" Mr. Robin, I'm wondering where you'll sleep tonight."

" Oh, anywhere—what does it matter ? "

" M' lord Viscount would be glad to——"

" Yes, but I'll not trouble him."

" He wouldn't think it a trouble, sir, not him ! But there's Jasper would——"

" True, but it's a goodish step to The Gun, so—no again."

" Then, sir, I could offer you a bed along o' me at Rotherhithe, which is nearer."

" Where are you living now, John ? "

" At the Angel, sir."

" A pretty riotous abode, old fellow ! "

" Not always, sir. And 'tis kept by two good folks. Tom Betts is an old shipmate o' mine, and his wife Anne is a wonderful good cook, and there's a spare room 'longside mine, a clean, snug berth, Master Robin."

" Good, then I'll take it ! Stay though ; let's see if I can and what I'm worth." And when he had searched every pocket, Robin said, with rueful laugh :

" Lookee, John—two shillings, one groat and a ha'penny. What little money I had by me is ashes yonder."

" No matter, sir, I can lend you enough till Sir Oliver sends——"

" He did, John, and I sent it back. Hereafter the money I spend I must earn, and I'm wondering if you can tell or, better, show me how."

" I can, sir, if you don't mind roughness and dirt."

" I'll welcome both, old fellow."

" Then, sir, you and me can work together."

" Excellent ! What at ? "

" Lading barges, Mr. Robin, if you can bring yourself to sich——"

" I can and will, John, with all my heart ! "

" Why then, Mr. Robin sir, I——"

" Hold hard, John ! If we are to be fellow-labourers as well as friends, have done with your ' sirs ' and ' misters '."

" Very good, sir, only I—never respected you more than I do at this here minute ! So now, if you're ready, shall we go ? "

" Where to ? "

" The Angel, sir, the room I spoke of—and a feather bed, Mr. Robin ! "

" Not so, John ! There shall be no room or bed for me this night—no, b' jingo ! After that horror of fire—the heat and suffocation—all I need is the open air."

" But, sir, you must have a roof to shelter you."

"Not I, old friend ! No, I shall go for a pull upriver, and if I want to sleep it shall be in some barn or on some fragrant rick. So, expect me at the Angel tomorrow night. And now, let me tell you this. Ever since I—we parted, I've missed and needed you very damnably ! And now that you've come back to me, I'm hoping you'll never leave me again, never, John ! Is it a promise ? "

" Yes, Master Robin, I'll stay with you to—the end o' my days, sir."

Here, with sudden gesture, Robin seized his hand, shook it, dropped it and, descending the old stairs, stepped aboard his boat and pulled away upstream while Black John stood to watch him out of sight.

And so, thus wonderfully alive, upriver went Robin, intending for a certain barn with the hope that thereabout tomorrow, when the day was young and glad, he might behold the woman whose prayer, he believed, had wrought his salvation.

CHAPTER XXXIV

In Which Father Thames Philosophises

" GOOD MORNING, Mrs. Brent ; I've come for the milk and butter and——"

" And I'm here to warn ee, my dearie miss, don't go anigh the barn ; there be a gurt blackymore, a dark-faced man wretch asleep there and snoring and grunting worse than our old sow ! "

" A blackamoor ? Do you really mean——? "

" A dark-faced nigger man, Miss Tracy ! So soon as our men come they shall rout him out wi' pitch-forks. He looks such a desprit, wicked villin and youm such a tempting armful o' loveliness, so come you indoors along o' me now, and hurry afore he wakes and catches sight of ee."

The " tempting armful " laughed but obeyed. . . . Then up started smiling Robin from the fragrant hay pile that had been his bed, to listen, glad-eyed, until voices and footsteps had died away ; and when he had brushed the clinging hay from his scorched garments and smoothed his hatless head, forth he went in a radiant morning and down to the river, where, drawn up close beside his own, lay the boat inscribed by those three magic letters—B.E.T.

So down he sat to wait and gaze at the murmurous river just now made glorious by the young sun's level beams. Thus presently he held communion with it (and himself) as usual, thus :

ROBIN : Tell me, Old Thing of wisdom, shall I or shan't I ? Is it too soon to speak, d'you suppose ?

THAMES (*throatily*) : Better too soon than too late.

Nothing venture, nothing win. Faint heart never won——

ROBIN : Yes, I know, but what I desire to win is so absolutely vast——

THAMES : Yet you might span it easily with one arm.

ROBIN : Lord love you, Old Thing, what a blessed thought —in one arm ! Yes, in that span is a very infinitude of happiness, a wonderment so vast it fills the universe.

THAMES : Yet goes on two legs like any other ordinary——

ROBIN (*fervently*) : No, damme ! Here is nothing ordinary ; on the contrary, here is the exception completely exempt and so rare, so very holy and truly sacred and perfectly divine that I——

THAMES (*bubbling derisively*) : Bub-bub-balderdash, bub-boy ! Can anything human be divine ? Not it, and especially a young woman ? No again, not she, certainly nowise and no when.

ROBIN (*more fervently*) : This one can be, she is and alway will be——

THAMES : Bub-bub——

ROBIN : Don't say balderdash !

THAMES : Ho ho, what I say is as how you are a bub-bub-besotted bub-boy bub-blinded by that unreasoning though necessary human passion called love.

ROBIN : On the contrary, I that was so blind now see ! Yes, by heaven, my eyes are wide open at last, because only a few hours ago I was very near my death, as you probably know.

THAMES : Ar ! Of course ! The fire.

ROBIN : Well, today by a miracle I am more alive than ever before.

THAMES : Because Black John beat down the door.

ROBIN : And because She prayed for me. Now don't bubble and mock, because I am perfectly convinced.

THAMES :   Because you are merely a young male animal
  newly in love, which is a quite ordinary, very common
  —not to say vulgar happening.
ROBIN (*indignantly*) :   This is neither ordinary nor
  common.
THAMES :   It's both ! It always was and will be.
ROBIN :   Oh no, never ! Never since Time began was
  there ever anything so altogether sacred, holy or marvellous as——
THAMES :   Bub-bub-bosh ! Love's a bodily disease, a
  commonly natural impulse implanted to the one sole
  purpose of——
ROBIN :   Nothing of the sort, Old Mud and Slime, no
  indeed ! True love is utterly unselfish, giving all but
  asking nothing, a power so nobly good that I am
  daunted by my own unworthiness.
THAMES :   Lord, Rob, you have took it bad, and if she
  takes you—oh, my eye ; you'll live in a fool's paradise !
ROBIN :   What do I care, so long as it is indeed paradise.
THAMES :   Rob, you moo like passion-blinded moon-
  calf.
ROBIN :   And you bubble and blither like the cynically
  soulless and sinful old runagate you are !
THAMES :   I'm all soul, Robin ; from source to sea
  nothing but soul to serve and sorrow for poor humanity
  as I have done through ages past and shall do in ages yet
  to be. ·And as for love, me lad, go to it bold-hearted.
  She's young and apt to wife, and motherhood—and
  for your unworthiness, do you but tell her of it
  and she, being so truly woman, will love you the better
  therefore.
ROBIN :   Oh, Father Thames, now indeed you are my
  comfort. Shall I—do you advise me to speak ?
THAMES :   As I says afore, better too soon than too
  late.

ROBIN :   Will the answer be " Yes " or " No " ?

THAMES :   Too-whoo, says the owl and so says I.

ROBIN :   Very well, then answer me this instead : do you
believe in the efficacy of prayer ?

THAMES :   For my answer—look behind you.

Robin obeyed and thus met the gaze of these eyes so
vividly blue, eyes that now widened to horrified stare, as :

" Oh ! " she exclaimed. " No wonder Mrs. Brent mistook
you for a blackamoor. Your face—so dark, Robin ! "

" B' George, yes, I—I forgot," he stammered ; " effect
of the smoke and—and so on."

" And your hair ! "

" A trifle singed, I expect."

" But how—what, oh, whatever has happened to you ? "

" Something so amazing that I don't know how to tell of
it."

" Ah," she whispered. " What—have they—done to
you ? "

" It was the fire," he answered. " But don't look so
frightfully distressed. It's nothing to matter ; it's all over
and done with now, so let's——"

" The—fire ! " she repeated and shuddered so violently
that she very nearly dropped her heavy-laden basket. So he
took it from her, saying with new reverence in voice and
look :

" Oh, Bet—you never-ending wonder ! Because of you I
am alive. You brought me out of that fiery hell to a new life,
a new belief and understanding ! Yes, in spite of all the
Powers of Darkness and Evil, here am I alive and well,
and all—because of you ! "

" Of me ? " she questioned in tremulous bewilderment.
" But—how ? What happened ? Tell me."

" Why, so I will. I'm yearning to tell you, though, as I
say, I don't know how—it was all so marvellous ! "

" What was ? "

"You!" he answered, gazing at her now with the reverent eyes of his "new understanding". "Last night you—performed a miracle!"

"How, Robin, how? Oh, tell me—tell me how I did it."

"No, this you should tell me, because the more I think of it, the less I am able to describe or speak of it."

"Then try beginning—at—the beginning."

"Very well!" said he, shaking his head dubiously, "Though now with this blessed old sun so bright about us, it will sound so wildly unreal and fantastic that you may doubt——"

"Oh, let me hear and judge for myself."

"You shall, and please believe if you can. It begins with me on the bed, very fast asleep and—in my boots! Now if you ask me why I didn't take them off, I don't know."

"Perhaps because of what Mr. Shrig said about not doing so?"

"Maybe, though I never thought of him. However, there I lay fully dressed, thank heaven, and quite lost in most profound and dreamless slumber. But, all at once—and, mind you, I was not dreaming—your voice came to me, faintly at first as if from a great distance, but gradually it became louder and nearer—and it was crying on me to wake. And then—ah, Bet—when I tried to wake—I couldn't; it seemed that some evil thing had me in its grip. I could neither wake nor move! Oh, most horrible! But still you called to me, louder, nearer, more insistently, and still I lay as though paralysed. Then you were beside me, pleading, telling me to rouse and fight for both our sakes and—our future. And so, inspired by your nearness and compelling voice, I—yes, I broke that accursed spell at last and awoke— only just in time, because the place all about me was on fire."

"And, oh," she exclaimed, clasping her hands, " I saw it —that terrible glow in the sky! I saw it—and wondered what was burning so fiercely!"

"The poor old Roost, Bet, flaming sky-high. And because of the furious wind it burnt all the fiercer and spread so rapidly that—it was touch and go with me ; yes, b'gad, at one time I thought it had me. That was a ghastly moment ! "

"And how—how did you escape ? " she enquired breathlessly. "Tell me, Robin ; tell me everything."

"Then sit down with me, here close beside Father Thames, our river of Destiny, and I'll do my poor best to describe all the horror and wonder of it."

Mutely she obeyed and as mutely listened, nor breathed a word until the tale was ended, then :

"Oh ! " she exclaimed. "That door ! That cruel, hateful door ! It was meant to—kill you."

"But I am very much alive, thanks to you ! So henceforth Robin Dale must be regarded as your ' brand plucked from the burning '—yours, Bet. For this fellow's liveliness you are now responsible, so pray what do you intend for him? What about the fellow ? "

"This," she replied with smile he thought all too brief, "will depend upon the fellow."

"Yes, but how ? "

"Is the fellow a hungry fellow ? "

"Dear soul, the poor fellow is famishing."

"Then if Robin Dale will bear me company he shall help me to feed the fellow."

"Aha, breakfast ? But must it be at the farm yonder ? "

"Oh no, in the alder bower as usual."

"Glory be ! Ah, but I haven't brought the wherewithal, kettle and so on."

"But I have ! "

"Well now," exclaimed Robin in glad surprise, "confound me if you aren't my perpetual wonder. Tell me, pray, are you goddess, witch or angel ? "

"Neither, sir. I am merely a woman."

"Which in your case is a compound of all three. And

you are not—a—woman, no, most certainly not ; you are—
the—woman, for in all this wide world there is only one
Bet, and she being so——"

" So extremely human, Robin, she also desires her breakfast ! Come then and go with her to——"

" To the end of the world, yes and of life itself, if she only
will ! " said he fervently.

CHAPTER XXXV

Some Account of a He and She Breakfast

NOW FOR some reason or other this breakfast of He and She (or Him and Her) begun thus joyously, and with such hearty appetite became gradually an unwontedly silent meal and not because of youthfully hungry gulping and devouring, most certainly not, for He, it seemed, was quickly satisfied while She ate scarcely anything.

Also, whenever She glanced at him, which was often, it was to see his brooding gaze turned riverwards ; and whenever He glanced at Her, which was even more frequently, it was to behold those very beautiful eyes looking everywhere except in his direction ; and yet it was She at last who broke this unusual silence, thus :

SHE : You are very thoughtful !

He : Yes, yes, I am ; and, for that matter, so are you.

SHE : Because I was thinking of the fire and that— murderous door.

HE : Well, forget the infernal thing.

SHE : I suppose it was of some such expected evil that Mr. Shrig hinted ?

HE : Forget him, too, and think of me.

SHE (*submissively*) : Very well, I will.

HE : Good ! Now look at me.

SHE : Not until you ask me properly.

HE : How, properly ?

SHE : Say " please ".

He : Will you please have the kindness to use your eyes on me.

SHE : Yes, Mr. Dale sir. (*She views him slowly from head to foot.*)

HE : Well now, what are you pleased to think of me—please ?

SHE (*surveying his every feature except his eyes*) : That your poor, smoky face needs washing and your——

HE (*ruefully*) : Yes, b' George—and shaving ! I must show rather more repulsive than usual ! Which, of course, makes what I have to say all the more confoundedly difficult.

SHE (*faintly surprised*) : Oh ? Why should it ?

HE (*beginning to flounder*) : Because to say what I have to say and wish to say properly I ought to say it at my best instead of worst, bristles, grime and so on, yet say it I must, because—well, I must.

SHE (*gently tolerant*) : Very well, I'm listening. Please go on.

HE (*scowling up fiercely at a lark soaring above them*) : Well now, deuce take me if I know how to say it as it should be said.

SHE (*maternally encouraging*) : You can only do your best, so try.

HE (*desperately*) : Then—here goes.

SHE (*as though bewildered*) : What goes where ?

HE (*suddenly suspicious*) : Bet, are you laughing at me, making game of me ?

SHE (*eyes wide and beautifully innocent*) : How can you think I ever would—or could ?

HE (*sighing*) : Very easily. But, indeed, you laugh all too seldom, so if you feel inclined to laugh at me, and Lord knows why, laugh away and I'll try to do the same, though what I have to say is no laughing matter, far from it.

SHE (*after trill of irrepressible laughter*) : Oh, good gracious me, Robin, whatever you have been trying

I

to say all this time, say it, for mercy's sake, and be done.

HE (*resolutely folding his arms*) : Good ! I will, hoping for the best. What I have to say is—are you listening ?

SHE (*with sound very like a titter*) : Yes, yes, of course I am.

HE (*grimly*) : Right ! It's this. I want you—for my wife.

Gone now was her laughter, for she was looking up at him very wistfully, as he at her, and neither speaking. Thus they gazed on one another eye to eye in a silence broken only by the faint, sweet song of the lark and the bubbling chuckle of Father Thames.

" Well," Robin demanded at last, " what have you to say ? "

" That you are as clumsy as you are sudden."

" Yes," he sighed, " yes, I am ! Being merely Robin Dale, I've muffed it as usual ! Of course I ought to have begun by telling you I love you, but I can't because my love is beyond the telling. All I know is that you are my very life . . . because we were made for each other, meant for each other, part of each other. Without you I shall never be anything better than I am ; with you I might become almost worthy of you—in time. And, oh, damme, if only I could make love properly—find the right words or knew how to say them ! But I feel too deeply for grace of speech or easy eloquence."

" I think you are doing very well, considering you are— merely Robin Dale."

" And consequently," said he dejectedly, " pretty certain of failure, as usual ! And, what's more, I have to inform you that just at present I'm a confounded pauper, so that I'm asking you to become the wife of a—a deuced labouring man, a loader of barges, though only for the time being— I hope. For if you are so very unwise and so nobly brave to dare the future with me, I know that with you to work for, as I will, and to love, as I do and always shall, we together would make a success of life, and, what's more——"

" Hush ! " she exclaimed with arresting gesture. " Someone is coming—listen ! " So saying, she drew on her hood swiftly, with an almost fearful haste, and bowed her head, as somewhere nearby was a rustle growing louder until the leafage parted and Mr. Shrig stood looking down upon them. He showed pale and haggard ; also he bore his left arm in a sling. But he smiled and his eyes were bright as ever as he touched his hat, which, like himself, showed signs of rough usage. . . . Down went Robin's plate and knife and fork and up he rose, saying :

" Jasper, Lord love you, what's the matter ? "

" Master Robin, if John hadn't tipped me the office, I should be peeking and pining werry grievous over your dewoted cinders among the ashes o' the Gamecock's——"

" Oh, deuce take the ashes, man ! What about you ? Sit down and tell us what happened. Yes, and have an egg or something, coffee and a rasher or so ; eh, Bet ? "

" Dear Mr. Jasper, of course ! " said she, busied with the coffee-pot. " Sit here by me ; I'll hold your cup or plate if your arm is too painful."

" Lady o' Lovesomeness," he answered, beaming, " my flipper looks worse than 'tis b' reason o' my Lady Rosamond abinding and slinging of it so careful."

" She would, bless her ! But how did it get hurt ? "

" The kiss of a knife, same being a stiletta and nothing to matter beyond a bit o' smart. Howsever, my birds is took and dooly caged. Vich reminds me to tell you, Master Rob, of your respected governor Sir O."

" Ah, is he in town, Jasper ? "

" At the ' Jolly Vaterman '—rode in last night and lost his precious life for your sake, or werry nearly."

" For my sake ? Good God, how, man, how ? "

" Seeing the Roost ablaze, there he goes along o' George and the bo'sun and 'twas all as they could do to keep him from wenturing into the flames, thinking you was perishing therein ; tried heavens hard——"

" Did he, Jasper ? Oh did he ? "

" Ar, fought and struggled he did, calling your name till Black John come along and told as you was safe."

" Oh, Bet—Bet, you hear ? He would have given his life—for me ! "

" So, Master Rob, by his vish I'm here to find you, vich I have, and, having found, to bid you to him at the ' Vaterman '."

" Then," said Robin, starting afoot all joyous eagerness, " I'll go to him at once ! I shall feel like begging his pardon on my knees. So, Bet, my lady, by your gracious leave, I'll be off, but——"

" ' 'Twill be labour in wain, seeing as how."

" As how what, Jasper ? "

Mr. Shrig emptied his coffee-cup thirstily, sighed blissfully and replied :

" He's wisiting the Duchess o' C. along o' the Wi-count. Sir O. expects you any time's arternoon."

" Good ! Did he give you any particular message for me?"

" Ar ! ' Pal Jarsper,' says he—ay, on occasion he calls me ' pal ', a Romany vord meaning ' brother '—' tell him '—meaning you, Master Rob—' as I'm hoping to welcome Robin Goodfellow,' says he."

" And he will, Jasper ; yes, by heaven, because Robert the Devil perished in the fire."

" Sure o' that ? "

" Certainly I am ! "

" Werry good ! So now talking o' marriage——"

" Eh ? Now what the—who—marriage ? "

" Another name for it is vedlock."

" Whose marriage ? "

" Yours, sir ; the Wi-count's idea is———"

" Ragworth ? Now what on earth———"

" Sir, as your lady aunt is binding my arm, he axes me to tell you as he hopes you'll bring it off on the same day and so make a double ewent of it."

" Bring what off ?"

" Your vedding."

" But—good great jingo, who—what—whom does he expect me to wed ? "

" Since you ax me so p'inted, I should respond—some bee-oo-tiful young female party as is villing to take you for better or vorse and make the best o' you, as—if she vould, she could."

" Who could ? "

" Aforesaid young fee———"

" Are you sure of this ? "

" Ar ! Certen sure ! "

" Then, name her."

" Not me, sir—no ! In my line o' business names is best un-spoke."

" But we're not talking ' business '."

" Howsever, I am ! "

" I see ! " said Robin, and, heedful of Mr. Shrig's bright, roving glance, enquired, though very diffidently :

" Bet, I—I'm wondering what you think of—of this ? "

And in the act of refilling Mr. Shrig's cup she answered :

" That depends on what you mean by ' this '."

" Jasper's young female party, of course."

" Oh, but you're forgetting the adjective, Robin ! "

" Well, do you think this beautiful young female could and would try to make the best of me ? What do you think ? "

" That it would be a very onerous task, Robin."

" Yes," he sighed, " it would be confoundedly hard work, I know, the work of a lifetime ! "

" Yet p'raps," Mr. Shrig suggested, " ar mebbe a—labour o' love."

" Ha, Jasper, my dear old boy, what a friend and comforter you are ! At the first opportunity I'll ask your young female par——"

" Hush ! " she exclaimed in sudden alarm. " Someone is—oh—running towards us ! "

Mute and still, all three, they listened and in some apprehension, for amid the neighbouring thickets a raging tempest seemed driving down upon them—and so came the man Daniel, breathless with more than mere haste, a man direly altered, whose meekness had given place to a stark ferocity, his very whiskers bristled malignantly as he panted :

" He's off, Jasper—he's away—number two ! they've let him—escape ! "

Very carefully Mr. Shrig set down his untasted (second) cup of coffee and rose, saying regretfully :

" A pity as I didn't pull trigger on him last night ! Oo's to blame, Dan'l ? "

" The Lewes officers ! He shammed sick—shed tears and —they took pity on him and——"

" Ar! " sighed Mr. Shrig mournfully. " And he took French leave. So it's us again, Dan'l—up and arter him, prompt."

" Too true, Jarsper ! But d'ye know where, or——"

" Ar! He'll follow wengeance and the money, but, first and foremost—wengeance ! So the sooner us is up and doing the better for all con-sarned ! Therefore, here ends my breakfast werry sudden——"

" Shall I go with you, old fellow ? "

" No, Master Rob ; here'll be no clean and honest fistplay—for there's a thing of evil broke loose, a thing

as looks human yet ain't rightly so ; a thing roaming at
large intent on Windictiveness wrote in capitals ! So, my
Lady o' Sunlight, tell Sergeant Ben to keep his pistols noo-
charged and sabre handy ! And you, Master Robin, most
especial, mind your eye, ar—keep both your peepers peeled
and kind fortun' to you both ! " With this hearty wish,
Mr. Shrig nodded to Daniel and departed at speed.

CHAPTER XXXVI

Of Sergeant-Major Tracy and Things Domestic

" WELL NOW," said Robin so soon as they were alone,
" confound Jasper for completely spoiling my breakfast
again ! But this time he has contrived to trouble me no end,
because he evidently thinks you also are in some danger, Bet.
I mean, his mention of Sergeant Ben and——"

" I think," said she, drawing on the hood of her cloak
suddenly and glancing as swiftly round about them, " I
must have told you Ben is my—uncle."

" Whom I have never met ! But—why the pistols ? "

" Ours is a—very lonely cottage——"

" Which I have never seen."

" Help me with the breakfast things and you shall. And
hurry, Robin, hurry ! "

" Certainly, but why the breathless haste ? "

" Because the sooner we are away from here, the
better."

" Why, Bet," he exclaimed, peering beneath her hood,
" you're frightfully pale ! Were you anyone else, I should
think you were afraid. But what on earth can possibly harm
you on such a glorious morning and with me beside you,
and, yes, by God, ready if necessary to die for you——"

" No ! " she gasped, shuddering violently. " Don't—
don't speak of—death ! Come away ! "

Very soon they were afloat, and it troubled him greatly
to see how unsteadily she plied her oars and with what
dreadful eyes watched the river and tree-shaded banks. And
so striving to comfort her he enquired at last :

"Bet, oh my dear, what is it you fear? If you are thinking of Jasper's hints, vindictiveness and so on, do pray forget and don't bother; he loves to be mysterious."

"But—oh, Robin, he was right about—the fire!"

"Anyhow, deuce take Jasper. Forget him and let's talk of ourselves! I'm still yearning for an answer to the greatest and most important question of my life, Bet. Will you become the sole property of a pauper? Will you become the adored wife of that—I mean this poor, solitary, miserable failure called Robin Dale? Are you brave enough, strong enough to undertake him as your life's work; to love him almost as much as he, the poor wretch, adores you; to inspire him to better purpose and make his life complete? Can you, dare you, oh—will you, Bet?"

Now at this she ceased rowing and, shaking back her hood, turned and looked at him; and her face, framed in its lustrous, raven hair, was no longer pale or fearful; also in those eyes so wonderfully blue was a light not of the sun, yet all she said was:

"Follow me!"

Then, with dexterous play of oars, she turned her light skiff very suddenly and urged it straight towards the lofty, bush-grown bank, and to his wonder he saw the stern of her boat with its letters B. E. T. vanish amid the dense leafage, and again she called softly:

"Follow me, Robin!"

"Now and forever!" he replied fervently, and, turning where and as she had done, heard the prow of his boat part this rustling, leafy screen; found himself in a close, green tunnel through which he glided, and so—out again into the sunshine and a broad, still backwater bowered in trees. And here, throned upon a bank and set within a garden where flowers bloomed, was a steep-thatched, roomy cottage.

"Oh, Ben—Uncle Ben!"

"Here, my——" A man's deep voice suddenly hushed as the speaker beheld Robin. A tall man this, very neat and trim as to person, whose stern features were rendered grimmer by the black patch beneath one shaggy eyebrow.

"Well, my—m' dear?"

"Yes," she replied as they stepped ashore, "this is Mr. Robin Dale of whom you have heard. Robin—my uncle, ex-Sergeant-Major Benjamin Edward Tracy of the Life Guards, who lost his eye, bless him, saving the life of my dear father in that frightful Battle of Waterloo."

"I'm very glad to meet you!" said Robin, proffering his hand.

"Honoured, sir!" quoth the sergeant, grasping it. "I've heard great things of you, sir, from Mr. Shrig."

"Ah, so you know Jasper, do you?"

"Quite well, sir; he often visits us to drink a cup or so of tea, or something stronger. I met him hereabouts fishing and we struck up an acquaintance which has ripened into friendship."

"Fishes, does he, Sergeant?"

"Now and then, sir, not often."

"Is he a good fisherman?"

"Well, sir," replied the sergeant, his stern face transfigured by quick radiant smile, "he's very patient and ever hopeful."

Robin laughed; then, becoming suddenly grave, enquired:

"Major Tracy, are you—do I understand you are Miss Tracy's sole guardian?"

"Yessir, you may, for I most certainly am."

"Then," said Robin, turning to front him, "I have to inform you I have asked her—your ward—to be my wife."

The sergeant's one bright eye blinked, glared, and blinked again; he threw out his chest, hemmed portentously, but all he said was:

"Oh? Ah? Indeed, sir! Is she willing?"

" The question is, Sergeant, are you ? "

" Sir, I am, if she is, so—is she ? "

" This I have yet to learn, when I can find her. Where in the world——? "

" Here ! " she called gaily. " In the kitchen, preparing dinner. Come in, both of you, and wash up these breakfast things for me."

" This way, sir ! " said the sergeant.

" At the double ! " answered Robin.

Enveloped in a large apron, but with round arms bared above dimpled elbows, she was doing marvels with dough and a rolling-pin—or so thought Robin, though all he really saw were those white and shapely arms made only the fairer by the flour that clung to them so lovingly—and no wonder ! thought Robin.

" Wash or wipe, sir ? " enquired the sergeant.

" Eh ? " exclaimed Robin, starting. " Oh, I see what you mean. I'll wipe."

" Right ! " said the sergeant, removing his coat and draping it carefully across a chair-back. " I'll wash ! " So saying, he rolled up snowy shirt-sleeves and together they fell to work with mop and cloth. . . .

But the arms, their beauty and graceful movements, so thralled Robin that, wiping a cup gazing at these, the cup, being wet and therefore restive, leapt from his lax grasp and splintered upon the floor. Whereat She glanced down at the fragments and up at Robin and said :

" There goes number one ! Uncle Ben, take care you don't equalise with a number two ! "

" Not likely, m' dear ! " he retorted. " I'm too well drilled for any such catas——" The milk jug he had brought to close action with the mop, splitting asunder, left him staring and speechless.

" Ah," sighed she, " number two came apart of its own accord, didn't it, Uncle Ben ? Never mind ! But when you finish with the few that will remain, I want you both to help me with the beans and potatoes. Uncle Ben, you have already invited our visitor to dine with us, of course ? "

" Well, no, m' dear, but I will. Sir, I do and right heartily."

" And right gratefully I accept ! " said Robin, wiping a plate very carefully.

Thus the washing and drying proceeded slowly but with no further accident, until all was done and each article bestowed cautiously in its proper place on hook or shelf.

It was now that the sergeant winked his bright, solitary eye at Robin, gestured furtively in a certain direction and stole out and away to his beloved garden.

And forthwith Robin attempted to put his thought into words :

" Oh, Bet—your arms——"

" Goodness ! " she exclaimed. " What's the matter with them ? I know they're all floury, but——"

" They are the loveliest, most beautiful I have ever seen."

" Oh ! Then—have you seen so many ? "

" Well, no, at least—not lately. And now that I see yours, I'm yearning to kiss them."

" Gracious goodness—what an idea ! "

" Especially the dimples in your elbows. May I ? "

" No ! No, you may not ! Robin, go away ; you make me feel quite shy and ridiculous ! "

" I never saw you look shy till now, and it makes you all the lovelier. So pray yield me your dimples, for——"

" Oh, Robin," she laughed, " instead of such nonsense think of the vegetables—and wherever is Uncle——? "

" Out and away, Bet ; he has left us to each other, which gives me a hope that he may not object to me as a nephew-in-law, if you will only do your part. So now—what is your answer ? " And busied now with the flour-dredger, she replied :

" I will tell you—this evening, after you have seen and been forgiven by your Sir Oliver."

" But suppose he—does not forgive me ? "

" You must wait until you have earned his forgiveness. And now tell me—so you like breast of veal, Robin, stuffed ? "

" Yes," he replied instinctively. " Yes, of course I do, but—oh, good great jingo, what a question to ask me when I'm asking you one so—so profoundly different, a question so confoundedly sacred as to be—yes, holy— and, b' George, you talk of—veal ! "

" Stuffed, Robin ! " she added, and, avoiding his eager (and expected) clasp very dexterously, leapt and fronted him across the table, grasping the flour-dredger defensively— all delicious provocation from defiant head to nimble feet, for though she contrived to frown, yet in her eyes was that which awed and humbled him, so that he murmured :

" How—beautiful you are ! "

" Oh, but, Robin, in spite of——"

" With your—glorious hair. Black is the one and only colour——"

At this moment the sergeant, venturing too near, was sighted and hailed commandingly :

" Uncle Ben, for shame to desert in face of the vegetables ! Come back and engage them at once, point and edge."

" Right, m' dear. I was only doing a bit of very necessary hoeing." Laying that implement aside, back he came, to wink his solitary eye at Robin and enquire :

" Which for you, Mr. Robin ? Will you peel or cut, sir ? "

" Either, if you'll show me how—like the good friend I prove you ? "

" Very good, sir. You take your bean, cut him tenderly front and rear, so—to remove his strings, you then slices him thin, so—that he may eat the better."

And now as they wrought together on bean and potato, Robin, seated near the table, glanced up frequently at Her ; and She, though busied with her pastry, glanced down as frequently (almost) at him. And presently he began to converse, thus :

ROBIN   (*slicing a bean more or less deftly*) : Sergeant Ben, your niece is my continual wonder.

SERGEANT   (*peeling a potato with experienced dexterity*) : No wonder, Mr. Robin, for she's mine, too, but why yours ?

ROBIN : Because she's so various ; yes, of infinite variety. For instance, she is not only so extremely decorative and most pleasing to the eye, but she can manage a boat with the utmost grace and dexterity.

SERGEANT : Very true, sir, and, if overboard, swims like a fish.

ROBIN : She would ! And graceful as a mermaid, of course——

SHE : Oh ? And how can you know, pray ?

ROBIN   (*plying knife vigorously*) : Simply because you are you.

SHE   (*pointing with rolling-pin*) : And you are hacking that poor bean to nothingness ! The idea is to leave as much of it as possible.

ROBIN : Madam, I'm aware of it. This knife becomes a trifle restive occasionally. May I ask what you are up to with all that doughy stickiness ?

SHE   (*kneading with both fists*) : Making—a—black-currant pudding—I hope !

ROBIN : Mag-nificent ! Ha, Sergeant Ben, it seems she can cook also.

SERGEANT : Sir, in pie, pudding or tart, fish, flesh or fowl, she can get more flavour than seems possible when you see 'em in the rough before she's handled and drilled 'em ! She'll take a raw carcase, slimy fish, or lump o' meat and transmogrify 'em into mouth-watering delicacies—toothsome, sir, toothsome.

SHE : Dear Uncle Benjamin ! Just for this, you shall have two servings of everything, and, yes, an extra tot of rum !

ROBIN : Now Lord love her, what a woman ! What a wife ! What a helpmate for a labouring man ! What an inspiration to any man ! How much better to be such capable woman than any too-dainty, languishing, do-nothing fine lady ; eh, Sergeant ?

The sergeant starts and actually drops a potato as he glances keenly at Robin, then at her, shakes his head and goes down after the potato, comes up with it and says :

" Ah, but you should see her on horseback."

" I should love to," said Robin with fervour, " and hope I shall—someday."

" Also, Mr. Robin, she can dance most graciously, play on the harp and sing to it."

" Can she, by jingo ! "

" Furthermore, sir, she talks French and I-talian like so many natives, and besides all these polite accomplish-ments she——"

" Enough ! " sighed Robin. " No more, Sergeant Ben, or I shall lose all hope ! For how can I expect such amazingly gifted creature to stoop for such graceless, commonplace fellow as poor Robin Dale ? How say you, my lady Bet ? "

And over her shoulder she replied :

" Like Mr. Shrig, I say ' ar ' ! Now please stand aside and let me get to the oven."

In due season they sat down to such meal as Robin was never to forget, not so much because of its excellence as for the hands, so slender yet so very capable, which had prepared, cooked and served it.

It was therefore a meal to linger over and, as it were, dwell upon. Robin did both. Indeed, long after the table was cleared and the crockery duly washed, wiped and put away he would have lingered still, had not Father Time, that most remorseless of tyrannical ancients, compelled him away.

"Almost two o'clock already, Robin, and Sir Oliver will be expecting you."

"Yes," he sighed, glancing from the vital beauty beside him to the fragrant loveliness around them, for they were in the garden. "Yes, I must go, of course. But, anyhow, and whatever happens, I shall return and soon as possible for your answer."

" 'Whatever happens' ? " she repeated, clasping her hands as she glanced around with that same look of horrified expectancy. "And such dreadful things may happen——"

"Well now, Lord love you !" he exclaimed, taking those nervous hands and kissing them. "All I mean is—should Sir Oliver refuse his forgiveness, as he well may, for, b'gad, he can be devilish stern on occasion and my offence was so altogether damnable—should he cast me off, I shall come crawling back, like any other lame dog, hoping you may prove more merciful or at least show a little pity. So why this sudden distress—and your dear clever hands all of a tremble—why ? What is it you find so very terrible ? "

And while her fearful eyes still glanced here and there, she answered, almost whispering :

"Jasper Shrig's warning—the Thing of Evil that looks human but—"

"Oh, deuce take Jasper ! This was only more of his infernal mysteries. I can guess just what and whom he meant and am perfectly able to tackle the detestable——"

"Ah no !" she gasped. "Don't be too foolishly sure, because even your strength and bravery may be of no avail. Instead—be watchful, and especially in lonely places—keep looking behind you."

" Now 'pon my life, Bet, you astound me! For however can you know——? "

" Oh, Robin, because I am—myself, I know you are in most deadly peril and this terrifies me because—you are you."

" Glory be ! " he exclaimed, looking down on her radiant-eyed. " For, oh, my dearest, it seems I must be—rather precious to you. And for this I should kiss—and kiss you—if I didn't love you quite so much—in such an odd passionately reverent sort of way, that I never shall until—the only proper time."

Here, very unwillingly, he stepped into his boat.

Standing on the bank above him, she enquired :

" When would be your 'proper time' ? "

And, glancing up at her with that same radiant look, he answered :

" When, of your own accord, you come into my arms and say, ' Now, my own Robin, kiss me.' I wonder if you ever will ? How say you ? "

And smiling very wistfully she replied :

" Like Mr. Shrig, I say—ekker alone responds. But as myself I pray, God protect you, Robin."

" And," said Robin, shipping his oars, " my prayer is this : ' O God, knowing how I love her, make her mine to be my joy and salvation, amen ! ' "

K

CHAPTER XXVII

Tells of Sir Oliver's Greeting

URGING his boat out and away from this secret and (for him) loveliest of all backwaters, Robin plied his oars vigorously, for the tide was against him; it was past two o'clock and his present anxious thought was of Sir Oliver Dale. . . . And now, as he pondered this approaching interview that was to affect his life thereafter so greatly, his oars faltered in their swing and lost their power as doubt assailed him, a nervous uncertainty akin to dread. Yes, he was indeed actually afraid of this meeting, and that he should thus dread to meet his beloved patient old Noll was most astonishing until he remembered this same gentle, great-hearted Noll, though his foster-father, was also Sir Oliver Dale, an aristocrat proud of his ancient name and unblemished honour. Could such a man be expected to forgive the ignominy of being struck, that dastard blow which had so nearly felled him—and before so many witnesses?

Robin burned with shame at the recollection. Oh, could any man, however magnanimous and long-suffering, pardon so public an affront of his dignity and manhood?

Robin ceased rowing. Appalled by his own unspoken question, he leaned on his oars, and, being thus troubled, sought comfort of his Father Thames.

" Oh, my dear Old Wise One, is even he capable of such unearthly goodness and mercy ? " And the river's babbling tide-race seemed to answer :

THAMES : For you he would have dared the fire !

ROBIN :   But that may have been only a momentary impulse. And remember he has so often forgiven me in the past——

THAMES :   Well, why not again in the present ?

ROBIN :   Because by now he may be tired of condoning my accursed faults, and especially this, the worst and most damnable of all.

THAMES :   Too true, my poor, passionate young egoist, always thinking of number one.

ROBIN :   Not always, because now I'm thinking of— him. And he is such a proud man, and sometimes can be sternly aloof, remote and out of my humble reach because he is a true-blue aristocrat.

THAMES :   But he is also a gentleman.

ROBIN :   Of course, as I say, he is a real aristocrat and——

THAMES :   I said " gentleman " !

ROBIN :   Yes ? Well, what is a gentleman ?

THAMES :   A man who dares be gentle to all, especially such as are weaker or less fortunate than himself.

ROBIN :   Ah ! Then you think he may possibly forgive——

THAMES :   This you must learn from him—instead of crouching there so fool-like while I drift you back'ards.

ROBIN :   You are no help or comfort to me.

THAMES :   Not I, and for why ? Because, Rob, none can help Robin but Robin. So, put your back into it and row, meet him and get it over.

ROBIN :   How will he greet me, d'you suppose ?

THAMES :   I don't suppose, I know.

ROBIN :   Well, how ?

THAMES :   Find out !

ROBIN :   Can't you be a little kinder to me ?

THAMES :   Oh yes, infinitely so—later on !

ROBIN :   How, later on ?

THAMES :　Wait and see.

ROBIN :　I've never known you so cursedly unsympathetic.

THAMES :　I've seldom known you so cursedly futile—cowering there, a pitiful do-nothing all adrift. Row, fool, row !

ROBIN :　Yes, I may as well. And thanks for—nothing !

THAMES :　You are heartily welcome. So make the best of it.

ROBIN :　Of what ?

THAMES :　Everything, of course, but just at present, your oars.

Robin did so ; and thus after some while beheld the old waterstairs and beyond—a blue haze rising from the still-smouldering ashes of his Gamecock's Roost. He could smell the acrid reek of it and therefore lengthened his stroke to leave this most woeful desolation behind more speedily, for it seemed to him just at present that his own life might become scarcely less grievous if Sir Oliver should refuse him and She (on whom all his dearest hopes now centred) should prove equally unkind—of which, in his present mental state, he was ready to believe—almost !

But these doubts and unhappy forebodings were suddenly interrupted by a familiar voice hailing cheerily, and, glancing over his shoulder, he beheld Viscount Ragworth waiting to greet him on that causeway leading across muddy foreshore to the spacious yard where stood the ancient now glorified tavern known from time immemorial as the " Jolly Young Waterman".

" Avast ! " cried the Viscount with hoarsely nautical bellow. " Bring to, yo-ho ; belay and—why, good God, Robin, what the dooce—— ? "

" I know ! " he sighed, looking up gloomily into the face above him. " Frightful spectacle, aren't I ? Scorched clothes, singed hair, and so on—and—I feel worse than I look! I'm low, Rags, dismally low—in the profoundest deeps of despond! No poor prodigal or destitute outcast could be lower. My spirits are in my confounded boots, old boy; I'm dejection personified!"

"And no wonder!" said the Viscount as they gripped hands. "I mean, considering all you've gone through, that hellish fire and——"

"It's not the fire," sighed Robin dismally. "That's past and done with, and I'm little the worse owing to—one who wrought a—stupendous miracle of which I shall tell you later on. But now my present trouble is my coming interview with old—I mean, Sir Oliver, my scorched phiz and most of all my accursed self. Consequently, my dear old Rags and Bones, to have you beside me in this dark hour comforts me no end!"

"Doocedly happy to know it, Robin. And to tell you I carted your traps and toggery here—I mean they're waiting you in bedchamber called ' Luff ' is it?"

"Good old Rags! I shall feel better for 'em, more able to face—him! I suppose he's expecting me?"

"And has been this half hour. You're late, you know."

"Yes, and thereby have probably set his stately back up somewhat already—eh, old boy?"

"Well, he shows a trifle on edge, old fellah, champing the bit and pawing the hoof somewhat."

"Which makes things all the worse for me, of course."

"My poor old Dev——"

"No!" said Robin with sigh like a groan. "No more o' that! Never call me that again, Rags. I got rid of Robert the Devil in the fire."

"Impossible, my dear Robin! Quite impossible!"

"In the fire, Rags, and forever!"

"If so, then peace to his ashes, for in our callow youth I admired him immensely."

"Then you must have been confoundedly callow, old boy. But now as regards my gov., Sir Oliver—I mean if possible to steal a march on him—with your help, of course."

"Of course, old fellah, but how?"

"You will scout around till you run him to earth, which done, you will pin him down, hold him in play while I steal indoors to more suitable garb. Is it a go?"

"It is. I'll do my best to entice him into the stables to judge my newest, a bay mare you haven't seen yet—if he will entice, which I doubt. However, I'll try."

"Thanks, old boy! Now off you go."

Away sped the Viscount and performed his mission so successfully that when Robin, after a tense period of waiting, peered cautiously into the stable-yard it appeared quite deserted; so across it he sped without a sound—only to be met on the inn's very threshold by Bo'sun Tom, who forthwith hailed him in loud and hearty greeting:

"Lord love you, Master Robin, you're right welcome! Step aboard, sir, for your governor's standing by wishful to —ah, there he be yonder!"

And—there he was indeed! For, summoned by the bo'sun's welcoming roar, out from a stable nearby stepped Sir Oliver Dale, tall, stately and immaculate as usual from lofty head to spurred heels. He advanced a leisurely pace or so, then halted to gaze at Robin, his hatless head, his scorched and rumpled garments; and Robin, all too conscious of this keen scrutiny, bowed his head lower than ever and, yearning to speak his remorse, was dumb. . . . And as they stood thus so still and mute, the bo'sun instinctively shrank away indoors, while Viscount Ragworth as silently retreated backwards into the stables. . . .

And still, uttering no word, Sir Oliver gazed at this stalwart, much distressed son of his adoption, who, waiting so humbly, stared dejectedly earthwards. Thus at last he saw

Sir Oliver's right hand lift slowly and come towards him, heard again this dearly familiar voice.

"Well, Robin, when are you coming to see—the—baby?"

Now, lifting his head, Robin grasped this hand in both his own for the precious thing it was, saying brokenly: "Sir, I . . . oh, Governor . . . dear old Noll. . . ."

CHAPTER XXXVIII

How Robin Explained and Went for Her Answer to the Question

IN THE small, triangular parlour called " Salamander ",
Lady Rosamond was dispensing that indispensable beverage
(at least to English folk), high tea. The cups being charged,
she handed them to the merry-eyed Viscount, who, glancing
from her to Robin and back again, lifted an enquiring eyebrow; to Sir Oliver, who, no longer stately or austere,
smiled at her so very youthfully and actually winked (his left
eye); and lastly to Robin, who, now suitably attired and
seated to the right of his foster-father, was gazing at him
as a son should. . . . And now, inspired by lifted eyebrow
and furtive wink, Lady Rosamond, having sipped her tea,
said :

" When Mr. Shrig informed me, I was naturally greatly
astonished, Robin my dear ! "

" Oh, but, Aunt," he replied above his brimming teacup,
" you know Jasper is a surprising person and loves to
astonish people. How did he do it this time ? "

" By telling me—her—hair is black, or, as he put it, 'dark
as a raven's wing ', though he said ' ving '."

Robin very nearly upset his tea and, setting down his cup
with a clatter, exclaimed in tone of vast relief :

" Ah, so good old Jasper has told you, has he ? Which
makes it easier for me. I've been wondering how and where
to begin ! Yes, she has the most gloriously beautiful hair
in the world."

" Oh, but, Robin dear—black ! Remembering your so
often expressed detestation for dark tresses and your
passionate admiration for——"

" Auburn ! " quoth Sir Oliver.

" Yellow ! " murmured the Viscount.

" Precisely ! " said Lady Rosamond. " So now, my dear boy, we are all surprised. And because we love you, are wondering how long this new choice, this astounding change in you will endure."

" Then don't wonder," said he fervently, " because it will endure so long as I breathe—and after, I hope ! For me the only and most beautiful hair is black and always will be— until it turns white, and then I shall only love it more, because she—I——" He stopped to glance round at these three intent faces, each so familiar and now dearer to him than ever.

" Well, my dear," his aunt enquired, " because——? "

" Because I love every individual hair because of the head it beautifies, and I adore the head because of the mind and soul that goes with it ! And now, pray let me tell you the who, how and why—yes, and all the wonder of her, if only I can." And so indeed he did, speaking from his very heart and therefore with a simple eloquence that was sufficiently convincing. . . . " So this," he ended, " is why I love her, though I can never tell you or her how deeply, because it is beyond all telling. . . . She called to me in that hell of fire, called me back not only to life but to a better self and under-standing of life and—and so on."

Here Robin paused again, and for a space none spoke.

" And does she, Miss—Tracy, return your——? "

" Oh, Governor, I don't know ; I can only hope—because it seems so utterly impossible she can feel the same for me, considering her beauty, her wit, her many accomplish-ments—and myself such a confounded miserable failure ! "

" You are quite confoundingly humble, Robin ! "

" Because, sir, I know myself at last ! Ever since you fathered me, God bless you, I have been your constant dis-appointment ; school, college and university—it was always the same waste of time and opportunity ! Today my only hope is her ! To live and work for her sake. With such wife I could succeed in some way or other."

" Suppose she refuses ? "

" I'll go for a soldier or join the navy."

" And if she blesses you with ' Yes ' ? "

" Then—oh, my dear, blessed old Noll, then I'll accept your offer of Stonyhurst and work for you, b'gad ! With her beside me and Black John to help, we'll make that worst of your farms blossom to prosperity. If that's impossible, we'll breed horses, a stud farm. Old John has a marvellous way with all animals ! Lord, what a glorious idea ! "

" When shall you know her will, one way or the other ? "

" This evening, sir ! Oh, Noll, she has promised to tell me the moment we meet, and if it's ' Yes '—oh, glory ! This is why, with Aunt's and your permission, sir, I'll be off."

" Yes, yes, away with you ! " said Lady Rosamond. " You shall go at once, but first—stoop, my dear boy—there, may this kiss be a prelude to others—more ardent, of course, but never more truly affectionate. Now go—to your happiness, I hope and—believe ! "

" And," said Sir Oliver, rising, " Rags and I will see you off."

So down to the river they went all three. And when Robin was seated in his boat, eager to be gone, Sir Oliver smiled down on him, saying :

" If, as I venture to prognosticate, the word is the ' Yes ' you hope for, the most joyful of welcomes awaits you both at Abbeymead, Robin—my Goodfellow."

" Dearest old sir and Noll," he answered rather hoarsely, " that will—crown everything most—most gloriously and make my happiness so absolutely—oh, I can't tell you——"

" Then don't try, old fellow ; and, Robin, pray, after the word is spoken, convey to her my hearty salutations and profound hope for united happiness."

" And, my dear old fellah," said the Viscount, " let's make it a double event, eh ? "

" Oh, Rags, old boy," sighed Robin, " if I only can ! " And so with their kindly faces and good wishes to hearten him, Robin pulled into mid-stream and rowed away to front the last and most dreadful of his trials.

CHAPTER XXXIX

Tells How the Question was Answered

AT A bend of the river where town and country met stood a cottage, upon the wicket gate of which hung this notice laboriously inscribed :

Froot and flours for sail.

" Aha, flowers, of course ! " said Robin aloud and, turning, forthwith urged his boat thitherward, ran it ashore, and, hurrying up a steep path, entered a well-tended garden and there gladdened the heart of a bearded ancient by purchasing a great armful of his choicest and most expensive blooms, though with a haste that left the old fellow beaming but breathless. So, bearing his fragrant burden, down to the riverside sped Robin and was about to step into his boat when he heard a shrill cry which, though distant, was so arresting that he turned to look, and thus avoided the unseen murder-stroke, yet so narrowly that, sorely smitten, he stumbled blindly forward, floundered into deep water and sank, leaving only a trail of bubbles and drifting flowers for his murderers to see, ere, having accomplished their dire work, they turned and fled.

Down went Robin, and down to greeny deeps where death waited with slimy tentacles to clutch and fetter struggling limbs. Aware of this menace, he waited like the experienced swimmer he was ; waited until the clinging weeds released him ; then, with lungs nearly bursting, rose to the surface and blessed air. . . . But now he was conscious of pain, also his right arm was useless, and the current was

sweeping him away. . . . Thus in his agonised helplessness he gasped :

" Oh, Father Thames, is this—the end ? Is this—my
finish ? If so, be kind and—let me—die soon."

" Are you so ready to die, Robin, and she waiting to fill
your arms—perhaps ? D'you wish to die ? "

" No ! " he gasped. " Ah, no—but if I must I'd rather
go along with you. Though life was never—so precious
as now."

" Well, you have one arm and me to help you."

" Or to drown me—Old Thing."

" Naturally I shall, if you lose faith in yourself and belief in
me."

" But my strength—is going ; I—shall sink."

" Because, m' lad, you ain't using me or your mind
properly. Turn on your back and float, y' fool, float."

" Of course—yes—thanks. I was—forgetting."

" There ! So, my boy, how are ye now ? "

" Very weak—faint."

" And no wonder ; you had a woundy rap. If you hadn't
turned your head It would have brained you."

" What would ? "

" The Evil Thing. But she screeched in time."

" Who did ? "

" Why, Her, of course ! Saved you again, she did. Nay,
now don't struggle or down you'll go. Trust to me."

" Yes, but—I think I am—going——"

" So you are—downstream along o' me."

" I'm growing—weaker—dying——"

" Not you ! Keep a stout heart, my son ! Help will come
—is coming, a boat, oars—can't you here 'em ? "

" No, I'm—deaf—blind—it's too late."

Thus when at last she came it was to find him helpless,
adrift and apparently without life. But with desperate hands
she clutched and, drawing him astern, strove with all her

might to drag him aboard. Finding this impossible, she lay full length to hold and keep his head above water, hoping and praying for help, yet all in vain, for at this twilit hour the river hereabout was deserted. So now she prayed that cramped hands and aching arms might endure and fail not. And even then her prayer, it seemed, was answered, for Robin stirred feebly, opened swooning eyes and, gazing up into the face so near his own, panted :

" Oh—you, most beloved—if this is death—and you here, I—shall love it more—than life ! "

" No no," she answered, breathless but thankful, " this is—life, I pray God."

" Life ? " he repeated. " Oh then, will you be my wife—yes or—no ? "

" Ah, my—dearest," she gasped in tone that was neither laugh nor sob, being something of both. " Robin, my dear—beloved man, my answer is yes and yes. I'm only living to be —your wife."

" Mar-vellous ! " he exclaimed breathlessly. " Now d'you think—you could manage—to kiss me ? " And most certainly she would have done had not a lusty shout and swift beat of oars arrested her. So to their relief came one, a sailorly man who with sundry yo-hos of self-encouragement and powerful arms lifted, hauled and eased half-swooning Robin into this ark of refuge, this right, tight craft bearing the letters B.E.T.

"Now," quoth the mariner, "heave ahead, lady. Give way and with a will. Home wi' him, strip him, bed him, dose him aplenty wi' rum hot, and he'll be all ataunto in the morning."

And row, indeed, she did, gazing down on half-drowned Robin, who, hovering on the borders of unconsciousness, murmured repeatedly :

" Mar-vellous ! " And later, rousing a little, " You haven't—kissed me—yet ! "

But her only thought was to get him safe indoors and, soon as possible, dry and warm.

Therefore although she contrived to smile down upon her shivering though doggedly-persistent, one-idea-ed mutterer, she saved breath and strength the faster to ply her oars, while Robin, closing his eyes again, seemed to slumber. " And yet how ghastly pale his face, and how terribly still his usually vigorous form! Oh, pray merciful God it is indeed sleep the restorer and not—oh, Divine Father, not—that ! "

With this unuttered supplication in her soul but growing anxiety in her harassed mind, she rowed the more desperately, straining every nerve, every muscle and sinew of her strong young body, until hard-driven flesh yearned for respite denied by resolute mind and merciless will. . . .

Thus when Robin next opened his eyes it was to find himself swathed with blankets on a couch in the comforting warmth of a blazing fire while seated at the open lattice, radiant with sunset, Sergeant Ben was busily engaged ; that is to say, in close action with a pair of very large wooden knitting-pins.

" Hallo ! " said Robin cheerily, whereat down went the sergeant's knitting and, reaching a jug from the hob, he filled a glass with a steamy fragrance which he tendered with the words :

" Rum, Master Robin ! There's nothing like rum afore going into action and after, and if hot with lemon peel and a clove or so, so much the better ! So drink hearty, sir, and no heel-taps ! "

Robin obeyed meekly, sighed blissfully, returned the empty glass, and enquired eagerly:

" Pray, Sergeant, where is—She ? "

" Resting, sir, and I hope fast asleep, for she was nigh foundered and ready to swound when she rowed you in."

" Then may she sleep well, God bless her ! You know, she saved my life again, Sergeant Ben—from the water this time."

" Yessir ! How are you now, sir ? "

" Fit as a fiddle and right as any trivet, except for my confounded arm."

" Painful, of course, sir ! Was afraid at first as your collar-bone was broke, but glad to say 'tis no more than a bruise, though an uncommon bad one as will trouble you for days to come. I've done my best for it, but Doctor Brook will do better—army surgeon, sir, Peninsular and Waterloo, very experienced. I know him well, and no better fisherman ever plied angle ! "

" However," Robin demurred, " we don't need to trouble him for my confounded bruise."

" Wisest course, sir. Besides, She so commands. Wherefore, I'll march so soon as your garments are dry and I've got you back into 'em."

" Eh ? Oh, good Lord, then I'm——"

" Naked as Adam, sir, except for one o' my nightshirts, flannel, best, which you fill as complete as I do."

" How on earth did you get me from the boat here ? "

" I carried you, Mr. Robin."

" Then, by jingo, you must be deuced strong ! "

" Yessir. They used to call me Atlas when I was younger, and—eh, what is it, sir ? "

" Her feet, Ben, overhead ! Her little precious feet ! She's up and about and mustn't find me lying here in your best flannel like the poor, sickly invalid I'm not. So bear a hand, like the good friend you are, and I'll dress."

With the sergeant's deft aid this awkward and painful manœuvre being excuted or business accomplished, Robin, disdaining the couch, sank gratefully into the nearest armchair ; and though his once modish garments were none the better for their recent soaking, he was glad to see they were better than expected, and straightway forgot them, since his thoughts were all of something so profoundly, infinitely, wonderfully . . .

"Sir," quoth the sergeant, "may I trouble you to look this way?"

Unwillingly Robin turned from watching the door, which, though apparently a quite ordinary sort of door, was soon to admit all that was to him loveliest and most adorable in the whole universe. However, Robin turned and thus beheld Sergeant Ben standing by a corner-cupboard, from a shelf of which he reached a brace of heavy, very formidable pistols, saying:

"These, Mr. Robin, are newly primed and charged. I show 'em to you—in case."

"Of what, Sergeant?"

"In-vasion, sir, any in-truder, this being such a very lonesome place. So I keep 'em handy in case, here upon the top shelf."

"Good!" said Robin. "But let me tell you, dear old Sergeant, she has now saved me from death three times— once by fire, once by water and once by a scream."

"Eh, a scream, sir?"

"Yes, because just as Murder struck she cried out. I turned my head, and the blow missed it and struck only my shoulder."

"Then whoever struck you must have heard her, too?"

"Yes, I suppose so."

"Ah!" exclaimed the sergeant in sudden anxiety. "Then, Mr. Robin——!" The pistols clicked as he cocked them, saying again as he did so: "In case!" Then, replacing these weapons, he closed the cupboard precisely, in which same moment the chamber door opened, and, glancing thither, Robin beheld her.

She was dressed rather more richly than usual, but all he

saw at first was the lovely oval of her face, the light in her black-lashed eyes, the full, ruddy lips that, curving to tender smile, now parted to exclaim :

" Oh, Ben. So our poor swooning misery is up ! "

" Madam, he is ! "

Rising to his feet, Robin made her a bow of agonising ceremony, yet contrived to say lightly :

" Most gracious of all ladies, your ' brand from the burning ' and now utterly devoted ' flotsam '—thanks to Ben's skill and a certain ' female party ', is able to greet your ladyship with, I hope, a becoming grace and——" His breath caught, weakness smote him and he sank back feebly into the armchair.

Then she was bending over him, all tender solicitude and motherly reproaches :

" There—there ! This cushion for your poor shoulder ! Oh, Robin, how foolish of you to defy nature ! Ah, Ben, how pale he is ! "

" Yes, 'twas the bow he made you as—wrenched his shoulder. What he needs is rum, my—m' dear, rum's the thing—here on the hob—dose him well. I'll fall in and march on the doctor."

" There's no need ! " said Robin, firmly as possible. " I'm better already ! " And to prove this he sat up and contrived to chuckle. " Oho, my beautiful, bewitching, bouncing Bet, I'm practically well."

" Hurry, Ben ! " she sighed. " Doctor Brook. I wish he lived nearer. Go now—no, first get our rebellious invalid back onto the couch for me."

So thither, despite his protests, the sergeant gently compelled him. Then with meaning look and furtive gesture towards the corner cupboard, Sergeant Ben strode out and away.

And now, though bitterly mortified to know himself so weak, Robin otherwise lay supremely content because she was sitting so very close beside him. . . . Therefore after some while :

" Bet," he sighed, gazing up at her very wistfully, " in my helplessness . . . up to my chin in the river, I asked you . . . the . . . question and the answer you gave me then . . . may have been inspired . . . only by your angelic pity. So now that I am so nearly well, thanks to glorious you . . . I ask you again, will you dare to be my wife ? "

She leaned nearer, stooping closer to look down into his pleading eyes as she said :

" Then now, Robin, I must tell you again I am living only to be your wife, because you are the only man I shall ever love. And if you ask me why—I must tell you, because I honour you for your clean, strong nature ; admire you for your strength and courage ; but—oh, I adore you for the dear, blundering, blind, silly, masculine male man that you are. So now, as you told me I must, I say—oh, Robin, dearest of men, kiss me."

Then just how Robin did needs no telling. And after some while she enquired rather breathlessly :

" Do you love me, Robin—very much ? "

" More than I can ever say ! "

" And you will—always ? "

" All my life—and beyond ! Yes, in the hereafter, I hope and pray."

" Well—now," she murmured, nestling closer, " tell me, Robin, who do you think—no, whom do you believe you are clasping so—so fervently—and in spite of your poor arm ? Who is she ? "

" My own most beautiful and precious property."

" Oh, she is ! But—who beside ? "

" The loveliest, wittiest, cleverest, most bewitching of witches——"

" Yes, my dearest, and do pray always believe me so ! But who else am I, and—what ? "

" The very perfection and epitome of womanhood."

" Oh, Robin, however can I live up to such an estimate ?
And yet I am something more, something you should have
guessed, something Jasper Shrig knew almost at once and
hinted to you so often ! Cannot you guess even yet—must I
tell you ? "

" Yes," he answered, kissing a strand of her silky hair
that had come loose, " yes, but only if you wish."

" Then—oh, Robin, my own beloved darling dolt, I am
your ' armful of filth ' ! "

His close embrace relaxed, he drew away, his grey eyes
widened to staring amazement, parting his lips to speak, he
was dumb, and thus—he gaped ; at which she laughed,
though with hint of tears, then, hiding her face against him,
continued rather brokenly : " Yes, I am the loathsome
burden dear Father Thames, refusing to drown, bore to your
arms ! I am the waif of this river of our destiny—and so—
because of our—beloved Old Father—I am lying here upon
your dear, strong heart. Father Thames has made us each
other's very own."

" Alas ! " sighed a pleasant voice in gentle mockery.
" Alas and alack, what pitiful delusion ! " And thus,
unseen and unheard until now, the Thing of Evil was with
them.

Now suddenly, as he gazed at this stealthy intruder,
Robin knew at last the reason for his instinctive loathing.
This slender, too-exquisitely dainty, soft-voiced creature
with too much grace in every supple movement and gesture,
this creature of inherent evil—ineffably malicious and—
abhorrently feminine !

CHAPTER XL

Thing of Evil, End of

" CLAUDE ! " she exclaimed, and with the word was afoot between Robin and this smiling menace.

" Myself ! " he tittered. " But who are you, I wonder ? Your form and features remind me woefully of Aramanthea, our beloved, rebellious Thea. But she is dead and buried ! Such very moving ceremony, too, glory of flowers, pealing organ and white-robed choristers to waft her soul heavenward on blended harmony."

" How absurdly you talk, Claude ! You know that I——"

" Most true, I know that you, my dear, being so extremely dead, have no right to speak and move as though yet living. This I shall rectify——"

" Oh, Claude, go away ! You know I was never afraid of you."

" And yet, thou ghostly one, I think you have dreaded me a little of late and venture to aver you will fear me even more——"

" You are more ridiculous than usual, Claude—talking such perfect nonsense."

" Oh, but, sweet ghost, how convincingly I shall perform, for—oh, look at these ! " As the words were uttered, each slim white hand was grasping a small though murderous-looking pistol.

" Do look at them ! " he pleaded. " Are they not beautiful ? So elegant, so light and yet so accurate ! I have tested them quite often lately for—this supreme occasion. No, please don't interrupt me by word or movement, either of you ; remain dumb and still, both of you, until I have gratified

283

myself by explaining to each of you what is to be and why.
See now, these fateful potencies you gaze upon are twin
brethren. This in my left hand is Damon, in my right is
Pythias. Presently Damon shall send thee back to thy grave,
thou resuscitated Thea; thus Pythias is for our Master
Robin Dale. Ha, yon great, coarse brute, yon vile animal
that dared outrage me so shamefully—I have waited and
sought him ever since that hour of utter shame and affliction.
Fire, it seems, will not consume his odious carcase; the
river refused his beastliness; ah, but Pythias shall not fail!
First—hush, be still, no interruptions—first your adored
Robin shall see his beloved perfected for the tomb, though
not until I——"

"The door—behind you!" cried Robin wildly, and as
those threatening weapons faltered, leapt towards them
desperately—at which moment through the open casement
gushed flame and smoke with a deafening report, followed,
after a moment of stunned quiet, by a shrill and very
dreadful screaming, the swift patter of light feet, and they
were alone, gazing down speechlessly at—Damon and
Pythias.

Then at that same window Mr. Shrig leaned in to peer
at them very round of eye and say:

"Lord love you, Master Rob; your precious life—a
werry narrer squeak that! I thought as my shot had took
you."

"No no, I'm all right, Jasper, but—he's off and away!
Ha, damme, d'you mean to let him escape? Eh, do you,
Jasper?"

"Ar!" he replied with slow nod. "But—Dan'l don't!
But, sir, dog bite my dewoted neck if you didn't give me a
turn—risking your life so desprit! If you hadn't fell down,
my ball might ha' took you through your tibby, or, as you
might say, napper."

"Well, it didn't—thank God! So now if you'll hop in

and lend me a hand I'll get up—my shoulder happens to be a trifle stiff."

But other hands did this for him, with tender arms to clasp and cherish; there were lips also to kiss his pain-wrinkled brow, and a voice to sigh:

" Oh, my Robin beloved, this time it was you saved me—to love you, if possible more than ever. Now, back with you on the couch, my dearest."

Observing all of which, Mr. Shrig silently withdrew, nodded, blew down the barrel of his pistol to clear it, thrust it into deep side-pocket and went his leisured way. Being come to the river, he paused to gaze down as if computing the speed and power of its ebb, then he ambled on again until he beheld the man Dan'l, who, propped against a tree, was also gazing pensively down at this ever-restless tide. And after a brief silence wherein his keen, roving glance seemed to question every ripple and eddy near and far, Mr. Shrig enquired:

" Fell in, eh, Dan'l?"

" With a splash, Jarsper. Sang out he did, once or twice, afore he went under—surprising shrill, too, like a woman!"

" Ah!" sighed Mr. Shrig. " Like a fee-male! Howsever, he's nice and quiet now, Dan'l."

" As death, Jarsper."

" Arter all, Dan'l, there's nothing like the old river to make a clean sweep."

" Also quick, sure and cheap, Governor."

" Werry true, Dan'l! He should come ashore at any o' the usual places 'bove bridge sometime tomorrer."

" Ay, thereabout."

" Remember to give the office to Bill Bartrum and t'others, Dan'l."

" Rightho, Jarsper! Where now?"

" London and the ' Vaterman '."

CHAPTER XLI

Wherein Old Father Thames Ends this Narrative

MORNING, with promise of another glorious day, and the three are seated at the breakfast table.

"My lady Aramanthea, ma'am," said Robin, pausing in the act of drinking to look at her instead. "Nevertheless and however, to me you are and ever will be—Bet. Yes, indeed, the most bewildering, beautiful and bewitching Bet that ever bounced."

"I hope," she demanded, "you are sufficiently informed to know that 'bouncing Bet' is a rather pretty flower, Mr. Dale sir."

"'Beautiful' is the adjective, my lady; 'tis flower beautiful and wild, or wildly beautiful, and generally grows upon old walls and aged ruins, hiding their scars and blemishes with her own loveliness, transforming them into things of beauty, making the best of the worst as you are doing with me. Hence, though to the generality you are Lady Aramanthea, to me, I repeat, you are Bet. Oho, Sergeant Ben, wherefore that throaty not to say ogreish chuckle ? "

"Tell him, Ben," sighed my lady, taking his cup to refill it. "Explain to my poor, self-deluding wretch how he has misnamed me from the very first."

"Well, Mr. Robin," said the sergeant obediently and repressing another chuckle, "the letters on my boat, B.E.T.——"

"Spell 'Bet', my dear old Ben."

"Very true, sir, but more rightly they spell and stand for me, Benjamin Edward Tracy, so that, d'ye see, all this time

286

you've been, in a manner of speaking, making love to and wooing—me ! Which strikes me as—well—comical."

"It is ! " laughed Robin. " I've thought so frequently of late——"

" Oh ? " enquired her ladyship. " How lately, pray ? "

" Since meeting your Uncle Ben, who is soon to be my uncle, too, per wedlock—eh, Uncle ? "

The sergeant very nearly dropped his coffee-cup, then set it down with elaborate care, saying :

" Well, Mr. Robin, what I say to that is—what do I say, my lady ? "

" Everything, Ben—no, I will ! Robin, our dear faithful Ben was first my father's valet, then his soldier-servant. Ben, as I told you, saved our father's life at Waterloo, but he could not save him from the result of his terrible head wound. Phyllinda and I were at our finishing school in Paris when I first heard of the Despards and of Father's strange infatuation for Count Hugo, and later how these strangers were imposing on his too good nature. So I insisted on returning home and found my poor father so completely dominated by Hugo and his—detestable brother that he had become their abject slave. He showered money upon them ; they had but to express a wish and it was granted. At their bidding Father even got rid of his devoted Ben, leaving himself entirely at their mercy—except for me, though my efforts were not of much avail. At their instigation Father bought a large estate in Italy and there we all went to live—in a great medieval castle, and there these Despards became more possessive and imperious than ever. . . . When Father died he bequeathed his Italian property to Hugo, but, what was so infinitely worse, had made Hugo our legal guardian, and we were helpless—and in Italy ! But somehow or other they lost or squandered this inherit- ance and so were compelled to return to England, thank God ! But now it became their purpose to compel Phyllinda

and myself to marry them. Their persecution became so—
so odious that I determined we must run away to one of
Father's oldest friends, the Duchess of Camberhurst. . . .
Well, we had launched the boat when vile Claude surprised
us ; he threw poor Phyl down and tried to stop me, but
I hit him with the oar and rowed away, telling Phyl she
should be rescued very soon. It was a very dark night and
I had rowed a long way when I ran into something, probably
a ship's anchor rope, and it swept me overboard—and, oh,
the horror of the cold, black water ! But I could always
swim, so I slipped off as many hampering clothes as possible
and—through that terror of darkness dear Father Thames
bore me at last—to you, Robin."

"Yes," said he, reaching to touch her hand, " to me,
thank God, and the ministering, angelic care of Aunt
Rosamond. But you stole away——"

"Of course, and you know why. And so, learning the
Duchess was not in London, I fled here to our trusty Ben,
who has uncled and aunted, fathered and mothered me ever
since, bless him ! "

Here the sergeant rose, saying :

" As you are to visit Lady Rosamond today, I thought a
few roses might please her." And out he marched into the
sunny garden.

" A grand fellow ! " said Robin, kissing the hand he
still held. " And today you are going to meet another grand
man, one of the noblest—I told you he'd forgiven me, did
I ? "

" Three times, if you mean Sir Oliver."

" Well, this very morning you will meet him and——"

" Oh, but I have."

" You—you have met my old Noll ? "

" Weeks ago ! Frequently——"

" Weeks ago !—old Noll ? "

" And Clia. I have even cuddled—the—baby ! "

" The ba—— Well, I'll be——"

" Don't say it; lean near and you shall be." Robin did and was.

" Now sit down again and finish your breakfast."

" I have."

" Then—just sit down."

" And now," said Robin, sitting obediently but urging his chair nearer, " you'll tell me you know old Rags and Bones."

" Of course ! He is marrying my sister."

" B' George, I'd forgotten her. I mean——"

" Robin ! How fickle of you ! Considering how you raved to me about her glorious yellow tresses and her name that was a small, sweet song. I'm afraid you can never call Aramanthea sweet or song-like."

" Well, it's somewhat of a mouthful—though delicious, of course, and needs thought and deliberate care to enunciate."

" However, your folks manage it easily enough."

" My folks—our folks ! And, b' jingo, they kept dark about knowing you, never a hint—and there was I raving about you no end ! "

" Raving, were you ? "

" Doing my best to tell why I love you and why I feared you never could possibly love me. And, by heaven, when I look at you and remember all you are and may be, I still hardly dare believe it."

" Not even yet, my poor Master Stalwart Humility, my lamb of seeming meekness, my dove of apparent mildness, my tame, for the moment—lion ? Then lean near again. Now," sighed she, " are you convinced ? "

" Yes—very nearly."

" Are you happy ? "

" Perfectly ! Absolutely ! Unutterably ! Almost ! "

" Oh ? Why, Robin, and what ? "

" One fly, most merciful loveliness, one confounded fly in the ointment, or, rather, wasp in the honey—your multitudinous money bags ! How can any man work for a wife who's able to buy anything she desires ? How, pray ? "

" Hard ! " said she, setting her chin at him. " My man shall work to his heart's content, for me and with—goodness gracious, look at the time ! Today being an occasion, I must prepare—but—will a woman look too ridiculous rowing a boat in silk robe and plumed bonnet ? "

" The woman will look the glorious angel she is ! "

" Ah no—no, Robin, with your beloved fluffy curls, she is indeed only—the merest woman, and, oh, how infinitely glad of it ! "

" Dearest of all women, do you mean—can you really mean——? "

" Yes ! " she replied ; then, eluding his good hand, fled away upstairs. . . .

High noon and Old Father Thames radiant with sunlight is singing his perennial song, but today he sings of love and life and the joy of it—of this Robin is perfectly certain as he listens to this long-familiar voice the which indeed breaks off every now and then to chuckle so knowingly in the shallows.

" Hallo, Rob ; ain't she the embodied perfection o' your dreams ? An armful o' warm, soft loveliness, ain't she ? She is ! Very well then, be dooly grateful to her for so being, to natur' for making the both o' ye, and to me, the old river, your pal and playmate, counsellor and comforter for refusing to drown the both o' ye. Oh, be very glad and vastly grateful, boy ! "

" I am indeed ! " said Robin.

" Eh, what are you, sir ? " enquired the sergeant, for Robin had spoken aloud.

" Very glad and vastly grateful ! "

"And there comes your lady, Master Robin!"

"My—lady?" he repeated. "Yes. Oh, Ben, dear old Sergeant, bless you for that possessive pronoun."

"Pronoun, sir——?"

"Tell me," says my lady, halting on the path above them, "am I too dressy, Robin? Please, how am I?"

And gazing up at her, he answered reverently:

"So truly the embodied perfection of my dreams that I am—very glad and vastly grateful."

"Then you think I shall do?"

"Till my last breath!"

Here Sergeant Ben, about to fix the boat's rudder, chuckled:

"B. E. T., Mr. Robin! To think as you fell in love with my name, leastways part of it, and wooed my lady as such! It is and so remains that comical!"

"Yes," said Robin. "But it's far more, Ben! For these magic, dearly familiar letters will remind me of a man to whom I shall always be deeply grateful for my lady's sake and honour for his own sake, Sergeant-Major Benjamin Edward Tracy. So, Ben, whatever the future may hold for us, we shall hold you in honoured and ever grateful memory."

"And, oh, Ben dear," exclaimed my ady, "isn't my Robin becoming eloquent in your praise, and so truly that I shall kiss you again!" Which she did forthwith. Then gathering frills and furbelows about her shapely loveliness with one capable hand, she gave the other to Robin and stepped lightly into the boat that was to bear them away downstream to the true blessedness of friendship, the joy of each other, and a new life.

And now as she took her place at the oars, silken petticoats (etc.) tucked close, silk-clad ankles apeep, and daintily shod feet posed together upon the stretcher, Robin exclaimed in awed and murmurous delight:

"Oh, Aramanthea, glorious Thea—my wonderful Bet is even more beautiful than I deemed possible. Those pretty feet, those lovely ankles, those bewitchingly kissable——"

"That'll do, young man, that'll—do!" exclaimed Bet, scowling at him beneath plumed bonnet. "Ketch 'old o' them tiller-lines and watch out where we're agoing of; keep them eyes o' yourn on the river 'stead o' me."

"Oh, Bet lass, for this I must kiss you."

"Don't ee dare—yet! Besides, you'd upset the boat. You have the tiller-lines so—steer instead of staring me out of countenance."

"But, my lady, it was not your countenance what so enthralled my adoring gaze; it was your bewitching——"

"Yes, I know. Well—don't!"

"Don't what, pray?"

"Be so odiously, personally—previous."

"Ah, the future!" he sighed.

"Yes, the future," she repeated. "There will be joy, and there will be sorrow, yet there will be you, my dear one."

"Yes, there will be me, and we shall have each other, and later on, which is a 'consummation devoutly to be wished'—there may be others! Devoutly and—very reverently, Bet!"

"Yes, Robin."

Very slowly, with leisurely dip of oars, they went downstream through this golden, never-to-be-forgotten morning, supremely content and so completely unaware of anything except one another that they both started at sound of a voice that hailed them; and, glancing (unwillingly) thitherward, they beheld a boat, two men and a hat flourished aloft.

"Jasper!" sighed Robin. "What can he be after now, confound him."

"I can guess," said my lady, smiling, "bless him!"

" Oh, and why the benediction, madam ? "

" Because he is—Jasper ! And I owe him so very much ; indeed, we both do."

" Yes, but on this of all mornings——"

" Fie, Mr. Dale ! Don't be a surly Robin. Pipe him a glee of welcome, a lay of gratitude."

" Oh well, beloved messmate, 'vast rowing, heave to, adored hearty, and wait. I'll warrant his first words will be : ' My Lady Bright, good morning.' "

" Yes, he always finds lovely titles for me—bless him again ! "

Very soon the weather-beaten though speedy boat was alongside, and Mr. Shrig saluting them hat in hand, he also beamed, saying :

" My Lady o' Sunlight and Lovesomeness and Master Rob, from information received, deedoocing as you'd be coming down on the ebb, I have took the liberty to run you aboard to vish you both J.O.Y. j'y—first a gal and then a b'y—and inform you as this here case is finished. Though much regretting as you refuse to prosecute Number Vun, Count H. But sich being so, so be it. Same now being a free man is on the bounding billow as is bounding him back to Italy."

" Good ! " exclaimed Robin. " But what of the other, what of that—that——? "

" Sir, talking o' rivers and our Old Thames in pertickler, same have took sich constant interest in the velfare of London Town and the huming beings therein, that he occasionally takes a hand in huming affairs, and taking matters into his own charge, deals according and acts— prompt. Vich so done, is—as nobody can't deny."

" Ha, Jasper, just what do you mean ? "

" Oh, Robin, my dear," sighed my lady, glancing down at the bright water and repressing a shudder, " Jasper means, of course, that 'echo alone will respond ' ! "

"Eggs-actly!" exclaimed Mr. Shrig, putting his hat on that he might take it off to her. "Ah, Master Robin, that bee-oo-tiful head, or, as you might say, tibby, ain't stuffed wi' sawdust! And so, till you next gladden my ogles, goodbye."

"So," murmured Robin when they were alone again, "it was the river!"

My lady merely nodded, thus was silence awhile except for the gentle plash and ripple of their progress. When next she spoke it was to propound this question:

"Do you suppose our dear Old Thames in all these hundreds and thousands of years has ever carried two people as happy as we? A few, I suppose, but a very, very few?"

"I doubt it!" said Robin. "No, b' jingo, I'm perfectly sure and absolutely certain our Thames never has and never will."

"Oh, but in thousands of years, Robin!"

"Nor in millions of æons, my Bet!"

"I wonder what Father Thames himself would say about it?"

"I'll find out!" said Robin, and forthwith asked the question:

"O, Ancient Wise One, my dear Old Thing, what say you about it?"

But the old river merely bubbled and laughed, though what he murmured was this very mysterious, most descriptive of all words:

"Pompholugopaphlasma!"